* * * * * *

    I knew better than to enter the mine as there could be a cave-in at any time. However, my curiosity got the best of me. I had no idea if there was anything in the box, but I had to know if there was something in it that might help me understand more about the mine and the miner who had dug for his riches.

    Being careful not to disturb anything for fear that the ceiling would cave in, I slowly and carefully moved toward the box. Reaching the box, I bent down to get a better look at it. I shined my flashlight around, but when it shined toward the box, I saw something that made me quickly jump away.

* * * * * *

Other titles by J.E. Terrall

Western Short Stories
   The Old West*
   The Frontier*
   Untamed Land*
   Tales from the Territory*
   Frontier Justice*
   Vanishing Wilderness*

Western Novels
   Conflict in Elkhorn Valley*
   Lazy A Ranch
     (A Modern Western)
   The Story of Joshua Higgins*
   The Valley Ranch War*
   Jake Murdock, Bounty Hunter*

Romance Novels
   Balboa Rendezvous
   Sing for Me*
   Return to Me*
   Forever Yours*

Mystery/Suspense/Thriller
   I Can See Clearly*
   The Return Home*
   The Inheritance

Bill Sparks Mysteries
   Murder in the Backcountry* Murder and the Gold Coins*

Nick McCord Mysteries
   Vol – 1 Murder at Gill's Point
   Vol – 2 Death of a Flower
   Vol – 3 A Dead Man's Treasure
   Vol – 4 Blackjack, A Game to Die For
   Vol – 5 Death on the Lakes
   Vol – 6 Secrets Can Get You Killed
   Vol – 7 Murder on the Racetrack

Peter Blackstone Mysteries
   Murder in the Foothills
   Murder on the Crystal Blue
   Murder of My Love
   Murder in the Dark of Night

Frank Tidsdale Mysteries
   Death by Design
   Death by Assassination

Non-Fiction books
   Two Brothers Go To War   (Letters from World War I)

*Also available in Large Print Editions

THE JOURNAL OF ISAAC MADISON 1861 to

by
J.E. Terrall

All rights reserved
Copyright © 2023 J.E. Terrall

ISBN: 979-8-9860262-2-0

No part of this book may be reproduced or transmitted in any form or by any means, electronic or mechanical, including photocopying, recording or by any information storage or retrieval system, in whole or in part, without the expressed written consent of the author.

This is a work of fiction. Names, characters, and incidents are either a product of the author's imagination or are used fictitiously, and any resemblance to actual persons, living or dead, is purely coincidental.

Printed in the United States of America

First Printing / 2023 – kdp.com

Cover: Front and back covers by author J.E. Terrall

Book Layout / Formatting: J.E, Terrall

Custer, South Dakota

THE JOURNAL OF ISAAC MADISON 1861 to

To
Norman Terrall,
my brother, who liked my
western stories, and who died too young.
We never got the chance to hike together even a
couple of trails in the Black Hills of South Dakota.

FORWARD
A LITTLE HISTORY

    It had been known for many years, even before the miners came to the Black Hills, that there was gold in the Black Hills. The Indians tried to keep it quiet, but news of gold in the hills was leaked out into the white man's world by traders who traded with the Indians, and by missionaries who tried to convert the savages to the white man's religion.

    Over time, the white man invaded the hills in numbers too great for the Indians to stop. The Army tried to keep the white man out of the hills, but they were unable to stop the miners. The area of the Black Hills was too large, and the area that had to be patrolled was too vast for the Army to cover with so few soldiers. The miners kept coming in search of the precious metal. The results were inevitable. Even Red Cloud, a great Sioux leader, understood that it was inevitable that the white man would keep coming.

    Over the years, I had heard many stories about the gold miners that had come into the Black Hills looking for the "yellow sand", as some of the Indians of the time were said to have called gold. A number of the stories were talked about, and written about, how the miners had snuck into the hills when it was illegal for the white man to be in the Black Hills. Many of the stories were true, but a lot of them were not. Many of those deemed not true may have been true, but had never been documented.

PROLOGUE
Present Day
Finding the Journal

I was hiking in the early spring in the backcountry in the Black Hills. It was in some of the same country that those long forgotten Black Hills gold miners had dug in the earth, panned in the streams, and walked through forests in search of gold. As I walked along, I began to think about those miners and what it must have been like for them almost two hundred years ago.

As I looked around while walking on a partially overgrown trail in the beautiful Black Hills, I could see places where there were still small amounts of snow on the ground. It was places where the sun rarely reached through the thick pines, or down into the steep canyons to melt it away.

The melting and freezing over the years had caused fissures in the rocks. It had caused the rocks to break loose and fall down the steep hillsides.

As I walked along, I noticed what looked like the entrance to a cave, or perhaps, an old mine just behind the pines. I knew that it is not safe to enter any of these old caves or mines as the rock might be very unstable.

When I got close enough to see inside, I discovered that it was the entrance to an old mine. The cliff above the mine had fallen down and covered the entrance many, many years ago. The freezing and thawing had eventually pushed the rocks on down the steep hillside away from the mine entrance, eventually reopening the mine. I was sure it had taken years for the rocks to fall away to reveal the entrance.

I carefully approached the mine, then bent down and looked inside. With the help of my flashlight, I could see what looked like a small box lying on the floor. It was only about ten feet inside the mine.

I knew better than to enter the mine because there could be a cave-in at any time. However, my curiosity got the best of me. I had no idea if there was anything in the box, but I had to know.

Being as careful as possible, I slowly and carefully moved toward the box. When I got close to the box, I took a minute to shine my flashlight around. I discovered something next to the box. There on the floor of the mine was the complete skeleton of a human.

I knelt down and began to look over the skeleton. There were what appeared to be fragments of cloth still clinging to a few of the bones. Around the waist of the skeleton was an old belt and holster with a rusty old gun in it. It looked to be an old Navy Colt, but I couldn't be sure because it was still in the holster and in very poor condition. I was sure that I had not only found an old gold mine, but I had found the miner as well.

My first thought was what had killed the miner. It didn't look as if the ceiling had fallen in on him because he was not covered with any rocks, nor were there any rocks near the body. However, the skeleton was covered with a fairly thick layer of dirt that indicated it had been there, undisturbed, for a very long time.

The skeleton was lying face down on the floor with one arm reaching out toward the metal box. Whatever had happened to him before he died, it had not stopped him from reaching for the box. It was obviously important to him.

I decided to look in the box to see what it was he was reaching for. I picked up the box. It was heavier than I had expected. The box was rusty but the rust had not gone through the metal. The box had been painted, which probably kept it from rusting through.

I brushed the dirt off the box and discovered it was an old metal tea box originally used to store tea. It took me a few minutes to pry it open because it was pretty well rusted shut. When I got it open, I discovered it had been well worth the effort.

Once I had the box open, I discovered three very interesting items inside the box. The first item was a small glass jar that seemed too heavy to be empty. The glass jar was painted on the inside so I was unable to see what was in the jar. It took a bit of effort, but I got it open. I found it contained several ounces of gold dust and a few small nuggets of gold. I wondered if that was what the miner was reaching for during his last moments of life.

I doubted the gold was what he was reaching for. If he knew he was dying, I wouldn't think the gold would be that important to him. I also wondered if the gold was the total sum of what he had given his life, for some reason I doubted it.

The second item in the box was a small tarnished silver frame. Behind the glass in the frame was a picture, but it was very hard to see. From what I could make out, it appeared to be a picture of a young woman. I glanced over at the skeleton. Was it a picture of his wife, or maybe it was a picture of a young woman who never knew why her man didn't return to her? There was no way for me to know who the woman was and what her connection to the miner might have been. I would probably never know even the names of either of them.

It was the third item in the metal box that came to be the most important and probably the most valuable item of all of them. It was a book.

I gently took it out of the box. It looked like it might be a journal. I decided to put it back in the box for now.

I took a minute to look around inside the mine for anything else that I might find to be of interest, being careful not to cause a cave-in, or to go too deep into the mine. I was looking for something that might tell me anything at all about the man whose remains lay on the floor of the mine. I found nothing but a few old rusty tools.

I hoped the book was a journal, and that it would provide me with information about the man and his life as a gold miner. I was also hoping it would tell me where he was from and a little about his life before he came to this place where his remains now lay.

I took the box with the book inside out of the mine into the sun. I sat down on a boulder and took the book out of the box. I opened the book very carefully and glanced through it. I soon found that it was a journal and it was almost full. It seemed a little ironic that he was so close to running out of pages when his life ended.

Since the journal was so old and delicate, I decided to take it along with the metal box and the items it had contained home where I could study the journal in a better environment. I put everything back in the tea box and headed for home.

Once I arrived home, I took my treasures into the den and placed them on my desk. I set the glass jar of gold on one of my bookshelves along with the metal box and the picture of the woman. I decided those items could wait until I had a chance to find out a little about who had written the journal. The journal was far more important and far more interesting than anything else to me. I wanted to know why the man had come here to mine for gold. I also hoped to find out what it was really like to be a gold miner in his time. I might also find out what it was that drove those men to risk their lives for riches in those early days.

After carefully setting the journal on my desk, I got a very lightly dampened cloth. Being very careful not to damage the journal, I gently wiped the dirt off the cover. There was something printed on the cover.

It read simply –

THE JOURNAL OF ISAAC MADISON 1861 to

I very carefully open the journal to the first page and began to read.

Isaac Madison

Just in case my journal should be read by someone other than myself, I will start out by writing a little about myself and my reason for leaving at this time.

I was born and raised in Richmond, Virginia. I had the good fortune to have been raised in a family that was well-educated. As a result, I was also well-educated and became a school teacher at the age of eighteen. I had been living and teaching in a small rural school in Otter Creek, Virginia, for two years which is why I started my journey from there.

Teaching had not satisfied my need to know the Frontier. In fact, it was the books and articles I had read about it that got me interested in the Frontier as a young boy. I was fascinated with the Frontier and dreamed about going out West to see what it was really like.

My serious thoughts of actually going to the Frontier began almost a year ago while I was on a trip to visit a friend of mine in Raleigh, North Carolina. I didn't start to form a plan in my head to go to the Frontier until I found a newspaper that had been left on a bench outside the train station in Raleigh, North Carolina. Since I had some time to waste before the train was to arrive that would take me back to Richmond, Virginia, I sat down and began reading the newspaper.

There were two articles in the newspaper that convinced me that now was the time for me to pack up my belongings and go west to see the Frontier for myself, and seek my fortune there.

The first article was fairly small and located on the fourth page of the newspaper. It was about the Black Hills located in a place that was called the Dakota Territory. In the article was only a brief mention of someone claiming to have talked to an Indian who said there was gold in the Black Hills. The claim of gold was quickly dismissed in the article saying the Indian was unreliable and drunk when he said it.

The second article was about the strong possibility of a war brewing between the North and the South. I'm no coward, but I had no desire to get involved. Some say the war was about State's Rights, some say it was about the south's dislike for Abraham Lincoln and some say it was about slavery. I had no interest in any of the reasons. I was neither for nor against slavery. I, nor anyone in my family, had ever owned a slave. I don't believe anyone in my family, including myself, had a problem with those who do. I was certainly not interested in having to take sides in the matter, even though it was beginning to look like people were already taking sides.

Most of those living in the eastern part of Virginia were in favor of Secession from the Union, while those living in the western part of Virginia, that part of the state west of the Allegheny Mountains, were against it. I felt it was a good time for me to leave so I didn't get forced into a conflict I had no interest in. I have no desire to die in a war when issues could be resolved if people would just sit down and talk about them. I'm twenty years old and would like to live to be an old man, so I'm leaving to fulfill my dream.

While I was in Richmond, I had said my goodbyes to my family. I wasn't sure how my father felt about me leaving, but I don't think he liked the idea very much. He never said anything about it, but I think he was leaning toward secession. I think it was more a case of loyalty to Virginia and the South than anything else.

April 19, 1861

It is the end of my first day of my journey to the West, also known as the Frontier. This is the first entry in what I hope will be a journal of my adventures into the Frontier. I had spent the last week preparing for my adventure to begin. It is on this day, I left Otter Creek to seek my fortune in an area called the Black Hills in the newly established Dakota Territory.

Although I left on my journey to the Frontier from Otter Creek, Virginia, in the Allegheny Mountains, that does not mean I am one of the hills people.

In the early morning of this day, I packed up my packhorse with the things I had gathered, and saddled my riding horse. I was ready to go by the time the sun came up. I swung up in the saddle. With a gun on my hip, a rifle on my saddle and supplies on my pack horse, I left the small mountain village for the Frontier.

During my first day of travel, it was cloudy and damp, but it didn't look like there was much chance of rain. It was cool as I rode through the woods heading west. I had my trip planned out with what maps I had been able to gather over the past few months. Most of them with any degree of accuracy went only as far as the Mississippi River. As best I could figure, it would take me the better part of the summer just to get to the Mississippi River. Having had no experience traveling long distance with just horses, it may not take that long. I had figured I could make about fifteen to eighteen miles a day, maybe more on a good day, without taxing my horses too much.

I had made only about eighteen miles on my first day. The road I was using was in the woods most of the time. It was very crooked as it followed a small creek that flowed down from the mountains. The further I went, the smaller the creek became. It was mostly uphill. I am spending my first night alongside the creek. It is a nice quiet place. The trees are just getting their leaves, and wildflowers are starting to show their colors.

As I sit leaning against a large oak tree to write the notes of my first day out, I find a certain peace within me. It is a feeling I have not experienced before. It seems to make everything around me prettier and more alive. I know I might not have this kind of peace all the time, but it feels good now. I am sure there will be times when I will question my decision to take this journey. But what good is having a dream if you don't do anything about it.

The light is growing dim as night approaches. Morning will come soon enough. It is time for me to put down my pen and journal, and turn in to get some sleep. I can see that my horses are already sleeping.

* * * * *

It was clear by Isaac's writings that he was a well-educated man for the times. His description of what he saw made it possible for me to visualize in my mind what he was seeing.

As much as I liked to read about his description of the things around him, I couldn't help thinking about what he might have thought was going to happen since the attack on Fort Sumter on April 12th. He may not have heard about it, as news traveled rather slowly in the mountains of Virginia in those days. It was clear that he was reasonably sure a Civil War would break out.

It was interesting that with a war looming on the horizon, he felt the need to leave. With his education, he would have probably ended up as an officer. He would also have been aware of the fact that officers led from in front of their men, which more than likely accounted for the large number of officers who lost their lives in many of the Civil War battles. There was little doubt that Isaac would have known the North had the manufacturing needed to build a well-armed Army, or at least a better armed Army than the South would be able to put together.

Although in current times, it is often believed by many that the only reason for the Civil War was slavery. Some historians and many politicians are partly to blame for this view as it became the major view of the North as the war went on.

To most of the people of the South, however, the principal reason for the war was States Rights. That is the right of each individual state to decide for themselves all issues that concerned them and affected them, including but certainly not limited to slavery.

Many in the South felt that the North had no business telling them what they could do and what they couldn't do. Most of the South felt the North had too much power. The Southern states wanted control over their own interests and their own destiny.

There was also a strong economical reason for the South to want to keep slavery. It needed the manpower to plant and harvest cotton, tobacco and other crops. There was no machinery to do most of the work at that time.

There was also a large faction of the South who hated Abraham Lincoln. Many felt he did not represent them, and catered to the powerful industrial leaders of the North.

My thoughts once again turned to Isaac's Journal. I began to read it. As I turned each page, I discovered that most of what he wrote over the next few days was some of his thoughts about the trip to the Frontier. Most of which had nothing to do with the Civil War. It was mostly about some of the things he hoped to see. He wanted to see the Indians, the buffalo and the wide-open plains, many of the things he had read about as a boy.

I had noticed in his Journal that he had skipped several days. I hoped to find out why in the next entry.

May 7, 1861

It has been several days since I have written in my journal. I will try to do better. I will take this opportunity to explain the lack of entries.

Everything before the above date has been pretty much the same. It has also been in an area of the mountains where I had spent a lot of time while I lived in Otter Creek. Lots of big old trees along narrow roads were about all there was to see. It was often hard to see more than a few hundred yards down the roads. Most of the time, it was almost like looking down a tunnel. The woods were so thick that to see into the woods more than twenty feet was difficult if not impossible. Most of the open areas were farms, some of them very small, while others were quite large.

However, it did tend to keep me vigilant for any danger that may befall me. The only good thing I could say about it was that there were a good many small animals that provided me with meat for several of my evening meals along the way. The rabbits were the best, but squirrels were tolerable. I even enjoyed a turkey for a couple of evenings.

I arrived in Lewisburg, Virginia on May third. However, since my arrival in Lewisburg, I have been unable to write in my journal due to what happened there. I'll explain.

I arrived in town about four in the afternoon on the third of May. The sun was shining and there was a gentle cool breeze out of the southwest. The weather had been very nice all day.

I rode up in front of the livery stable and stepped out of the saddle. The owner of the stable told me where I could get something to eat and lodging for the night. After putting up my horses, I started off across the street to the saloon where I had been told a good meal could be purchased. I had gotten only about halfway across the street when a man came out of the saloon waving a gun around and shouting something about dividing the state of Virginia. He was so drunk I had no idea what he had been talking about. It was clear he was looking for a fight. I had no desire to accommodate him, but he didn't seem to see it that way.

The man, who I had never seen before in my life, decided he was going to challenge me to a gunfight right there in the street. I tried to talk him out of it, but he was too drunk to listen. All I could understand was he didn't seem to like anyone from the eastern side of the Allegheny Mountains.

I had never been in a gunfight before, but it soon became clear he was not about to let me walk away from this one. I was going to have to fight him, or he would simply shoot me down in the street. I knew how to handle a rifle pretty well, but a pistol was a different matter.

With nothing left for me to do, I mentally prepared myself as best I could to draw against him. I was afraid he might get the best of me, but I didn't have a lot of time to think about it. He put his gun in his holster, then set himself to draw. I was no gunfighter, and had no desire to become one, but he left me with no choice.

Suddenly, he started to move as if going for his gun. I drew as fast as I could and fired. I think when my gun went off, I had my eyes closed. I'm not really sure. All I really knew at that moment was I was scared.

The next thing I knew was I had a sharp pain in my side and I was falling to the ground. The last thing I saw before I passed out was the man still standing in the street with his gun at his side looking at me.

The next thing I remember was waking up in a nice big featherbed. There was a young woman sitting in a chair next to the window reading a book. My first thought was she was an angel, especially when she looked over at me and smiled.

She took care of me for the next couple of days. She told me that I had shot and killed the man who had challenged me in the street. I wasn't sure if I believed her until the town marshal came to visit me. He told me the man I had killed was a local bully, and that he had not been able to arrest him as all his fights had the appearance of being fair fights. He also told me that the man was upset about the possibility that Virginia would be split up into two states, which was something I had heard rumors about back in Richmond. I had no idea if it might actually happen.

To-day, I was sitting up in bed and beginning to feel pretty good. I still had a considerable amount of pain in my side when I tried to move too much or too fast. Alice, my angel, did help me get out of bed. I got tired pretty easy, but I did manage to walk around the room a little bit before I laid down again.

Later in the day, she was nice enough to bring me my journal from my things at my request. After she left for a while to do whatever she had to do, I spent time bringing my Journal up to date. It is now getting late, and I am getting tired. I'll close my journal for to-day and get some rest.

* * * * *

Isaac had survived a gunfight. It must have been quite an experience for him. I had no idea how much Isaac had used a gun except for hunting, but he was either very fast with a pistol, or the other man was so drunk that he was terribly slow. Maybe it was a little of both.

The only thing I could think of at the moment was that he had a lot of courage to face a gunfighter in the streets. Although gunfights were not as common as some people tend to think, they were often tolerated by the local law officers as a way to settle disputes, as long as it was "a fair fight". The term "fair" in this case had nothing to do with experience in the use of firearms. All that was needed to make it "a fair fight" was for the two participants to each have a gun, or whatever other weapon was chosen.

As I thought about what he had written, I began to think about Lewisburg. It crossed my mind that Lewisburg was actually in West Virginia, not in Virginia. It was a fair size town at the time Isaac would have been there.

Somewhere in the back of my mind, I remembered that West Virginia had broken away from Virginia. I quickly looked up West Virginia on my computer and discovered that it had been part of Virginia. It seems that the western part of Virginia broke away over a difference in the attitudes of the people, primarily over slavery and secession.

The eastern side of Virginia was strongly plantations where slaves were needed to work the large fields. While in the western part of the state, the area on the western side of the Alleghany Mountains, there were much smaller farms and very few of them had slaves. My research showed that West Virginia became its own state during the Civil War. It was the only state to be formed by seceding from the Confederate States.

I found another interesting thing. He had mentioned the girl. He called her an angel, which indicated he might have thought of her as a rather nice-looking young woman. It was also possible he called her an angel because she cared for him in his time of need. Somewhere in that journal I would find out who the woman was, I was sure of it.

Looking at the picture, I wondered how did the woman fit into Isaac's life? Who was she and what did she mean to him? The only way I was going to find out was to continue to read the journal. I very carefully turned to the next page.

May 12, 1861

I once again find myself falling behind in the writing of my journal. There has not been very much to write about in the past few days. Everyday seemed to be about the same. I would eat breakfast, then Alice would help me get out of bed and we would go for a walk along the main street of town.

She is very kind to me and seems to like to spend time with me. I wasn't sure if it was because I needed help, and she was the kind of person who would help anyone in need, or if it was more than that.

The first day that I was able to walk outside, the weather was warm and pleasant. The sun was shining and there was a gentle breeze out of the west. We didn't go very far and walked kind of slow the first morning, but it was nice to have someone to talk to while walking.

I only got as far as the livery stable the first day we walked outside. I felt the need to check on my horses. The stable owner had taken good care of them. I did suggest he exercise them so they didn't get too much out of shape. He told me that Alice had been coming by every morning and would take them out for a ride.

I looked at Alice. I'm sure she could see the surprised look on my face. She smiled and said, "It only made sense that if you needed to exercise to get back in shape, your horses needed it in order to stay in shape." I was beginning to think she was not only an angel, but she was also a very smart woman.

In the days that followed, my strength continued to improve. I was getting much better and was able to walk from one end of the town to the other without much difficulty. I knew I would be able to continue on my journey before much longer. That thought saddened me a little. I had grown to like spending time with Alice. I think she enjoyed spending time with me, too.

If my desire to see the Frontier, and to make my fortune, did not lie in the Frontier, I might have considered staying in Lewisburg. It would not have been a bad place to live, especially if I were to live there with Alice.

I was beginning to think it might be best for me to move on soon rather than to break her heart by having her get any more attached to me. It crossed my mind on several occasions that I was afraid I might be falling in love with her. If I fell in love with her, I might never be able to seek my fortune in the Frontier.

I had no other skills than that of a school teacher. A school teacher never made enough to support a family.

I need to put my journal up and get some rest.

* * * * *

It was not difficult for me to understand what was happening to Isaac. He had found someone who wanted to spend time with him, to be near him. He may have even felt obligated to her for caring for him and helping him regain his strength.

The one thing that came out of his writings was that he was developing a real attachment, maybe even love for Alice. There was no doubt he had feelings for the young woman, but at that point in time his feelings for her were not strong enough to get him to stay.

I had to agree with his assessment of the situation. It was probably better that he left sooner rather than to break her heart by staying much longer.

I carefully turned to the next page and continued to read the Journal.

May 15, 1861

The time had come for me to continue my journey to the Frontier. I had told Alice last evening I would be moving on. She ran off with tears in her eyes when I told her. I was sure I had hurt her, but I had made no promises to her that I had any other intentions.

I looked for her before I left town on my way to the Ohio River, but I didn't see her. I have to admit that I thought about going back, but I had nothing to offer her. Teachers made very little, and there was little future for them in the hills of Virginia. I had no other skills from which to make a living.

I only made about ten miles to-day. The injury I had suffered became rather painful with the jarring my horse caused me. There were a couple of times when I got off my horse and walked as I found it more comfortable than riding. It was also difficult for me to load and unload my supplies from my horses without pain.

The weather was not as nice as I would have liked. It had turned cold during the day. It was also overcast all afternoon. I decided it would be a good idea for me to find a place where I could set up camp and get some much needed rest.

I found a place along a narrow river with a lot of big trees. I hobbled my horses near the river's edge and took my time getting my supplies off my packhorse. Once I had them on the ground, I sat down to take a breather.

After a short time, I built myself a lean-to and laid out my bedroll. I gathered some wood and made a fire to cook my supper over. I had gotten some coffee, salt pork and makings for biscuits before I left Lewisburg. I used it to make my supper. It was just getting dark when it began to rain. I sat under my lean-to and listened to the rain. It didn't rain very hard, but it was enough that it was running off the canvas I used to make my lean-to.

It is getting dark and my fire will not last much longer. I'll put my journal aside for tonight. I am sure I will think of Alice before I fall asleep.

* * * * *

It appeared Isaac's wound had not completely healed, or at least hadn't healed enough for him to be traveling. It seemed his injury had been more severe than was originally thought.

I also began to think about what consequence his injury had on his travel plans. Would he be able to go on, or did he have to find a place to hold up until he was in better condition to continue?

Since he didn't wait until he was completely healed, I wondered how much damage had he done to himself.

If he continued on his journey, there was a strong possibility he would do even more damage to himself. Should that occur, it could cause him to be delayed for some time.

May 18. 1861

    I spent the last couple of days camped by the river due to my injury. My horses were enjoying the rich green grass and the cool clear water of the river. They were getting a lot of rest and seemed to be enjoying a little time off the road. I, on the other hand, had been pretty much laid up for the past three days.

    When I woke on the morning of the sixteenth, my side was burning as if it were on fire. I could hardly move without causing a severe increase in pain. I spent most of the day trying not to move too much. I had my canteen next to me which provided me with water to drink. It didn't matter that I had nothing close by to eat as I didn't feel like eating.

    The worst part was I didn't know if I would get better or if I would end up dying alongside the river with no one at my side. Most of the pain was around the area where I had been shot. I was sure I had at least a touch of a fever.

    I had difficulty seeing if my wound had gotten infected. I could only hope it had not, because I wasn't sure if I could fight an infection. I was feeling very weak and found it hard to move. I spent the better part of the day just resting and trying to get as much sleep as I could.

    The morning of the seventeenth I was feeling a little better. The pain was still there, but not nearly as bad. I was able to move around a little better. I managed to gather a little wood to make a fire, although it took me awhile to get it together. I made a fire in front of my lean-to and made a cup of coffee. I spent the next half hour or so sipping on the hot liquid. It felt good as it slowly warmed my stomach.

    Once I was finished, I laid down to rest beside the fire. I must have fallen asleep as the sun was high in the sky when I opened my eyes again. I again gathered some more wood and built another fire. This time I was able to get to my supplies. I cut a piece of salt pork from the slab. It tasted very good after not eating for over a day and a half.

Since my horses were not in need of anything, I laid back down and rested again. I was beginning to think I was going to be all right if I didn't overdo it. I felt another day here would be best for me. I had everything I needed, at least for now.

The morning of the eighteenth, I woke with very little pain. I thought about packing up my supplies and moving on, but after what had happened before, I decided it was probably not what I should do. I had made the mistake of leaving Lewisburg before my body was ready for the rigors of travel. One more day, maybe two, would certainly not hurt me. In fact, it was probably the best thing for me.

I spent a good part of the day working around my campsite. I gathered enough wood to supply me with fuel for an evening fire as well as a fire for breakfast. I checked my supplies, cooked a meal, made coffee during the day and rested a lot.

I found it was not a bad place to spend a day or two. It was nice to see the sun shine down through the leaves of the trees and listen to the sounds of the river as it flowed by. There were a number of different songbirds that sang in the trees as well.

During the afternoon, I walked down to the edge of the river and took off my clothes. I waded into the river for a bath. The water was cool and felt good on my side. After I finished bathing, I washed out my clothes and hung them on a couple of tree branches to dry.

It felt good to have had a bath. For the first time in several days, I felt clean and refreshed. Putting on clean clothes helped improve the way I felt, too. Once the rest of my clothes were dry, I packed them in my pack and sat down to make dinner. After dinner, I pack up everything except my bedroll and the canvas for my lean-to. I then sat down and wrote this account of what had happened over the past few days.

It is getting dark. It is time to put my pen and journal away for the day.

* * * * *

The one thing I can say about the journal; it was providing me a bit of insight into one man's life, a man who lived over a hundred and fifty years ago. Well, at least a part of his life.

I had to wonder if there was something in Isaac's old mine I had missed. Something that might tell me more about Isaac Madison. I decided I would take another hike up there tomorrow and look around again.

May 19, 1861

It was a beautiful day when I started out again on my journey to the Frontier. The sun was shining and shone bright all day. It was perfect weather for traveling, not too hot, not too cold.

It took me much longer to pack my horses than it had in the past, but I was being very careful not to reopen my wound or to inflame it by putting too much pressure on it. I found it a little painful getting into the saddle, but once I was seated in the saddle the pain went away. Once in the saddle, I decided I would simply let the horse walk in order to avoid any unnecessary jiggling around.

The horses were ready to leave and get back on the road, but I don't know why. They had all the food and water they could want where I had camped. They didn't have to do anything but eat, drink and sleep.

I made it a point of staying in the saddle as much as possible as it was a bit painful to get back into the saddle once I got out of it. Since the horses were walking, the one I was riding didn't seem to mind. I did get out of the saddle for a break around midday. I sat down on the ground and leaned back against a tree while the horses grazed a little while I had a couple of biscuits and some water.

After I ate, I dozed off for a little while. I don't think I slept very long, but it was long enough to be refreshing.

Once I was back in the saddle, we moved on. It was a little easier going as the road was fairly straight and level.

I passed a few farms along the way. Some of the fields had men working in them. I don't know what they were planting, but they were working hard at it.

By late afternoon, I had ridden about as far as I wanted to go for the day. I found a small creek with several trees close to its banks. I decided I would camp there for the night.

I had no more than settled in when I heard the sound of horses running along the road. At first, I wasn't sure what was going on, but soon I saw about fifteen mounted soldiers riding by rather fast. It looked as if they knew where they were going and had to get there in a hurry. It was the first time I had seen any soldiers since the start of my journey. It made me wonder how the war was going.

It is getting dark so I will put up my pen and journal, and get some much-needed rest. I hope to-morrow I will come to a town where I can get some supplies.

* * * * *

It was clear from what he wrote that he knew there was a war going on. He did not mention enough about the soldiers for me to know if they were Union troops or Confederate troops. Nor did he mention what direction they were traveling. It might have helped if I knew what road he was using. He did however mention there were fifteen of them. With those few men, it could have been just a small patrol, or they had recently been formed and were on their way to join up with some other troops. With so little information, it was impossible to know what was going on.

Just from what he wrote, I got the impression he had no interest in whether the troops that rode past his camp were Union or Confederate troops; but I should not have been. He had shown a lack of interest in the war at the very beginnings of his journal.

I understood that he lived in a different time than I, and people had different values and different things to worry about. They also had different attitudes about all sorts of things, from state's rights, to their feelings about Lincoln and about slavery. In fact, there were some that thought once the two armies clashed, the whole idea of war would end. While many believed it would not last past the next fall. Once winter set in, they would all go home, returning to the jobs they had worked before the war started. Isaac might have felt differently.

I wondered what would happen to him if some recruiter happened to see him and was curious why a strong young man as he appeared to be had not joined up to fight. Would he be forced to fight for whichever side caught him first, or would he be imprisoned for running away, or would he be shot as a deserter? Isaac was still a long way from the Mississippi River. If he could get across the Mississippi River before he was caught, he might be able to realize his dream of seeing the Frontier and making his fortune there. The one thing I knew from the fact I had found his body was whatever happened to him over the years, he had either survived the Civil War, or got to the Frontier without being caught. Whether he had fought in it was something I would probably find out as I continued to read his journal.

My plan was to go visit the mine again. I wanted to see if I could find anything else that might help me understand Isaac Madison better.

When morning came, I took a few minutes to read a little more of the journal. I convinced myself it would help me focus on Isaac while I searched the mine for more things of interest.

May 20, 1861

The early part of the day had been rather pleasant as I rode on west. My injury was not bothering me very much. In fact, I was feeling as if I could make a good number of miles to-day. The weather was good during the morning, but by mid-afternoon it was looking as if it might rain. It looked as if the weather was going to cut my day short and I would not make as many miles as I had hoped.

As the clouds moved in and the wind started to come up, I began looking for a place where I could hole up at least until the storm blew over. I noticed what appeared to be an abandoned barn not too far off the road. Since there was no house anywhere near the barn, I thought it might provide me with at least some protection from the storm.

I rode over to the barn, got off my horse and tied them to a fence post. I opened the door to the barn and looked in. The barn was empty except for a few bales of straw. When I stepped inside, I disturbed an owl that had made his home in the barn. I saw no other critters. I seriously doubted that there were very many mice or rats living there with an owl as the largest and most dangerous resident. I saw nothing else in the barn.

I led my horses into the barn and put each of them in a stall. I had no more than taken my saddle off my horse when it started to rain. My horses were pleased to be in out of the rain. As for me, I found a pile of straw that looked like it might be a rather comfortable place to lay out my bedroll.

The barn was rather drafty, but the roof appeared to be solid. At least it didn't leak. With all the dry straw in the barn, I decided to build a fire inside the barn was not a good idea. Since the rain was coming in from the northwest, I went to the southeast corner of the barn and looked out the small door. There was an open lean-to built on the south side of the barn and away from the wind. The floor was dirt and there was nothing in the lean-to. It would make a good place to build a small fire to cook my dinner.

I gathered up several pieces of wood that were under the lean-to and built a small fire. I had biscuits, salt pork and water for dinner. I was getting a little tired of salt pork, but I had not come to a village where I might be able to get a hot home cooked meal.

After eating my meal, I again looked around the barn. I found a bale of hay in the loft. I pushed it out of the loft to the dirt floor below then fed it to my horses.

As it began to grow dark, I sat down on my bedroll to bring my journal up to date. Since it is growing too dark to continue, I will put up my pen and journal and get some rest.

* * * * *

After reading the May 20, 1861 entry, I left the house for a trip to Isaac's mine. His last entry was pretty routine. I found nothing of any real interest. From what he said, it sounded like something I would have done under similar circumstances. It also sounded as if he was feeling much better.

I left my house and drove to where I had parked my pickup truck the last time I had been to the mine. After putting my backpack on, I began the walk into the hills. It took me the better part of an hour to find the narrow, almost invisible, trail that had taken me to Isaac's mine. I was beginning to think I might not be able to find my way back to the mine. It took me another hour to find the place where I could see the mine through the trees and where the rocks had fallen away from the side of the hill exposing the entrance to the mine.

When I finally got to the entrance, I took my flashlight out of my pack and began looking over the entrance. I was looking for any signs of weakness in the rocks that might have occurred since the last time I was there, and caused rocks to fall. I couldn't find any problems that might cause me harm, but I knew I was still taking a risk going into the mine.

I slowly and carefully entered the mine, being very careful not to disturb anything. This time I had brought with me a digital camera. I wanted pictures of the inside of the mine for future reference and so I could study the details of the mine once I returned home. With each step into the mine, I would take pictures of the walls, ceiling and floor.

When I got to the location in the mine where Isaac's body was, I took a number of pictures of him from several different angles. I took close-ups of his gun and gun belt, of his skeleton and of what remained of his clothes. I took a lot of pictures as I might want to study them in detail on my computer. I could make them large enough on the computer that I could see every little detail.

It was while I was taking pictures of his skull that I noticed what looked like a crack in the back of his skull. I had not noticed it the last time I was there. It was obvious he had been struck in the back of the head. I had no idea what might have caused the injury. However, it was probably an injury that had occurred shortly before he died since there was no sign of calcification on the bones.

Finding the head injury made we want to take a closer look at the rest of the skeleton. On closer examination of his skeleton, I found an old injury to one of the lower ribs on his left side. I took a picture of it. I knew it was old because it had healed and was calcified. My first thought was the old injury might have been from his shoot-out in Lewisburg in May of 1861.

I continued to look for other injuries and took pictures of those I found. I discovered that he had signs of several broken bones in his left hand, a broken bone in his lower right arm and what looked like a serious break to the femur of his right leg. It was fast becoming clear that Isaac had led a hard life. I had no idea how he got so many broken bones. I was hoping that his journal would clear up at least some of them for me.

When I had found out as much as I could from the skeleton, I started looking over the area around the skeleton. In the area where I had found the skeleton and the metal box, I found several old one-quart jars. I actually found them by accident. They had been hidden behind rocks on narrow rock shelves carefully carved into the rocky walls. It looked as if the rocks had been set in front of them to hide the jars. It was only because of the flash of my camera when I took pictures of the area that I discovered them. I found three jars in all. Two of the jars were full of gold dust and small nuggets, and one was only about half full. It quickly became obvious Isaac had struck it rich. He had found the fortune he had set out to find. However, it was also beginning to look like he had not lived long enough to enjoy it.

I slowly began to move back deeper into the mine being very careful not to disturb anything. The last thing I wanted was the roof to fall in on me. The further I got from the entrance, the more nervous I felt about being in the mine.

When I was about forty feet deep into the mine, I found a fairly large box. It looked like a wooden chest. It appeared to be in pretty good shape. When I thought about it, it was not so surprising. The mine was dry. We had had a very wet spring, yet this far back in the mine everything was dry. I took a number of pictures of it from several different angles. After giving it a good looking over, I pried the chest open. I was rather surprised at what I found.

Inside the chest were a couple of rock picks, a coil of fuse, and several small glass jars of a pale, yellow liquid. The glass jars looked as if they had been packed in straw. With the other things in the chest, it didn't take a genius to figure out what was in the jars. It was nitroglycerin. I don't know much about nitroglycerin, but I had heard, or read somewhere, that it only gets better with age. Meaning it became even more unstable the longer it set around. It was clear that it had been in this mine for a very long time. It was not something I wanted to move or even touch.

My first thought was to notify the authorities immediately, but I hesitated. I didn't want them to come in here and disturb everything before I had a chance to find out as much as I could about the mine and the man who had mined here. I seriously doubted anyone else would find it, but then I had stumbled on it by accident. That being the case, someone else could stumble on it, too. There was only one thing for me to do. That was to get out of the mine everything that was important to discovering who Isaac Madison was, and anything of real or historic value.

While taking all the pictures I wanted, I discovered another small metal box. It was hidden under some loose rocks. I never would have found it if I hadn't tripped over a couple of the rocks which moved them away from the box. I decided not to spend any more time than was necessary in the mine. I took the metal box and the three jars of gold and put them in my backpack. I took one more look around, then left the mine. I would notify the authorities of the explosives in the mine and even show them where it was, if they ask. I could think of no other reason to return.

As I was walking back to my pickup truck, I got to thinking about Isaac. I thought it would be a nice gesture to find Isaac a nicer resting spot. I also got to thinking about his journal and some of the things I had taken from the mine. If I told anyone about the things I found in the mine, they might end up taking them away from me before I found out all there was to know about Isaac Madison. Once the mine was made public, which would happen if the authorities found out about it, people would be crawling all over the hills looking for the mine. I couldn't help thinking of the old adage, "Three can keep a secret if two are dead". In this case, one was dead, and as far as I knew I was the only other person who knew about the mine. I began to think it would be better not to tell anyone, at least for now. Maybe I could think of some way to close off the mine forever, by myself.

I returned home with my pictures, the jars of gold and the small metal box. I put the jars on one of my bookshelves, behind some books. The small metal box, I set on the shelf with the other metal box. I would wait to open it until I had some more information on Isaac's life. I was tired and hungry after my day of hiking to the mine and exploring it. My return to the pickup truck from the mine had been hard with my backpack being very heavy. In fact, it had taken me a couple of trips to the mine and back to get the jars full of gold to my pickup. It was time for me to get a shower and something to eat, then head off to bed.

When the morning sun started to shine in my window, I woke up. There was no doubt I had put in a hard day yesterday. My muscles were letting me know just how hard a day it had been. I got up and had my breakfast before I went into my den to continue to read Isaac Madison's journal. I sat down at my desk and carefully open the journal.

May 21, 1861

This morning, I woke to a less than pleasant day. There was a thick fog hanging over the fields and woods surrounding the barn where I had spent the night. The air had a chill to it that went clear to the bone. I had hoped for a better day, but at least it was not raining.

When I tried to get up, I suddenly felt sick to my stomach. The only thing I could think of was the wound in my side had been irritated by yesterday's travel. Since my horses didn't seem to be in need of anything at the moment, I laid back down to rest in the hope I would feel better later.

I don't know how long I slept, but when I woke up there was a young woman standing next to me. She was just looking down at me as if I was some strange sort of creature. I had no idea where she had come from or who she was. All I could think of was to say "Hi".

She didn't reply. She simply turned and looked back toward the door as if she had heard something. I heard what sounded like footsteps. Suddenly there was a man walking into the barn. He was a rather tall and very nice-looking man. He appeared to be some years older than the woman, old enough to be her father. He looked down at me for a moment then looked at the young woman. The look on his face caused me to worry about what he might do. I had no idea who he was.

The man asked me what I was doing in the barn. I tried to explain that I had taken shelter from last evening's storm in the barn, and I would gladly pay for the hay my horses ate.

The man asked if I was a deserter. He didn't ask from which army I might have deserted. I tried to explain that I was not, but I wasn't sure he believed me. I certainly didn't want him to see the bullet wound in my side. It would surely convince him that I lied and that I was really a deserter.

The young woman told the man that I didn't look well. He quickly agreed, and suggested they take me up to their *house where they could help me. I didn't want to go, but had little choice in the matter. I was not only feeling sick; I was feeling rather weak.*

The man left the barn while the young woman stayed behind. She asked me how I was feeling and what I thought was wrong. I told her how I felt and that I had been shot awhile back. She seemed to get concerned.

When the man returned with a wagon, she told him everything I had told her about my injury. He looked at me with suspicion in his eyes. That was when he asked me if I was a deserter again. I told him how I had come to be shot, but I doubted he believed me.

It wasn't until they got me in the wagon and took me to their home that I began to understand his suspicions. On a small round table in the bedroom where they put me was the picture of a man in a Union Army uniform. It was a picture of the man I met in the barn.

I was not feeling well and I was beginning to feel as if I had a fever. I told the young woman I was tired and would like to rest. When I closed my eyes, I heard the young woman leave the room. As soon as she was gone, I wrote what had been going on during the day. I had no idea if they would take my journal away from me or not, but my plan was to get as much rest as I could during the day, then sneak away when it was dark. If they read my journal, maybe they would believe I had been shot in a gunfight, but they would also find out I had left for The Frontier to avoid having to fight in a war I didn't want any part of.

Now that I have finished writing these notes, I will hide my journal in my clothes while I wait for darkness to come.

* * * * *

I found it interesting there was a Union officer living in that part of what was Virginia at that time. However, the western part of Virginia was not happy about the secession of

Virginia from the Union. The fact there was no mention of the man being in uniform when Isaac was discovered in the barn, might indicate he was either a retired officer and had not been called back to duty. There was also the possibility he had been a Union officer, but chose to take the side of the Confederates as did a number of the U. S. officers who were originally from the South.

It was clear that Isaac was about to find himself in the middle between two armies. If he had a fever and passed out, it was likely that either the man or the young woman would find the bullet wound in his side. Although Isaac had told them about the bullet wound, it could prove hard for Isaac to convince them he got the wound in a gunfight on a street in Lewisburg.

Isaac was going to have a hard time over the next few days. From his writings, it appeared the wound in Isaac's side had once again flared up. There might have been something left in the wound that caused the infection to keep coming back. If it was not taken care of, it could fester and cause him problems for a very long time.

I decided I would take a break and take a look at some of the pictures I had taken in the mine. Once I had the pictures loaded into my computer, I began looking through them. It was a little strange to me how much the pictures showed what I had missed seeing with the naked eye. The fact I could enlarge them on the computer screen helped.

In several of the pictures, I noticed little things that shined from the flash of my camera. Some of them I could recognize, some of them I couldn't. When I enlarged the picture, I could see little specks of either mica or gold in the rock walls. I was sure that most of them were mica.

I did notice one thing that I had not seen while in the mine. One of the photos of the large box containing the mining supplies showed the letters U.S.A. The letters were badly faded and very hard to read, but that was what had been defiantly printed on the side of the box. I had seen boxes like it before. It was actually a U.S. Army chest commonly used by soldiers, especially officers.

After spending several hours studying the pictures, I decided it was time to take a break. After I finished my lunch, I turned to the next page and was surprised to see the date.

May 27, 1861

I woke up with the sun shining in the window. I looked around the room. It was a beautiful bedroom with lace doilies on the table next to the bed along with a lamp and a bible. The first thing that came to mind was I had slept all the way through the night.

It wasn't until the pretty young woman came into the room. I recognized her as the woman from the barn. It had been her and her father who had brought me to this house. I could remember them from the barn, but that was about all. It wasn't until she explained what had happened to me over the past six days that I realized just how sick I really was. She also told me what her name was. It was Susan McHenry.

According to Susan, the wound in my side had flared up and was infected. Her father had called the local doctor. He reopened the wound and found it had not been cleaned out as well as it should have been. She said he had found small pieces of cloth in the wound that caused the infection to flare up. The doctor cut away the infected tissue then cleaned the wound. He left the wound open to allow it to heal better. During the past six days I had run a fever as I tried to fight off the infection.

She also told me that her father knew the wound was from a bullet, and he thought I might have gotten shot while trying to desert from the army. It was easy to understand why he might think that.

She asked me if I was a deserter from the Confederate Army. I told her I was not and how I got the wound, again. From the look on her face, I wasn't sure she believed me. She even said it was okay if I had deserted, and they would not turn me in.

Later in the afternoon, Susan's father came in the room to have a talk with me. We talked about the war going on in the east and that it was spilling over into the area. Most of the people living in the area of Mr. McHenry's farm tended to *favor the Union. However, there were some who leaned toward the South.*

He talked about the importance of keeping the Union together, something I had not thought much about. I listened to him. The more he talked, the more I came to see his point of view.

During the day, Susan had brought me meals and sat with me while I ate. We talked about what might happen to the country, and to Virginia, if the Union split. She told me about the talk that Virginia might be split up into Virginia in the east and West Virginia in the west. She wasn't too sure how she felt about it, but she appeared to understand why it might be a good thing.

When it was starting to get dark, she left me alone. I wrote in my Journal, in an effort to keep it as current as possible. I had a lot to think about.

I had to wonder what our country would be like if the Confederacy should win. Would we end up being two different countries? It was already beginning to look like Virginia would be split, probably along the Allegheny Mountains ridge. Or would it be one country with the South being the leaders?

What would happen to this country if the North won? How would the North treat the South for seceding?

There were so many questions to be answered. I had to think about what I believed in. It would not be easy, but once I figured it out, I would have to make a stand. For the first time it didn't seem right to run off when my country needed me. I just had to decide which side I needed to be on. I was a Southerner, born and raised, but I didn't agree with a lot of the things the South stood for. I also didn't think the South was doing the right thing by seceding from the Union.

It is getting late, and I am tired. I need some rest. I will take my time deciding what I need to do while my body heals. But for now, I will put my journal aside and get some rest.

*****

I found Isaac's last few comments to be rather interesting. He had started out his Journal wanting to escape from having anything to do with the war.

He was now feeling the need to possibly rethink his position. Maybe it was a sign of him starting to mature. I wondered if his decision to rethink how he felt about the war, and what was happening in Virginia, was due to the young lady he had just met. Whatever the reason, Isaac had some serious thinking to do, and some serious decisions to make.

If Isaac was to make the decision to join an army to fight, it would be my guess he would join the Union Army. But right now, he had to give himself a chance to heal. He had been very lucky he was found by the young woman. If he had been found by the troops that rode by the other day, he might have been arrested as a deserter. They might not have believed the bullet hole in his side was from a gunfight.

It was my guess the troops Isaac had seen had been Confederates. The reason for that thought was the fact at the time the southeastern part of what was to become West Virginia was still leaning toward the South.

Secondly, I got the impression they were headed east which was where the most serious fighting was likely to be. They also seemed to be in a very big hurry. That, along with the direction they were headed, made me think they might be headed east to join up with others to form a large force in the east in preparation for battle after the battle of Bull Run.

If I remember my history, the major part of the Civil War began primarily in the east, in northern Virginia. I know the attack on Fort Sumter in South Carolina was on April 12, 1861 and was the first act of any real hostility by the South.

The first major infantry fighting was the first battle of Manassas, or Bull Run, on July 21, 1861, in northern Virginia near Washington DC. That was less than two months away from the date on Isaac's previous entry. It only made sense that what troops were in the west would have been called to arms in the hope of winning the first battle and thereby shortening any possibility of a long conflict.

Right now, the only thing Isaac had to worry about was to get himself fit to do whatever he decided to do. If he was to continue his westward track, he would have to be in good health. He would also have to be careful to avoid contact with any military unit from either side. If he was to join the army, either one, he would have to be fit enough to fight. I couldn't help but think he would get into the fight. I had a feeling that if he decided to join the fight, the side he would be on might be partly influenced by Susan, and maybe by Mr. McHenry.

The only way I was going to find out what his decision would be was to read on in his journal. I leaned forward in my desk chair and turned the page.

June 1, 1861

I have spent the past few days walking around the McHenry farm. It is a very nice place. Susan has spent a good deal of the time with me. She is a very lovely girl. I can't help but feel a fondness for her.

To-day, I have been walking around the farm alone as I have a lot to think about. Mr. McHenry has asked me to join him. He had offered his services to the Union Army as an artillery officer, a position he held until about five years ago. He had received a letter telling him where and when to report. He asked me to be his adjutant and he would recommend I be made a lieutenant. Mr. McHenry was a colonel. I knew very little about the military, let alone about artillery, but he said he would teach me all I needed to know. He smiled when he said all I needed to know was how to take orders from him. We laughed about it, but he did agree to help me learn the basics of being in the military and being an officer before we would go. I would learn about artillery later.

During our talks together, I did find out his first name was Patrick. He said it was a good old fashioned Irish name, and I could call him Patrick when there was no one else around who could hear us, otherwise I was to call him, Colonel. Patrick said he had an officer's manual I could study while I was recovering from my injury. He promised to give it to me after dinner.

It was strange, but I found myself looking forward to getting the manual from him. Although I had not actually told myself I would join the Union Army with him, I think in my mind I had already made the decision to join with him.

When it was time for dinner, Susan came looking for me. She found me sitting under a tree behind the house. I was thinking about what she would think of me joining her father and going off to war with him. I didn't actually think much about the war for there was much optimism that the war would not last long.

I took Susan's hand in mine as we walked back to the house for dinner. She appeared pleased that I was showing her a little attention, but then I had grown quite fond of her. It had passed through my mind that once we got to know each other better, we might fall in love. I wasn't sure, but I might have fallen in love with her already. However, I didn't feel it was a good time for me to make my feelings for her known with a war growing on the horizon, a war I intended to be a part of.

We sat at the table and enjoyed a very good roast pork dinner with all the things that went with such a dinner. There were potatoes and gravy, corn, and cornbread with thick rich butter and apple butter. Patrick also broke open a nice bottle of wine as he said it was sort of a celebration.

After dinner, Patrick and I excused ourselves and went into the parlor. Once we were there, Patrick gave me a book. It was an artillery officer's field manual. He suggested I get started learning what was in it as soon as possible. I assured him I would, and I would also ask him about anything I didn't understand. We talked for a little while before he excused himself and left the parlor.

It was only a few minutes after he left before Susan came into the parlor. We sat and talked for awhile. She was obviously worried about my going off to war with her father, but she did a pretty good job of hiding it. I told her that I was getting tired. She suggested I go ahead and go to bed to get some rest.

I smiled at her, then turned and left the room after telling her goodnight. I went directly to my room and began reading the manual. I found it rather interesting. It turned out to be very late by the time I put the book down. I made my entry in my journal before putting out the light, and turning in for the night.

* * * * *

There it is. Isaac had made a decision to join the army. I was sure Colonel McHenry would get him in as his adjutant. At that time in history and with the pressure of a pending war, it would have been relatively easy for someone with the rank of colonel to pick his own adjutant. It might take a bit of exaggeration on the colonel's part, but he could pull it off. It would make it easier since Isaac was well-educated.

It was interesting to see the change in Isaac as he spent time with the colonel and his daughter. He was not only convinced he should do his part to keep the Union intact, but he had grown fond of Susan, too.

I was not familiar with the manual the colonel had loaned Isaac, but I am sure it gave instructions on such things as the order of command, how to treat fellow officers, and how to direct or give orders to those of lower rank.

Since it appeared that the manual was for artillery officers, I was sure it gave instruction on proven uses of canons, such as placement of them, and how to use them effectively in battle. I would think it would have been a very detailed book in the use of different types of canons of the day.

The fact Isaac found it very interesting might have been due to the fact he had probably never even seen such a book before. The manual showing how and where to position the canons would have been of great interest to him. However, as an adjutant, he would most likely spend most of his time working very closely to the colonel and might have time to learn more about the uses of canons in the field.

I could hardly wait to see how things worked out for him. I sat there looking at the journal for several minutes before I turned the page.

I read the next few pages in the Journal. Each entry was fairly short and really didn't give a lot of information. Most of it showed that Isaac was doing a lot of reading and a lot of exercises to get back in shape. It also indicated his wound was healing well.

There were also a few sentences about his feelings for Susan. Their feelings for each other had apparently grown fairly fast. I had to wonder what would happen when it was time for him to leave for war.

I finally came to the entry for the day just before he was to leave with the colonel for war. I took a great deal of interest in the entry.

June 10, 1861

To-day, Colonel McHenry got our orders to report to the nearest railroad station as soon as possible. Our orders were to take the train to Philippi where we were to join up with General Robert Patterson's Division and take command of one of his artillery companies. The orders told of the defeat of the Confederates at the Battle of Philippi on June third. We were to join up and provide support for the infantry that was there to protect the railroad. It was the first time I really began to think we would actually be getting into a war.

When I first heard the orders from the colonel, I didn't know what to say. I had wondered how Susan would take the news. As for myself, I felt I was ready. I had regained most of my strength, and I was no longer having any pain. The infection was gone and I had healed very well. I felt I was also ready to put into practice what I had learned from the manual Colonel McHenry had given me.

Shortly after dinner, the colonel gave me a package that had arrived several days ago. He told me to open it. Inside were brand new uniforms. Included were lieutenant bars for the shoulders. He suggested I go try them on and that Susan might like to put the bars on my shoulders for me after he swore me in.

I could hardly wait to try it on. I took the package up to my room, took out one uniform and put it on. I stood looking at myself in the mirror in the corner of the room. I don't know why, but I felt as if I had done something very important in my life.

I returned to the dining room and found Susan and the colonel were gone. I quickly discovered they had gone into the parlor. When I walked in, I found them waiting for me. The colonel had changed into his uniform and was standing next to the fireplace with a bible in his hand.

He told me where he wanted me to stand. I stood in front of him. Susan stood at his side. He held out the bible and I put my hand on it. In a very serious and formal manner, he had me swear my allegiance to the United States of America. He then told me that I was to be a lieutenant, and asked Susan to pin the bars on my shoulders. And just like that, I was a first lieutenant in the United States Army.

Susan rose up on her tiptoes and kissed me on the lips, and the colonel saluted me. I returned the salute to the colonel, then kissed Susan.

The colonel also gave me an officer's sword. He said "no officer should be without one". It was only then that the colonel told me that we would be leaving in the morning. That statement sort of took the wind out of me. I looked at Susan and she looked at me. I had hoped I would have a couple of days before we would have to leave.

The colonel excused himself from the parlor leaving Susan and me alone. As soon as he was gone, Susan threw her arms around my neck and kissed me hard. I wrapped her in my arms and held her close. I had never felt the way I did at that moment for anyone. I had never been kissed like that, either.

The fact I was going to have to leave Susan seemed to override everything else. What should have been something very special had become the one thing that spoiled the day.

I spent most of the evening with Susan. We sat and talked and cried. I was going to miss her. It took us a long time to say goodnight. It was late when I got back to my room. I had told her that I would write to her, and I will. She promised to write me every day. She said she would keep my letters as a journal of what was going on. She wanted me to write my letters like I wrote my journal so she could read about what I was doing and how I felt and what I thought. I promised her I would. She made me promise to let her read my journal when the war was over.

I kissed her several times at the door to my room. It was getting very late and I had to leave in the morning. I finally *watched her as she went down the hall to her room. As soon as she was out of sight, I went in my room and wrote this.*

* * * * *

I thought about what Isaac had written. He was now an artillery officer. It was a little safer place to be than in the infantry. He was not as likely to get into any hand-to-hand combat fighting, but the enemy's artillery was likely to be trying to put his artillery out of action. That was the way things were done.

The fact Isaac had lived to become a gold miner showed me that he had survived the war. Having seen his skeleton, I had no idea if any of the broken bones his skeleton showed were from his time in the army. I had no idea if he had been injured during the war, if he had been a prisoner during the war, or if he had made it through the war without a scratch.

The only way I was to get answers to the many questions that came to mind was to continue to read his journal. I read several more pages about what he was doing.

June 15, 1861

We finally arrived at Philippi this morning by train. We were immediately given orders as to where we were to set up our camp and the area that General Patterson wanted us to position our guns. As soon as we got our camp set up and had our guns in position, the colonel and I went to report that our position was set and get further orders.

The general told us that we were assigned to a newly formed artillery battery and to assist in guarding the railroad. We were to begin training our men for battle immediately. It was then that I found out that most of the men in our artillery battery were no better trained than I. It was also when I found out that I would be responsible for the training of the men, and would be in command of one of the batteries. That bit of information made me a little concerned. The only thing I knew about artillery was what I had learned from the manual the colonel had given me. I wanted more than anything to show the colonel that I was up to the task.

Fortunately for me, one of the sergeants, Sergeant Whitmore, who was assigned to my battery knew a good deal about the use and positioning of artillery. I took him aside and we had a very nice talk. He was a very understanding man and we hit it off right away. He agreed to help me learn what I needed to know, and help train the other men.

After talking to Colonel McHenry about the sergeant, he agreed to have him assigned directly to me. I would be spending a lot of time watching him as he instructed the men, and then he would spend extra time with me showing me how to set up and position artillery. I assured him it would get him an extra stripe if we did a good job.

Another of our duties was to help with the guarding of the railroad. Since we would also be in training, so to speak, the general limited our guard duties to the area closest to the railroad station, switching yard and the location of our battery. We had enough men that we could split up the guard duty into two shifts, thus giving our men time for the training they needed and still provide protection for the railroad station and switchyard.

I made rounds of the switchyard and railroad station with Sergeant Whitmore to make sure that we had the place well covered. We had been told there was a strong possibility that there were Confederate spies in the area and we should put out guards to protect the artillery as well. I made up a quick schedule for guard duty and posted it.

I just finished my rounds and it is late. It is time for me to put my pen and journal away for tonight. It has been a very long day.

* * * * *

Most of what I read over the next few entries had to do with the daily routine of being a soldier doing guard duty and training. Isaac was even getting some training on the use of cannons and was doing pretty well.

From several of his writings, the guarding of the railroad was apparently a rather boring job. I was sure it was for an artillery unit. After all, most of the action in that part of the country in the early days of the war was mostly guerrilla warfare.

It appears that Isaac got lucky. In among the men that he was to train was a man who knew what he was doing and was willing to help train them. Many of the recruits were men who had just come off the farm and had never been very far from home. There was a rush to build up a fighting force. Most of the recruits had only a minimal amount of any kind of training. They had learned how to use a rifle, which most of them knew how to do before they joined up. They had learned how to march, how to wear their uniforms, a few basics on how to fight as a group, and most of all, how to take orders. They were rushed through training as fast as possible, then placed with a unit. The same thing had been done at the time of other wars like WWI and WWII.

Most of those placed with artillery units had never used a cannon before. Some probably had not even seen one up close, if at all. The job of training them as artillery men was now the job of First Lieutenant Isaac Madison.

When he first was told he would have to teach them what they needed to know, I would think he was probably wondering what he had gotten himself into. I imagine it would have scared him half to death. I could only imagine the relief he must have felt when he discovered he had a man under his command who knew all about cannons and how to use them effectively. But more importantly, he was willing to teach the men as well as Isaac.

I was sure it would not take Isaac very long to catch on as he was a fairly smart young man. He had the advantage of being able to read. Many of the men joining up during the Civil War had not had more than a fifth grade education, and many of them lacked any kind of formal education at all. If they had grown up on a farm in the hill country of Virginia or anywhere in the Alleghany Mountains Region, most of them had to work on the farm as soon as they were old enough to help.

All I could think about was that Isaac had his hands full if he and his sergeant were going to turn the small group of men into a well-trained fighting unit. And if I had to guess, they didn't have a lot of time to get it done.

The next few entries in the Journal were filled with some of the problems they encountered in training the men, but over all the men apparently were able to catch on pretty well. I noticed he didn't write every day, and when he did, it was short.

June 20, 1861

I have been very busy with the training of the men I have been given. I have been working from sun up to well after dark. Most of my time had been in the training of the troops in the use of the cannons. My sergeant has been a godsend.

After to-day's morning training session, we are showing some very good improvement as horse artillery, as we are often called. They have learned to load and make ready to fire within a good time. They are not the fastest, but they have very good reload times.

This afternoon we practiced going from horse artillery on the road, to ready to fire the cannons. That is, the time it took us to unhook the cannon from the caisson and limber, and have it ready to fire were very good times. We did it several times which also helped us with our times required to move out quickly. These exercises were important for changing positions when required as the battle changes.

The men are working hard, but they seem to understand that doing well here may very well save their lives in battle, and the lives of others such as those in the infantry. I continually let them know that. I think the men are beginning to look up to me. That might be because I get right in there and work beside them. They see I'm not afraid of hard work.

By the end of the day, we are all tired and need some rest, but my day is not done. After the evening meal, which I often take with my men, I have a meeting with the colonel to report on the progress of my battery. Thank goodness, it is often a rather short meeting.

After the meeting, I make rounds of the guards that are on duty around the railroad station and switchyard. When all is done, I'm pretty tired. I don't often feel like writing in my journal. I am tired now, but will write tonight as I have missed several days. But I will keep this short and get some sleep.

* * * * *

It seems that Isaac is doing well. It looks like he is shaping his men into a well-trained fighting force. I get the impression they are a little short of artillery officers. Isaac was supposed to be an adjutant to Colonel McHenry, but now he is a lieutenant in command of an artillery battery.

Not knowing how artillery units were formed in those days, I went to my computer to find out. After reading about the formation of the components of Union artillery at the time of the Civil War, I found that it was a little strange that Isaac would be in command of a battery.

The basic unit of Union artillery during the Civil War was the battery, which usually consisted of six guns. The battery of six guns was normally commanded by a captain. Usually, a section consisting of two guns was under the control of a lieutenant. Artillery brigades were usually composed of five batteries which were commanded by colonels.

This bit of information confirmed the fact that they had a shortage of officers. Even so, Isaac seemed to be making the best of it.

The next few entries indicated his artillery battery was steadily improving and his days were busy from sunup to past sundown. It wasn't until I got to the entry dated in early July when it really got interesting. It looked as if things were going to begin to change rapidly for him now.

July 5, 1861

To-day we received orders to move out and head for Berkeley County. We are to join up with General George McClellan there. It could be that there is going to be a big push east to stop the Confederates from moving into the southern part of Pennsylvania and into Maryland. We would be going there to help protect Pennsylvania and Maryland from the Confederates. The orders were not clear as to what our duties are except to get there as soon as possible. It means we will be on the move for several days.

It seems we missed out on a skirmish. It was somewhere near Hoke's Run from what I have heard. Reports about what happened are not very good. What we have heard was a Confederate Officer by the name of Thomas Jackson raided the Baltimore and Ohio railroad terminal. He apparently captured some railroad locomotives and rolling stock. I'm not sure what happened as far as the outcome of his attack on the railroad.

I have missed Susan so much. I don't know why, but I feel homesick although I have not had a lot of time to think about it. I have not been homesick for my family, but homesick for Susan. It might have something to do with where we are headed and why. We will be moving further away from Colonel McHenry's farm and Susan. It also looks like we might be getting into our very first encounter with the Confederate Army.

I have just been called to Colonel McHenry's tent. Will continue this later.

I just got back from a briefing. It seems we are going in a different direction than I wrote about earlier, but that's the way things go around here.

We are going to head for Barbour County. I have no idea what is going on there. I have to put this up and get some sleep. Colonel McHenry said we will be leaving at dawn.

*****

It looked as if Isaac was finally going to see some action. I had no idea where they were headed in Barbour County. In fact, I had no idea where Barbour County was located. I was also not very familiar with the early parts of the war, especially those in the western counties of what was then still Virginia. I took a few minutes to look it up on my computer and to find out what had been taking place in that part of the country during the very early part of the war.

After a few minutes on my computer to find out a little about the war in the western part of Virginia, I discovered they were probably headed for the Battle of Laurel Hill. The battle covered a fair part of Barbour County, from Martinsburg to Hinesville. The actual battle went on from July seventh thru the eleventh of 1861. Apparently, a Union Officer named Morris got the best of the Confederate forces in the five days of skirmishing at Belington.

In looking at the map, there were a good number of small skirmishes in what was to become West Virginia in the early part of the war.

Isaac may have joined up with a unit that would be moving around the western side of the Alleghany Mountains quite a bit. There was always the possibility he would be sent back to join McClellan in the northern part of Virginia.

I decided I would do a little studying of the battles in West Virginia. It seems that there were a number of conflicts in what is now West Virginia, a lot more than I knew about. Most of the battles were not what some would consider major battles. I noticed that General Jackson was involved in a number of them. In the early years of the war, the Confederacy seemed to win most of the battles.

I found the names of the battles to be interesting. There was the Battle of Camp Allegheny in December of 1861, the Battle of Hancock in January of 1862, the Battle of the Henry

Clark House in May of 1862, the Battle of Princeton Courthouse in 1862, the Battle of Harpers Ferry, the Battle of Charleston in September of 1862, and so on.

Many of the battles revolved around controlling the railroads. That only made sense as the quick movement of troops and equipment was often very important to winning a battle. Without the railroads, it would be difficult to move things rapidly from one place to another. A battle could quickly be won or lost on the ability to move men and equipment quickly. The rail system was the ideal way to move things quickly at that time in our country's history.

It was time to read some more of Isaac's Journal to see what happened to him. Did he actually go to Barbour County, or did he end up going somewhere else? I turned the page and found the very next day he had written in his Journal.

July 6, 1861

Early this morning we received a new set of orders. Our entire Artillery Brigade led by Colonel McHenry was reassigned to join up with the Seventh West Virginia Volunteer Infantry Regiment. The Seventh had been assigned to guard the railroads and we were to join up with them at Morgantown. It looks like our duties will remain the same, that is, we will be providing support for the Seventh Volunteer Infantry. We will all be assigned to the Railroad District of Western Virginia to provide guard duty for the railroads against Confederate raids. We had had this kind of duty before. However, it is my understanding that the raids are becoming more frequent and with greater numbers of troops.

Since we were ready to move out, we started toward Morgantown to-day. It is beginning to look like we are going to really get into the war. It has been a long day. All the men and animals are tired. We should join up with the Seventh the day after tomorrow.

I have finished my rounds to make sure everything is secure. The horses are showing the wear of the days of hard travel. I am hoping we will be able to give them some well needed rest when we get to Morgantown. The men are faring pretty well. I have had to remind a couple of them to be sure to take time to eat something. There were several of them that decided they want to sleep instead of eat, but that will hurt them in the march to Morgantown. They have to eat.

Just a personal note before I turn in for the night. I have not received a letter from Susan for over a week. That is probably due to our moving around so much, but I am sure her letters will catch up with me soon, but I miss reading them.

* * * * *

It is becoming clear that Isaac is turning out to be an officer who is concerned with the welfare of the men and the animals assigned to his artillery battery. It is important for him to do that as their lives may depend on it.

I took a few minutes to look into the Seventh West Virginia Volunteer Infantry Regiment. I discovered Isaac is in for some of the most famous and bloodiest battles of the Civil War as he moved around with the Seventh. I also noted that the Seventh West Virginia Regiment spent most of the fall of 1861 under the Railroad District command. The Seventh Volunteer Infantry Regiment were involved in a number of skirmishes in what is now West Virginia during the remainder of the year, 1861.

In 1862, the Seventh fought in the Valley Campaign in Nathaniel Bank's V Corps, seeing action in a number of small and lesser-known engagements before fighting in the Battle of Port Republic in late May, of 1862.

The Seventh was reassigned to the II Corps and remained with them until the end of the war. Isaac's artillery battery was still assigned to the Seventh and put under the command of Nathan Kimball's Brigade.

In my search for information on Kimball's Brigade, I discovered that during the September 1862 Maryland Campaign, the Seventh Virginia took part in the attack on the Sunken Road at Antietam, also known as the Battle of Sharpsburg, or the Battle of Amtietam.

Since I had no information on Kimball's Brigade in that fight, I was not sure how Isaac fared. I had not gotten that far in his journal. The only information I had from his journal so far was they were headed in that general direction. I was still some time away from the Battle of Antietam in his journal.

I once again turned to the journal and began to read. Isaac's writings were interesting, but didn't shine much light on him as a person. I wanted to know Isaac, the man and what it was that compelled him to become a gold miner. I also wanted to know what things in his life forged the man into what he became. It was obvious his time in the Army did a lot to mature him and give him some direction he didn't have when he started out on his quest to the west.

However, I did find his account of the war interesting. I did find out from his almost daily writings that he had become not only a good soldier, but he was a man who had a deep concern for his men. He wrote little about the battles, but more about the men. He no longer wrote about himself and his feelings. His apparent view of the battles was from a limited point of view. He could often not see much of what was going on except for right around his position and from what information he could pick up from others and from the messages he would receive from the messengers.

Since I had found out Kimball's Brigade had fought at Antietam, I was very much interested in getting to that part of Isaac's journal. I needed to know how he did in a big battle. I also wondered if Colonel McHenry survived the battle. There had been very little mention of him in Isaac's journal for some time. I knew Isaac survived the war because he died in his mine well after the war was over, but I didn't know what happened to Colonel McHenry.

Once again I began turning pages and reading his journal. He apparently spent a lot of time moving from one position to another all over the northeast part of what was to become West Virginia. He was in several skirmishes and a few small battles over the next several months.

His time during the winter months seemed to drag on. His entries were mostly about the boredom that came with guard duty and the slower pace.

With all the moving around, and a lot of very short entries in his journal and a number of skipped days, it was some time before I found an entry that was very interesting. It was his entry of September the fourteenth of 1862.

September 14, 1862

From what we have been told, we got into a fight with General Robert E. Lee and his Army of Northern Virginia today. We ran into a large detachment of Lee's army. I was not sure where we were, but it seemed we were shooting then moving, shooting then moving all day long. It seemed like we were scrapping over and around several gaps in the mountains. The fight lasted most of the day without either side making much headway. We needed to get though the gap in order to really get at Lee and his troops, but nothing seemed to work in our effort to break through. At the end of the day, Lee withdrew and entered Maryland.

It was difficult fighting for us. Getting a position that would help the infantry was hard in the narrow gaps in the mountains. I haven't heard how it went with the other Brigades, but we lost a lot of men. My artillery battery had suffered only two casualties. However, the infantry had a good number of losses, from what I have heard.

Lee withdrew late in the day after putting up a good fight. I thought we should continue to go after him, but the General had us hold our ground. He might have thought that if we went deep into the gap so late in the day we would be trapped there. I have no idea what was going through the minds of our commanding officers. I guess only time will tell if the choices they made were the right ones. I'm just glad I'm not the one making life and death decisions for so many men. It's hard enough making those kinds of decisions for the men in my battery.

September 15, 1862

To-day we spent getting re-organized while keeping watch over the area we were assigned to cover. The Seventh Volunteers Regiment had held their ground against the Confederate forces, but had lost a large number of infantrymen.

Up to now, I had not seen very many casualties from where we were positioned. We spent most of our time behind the lines giving the infantry support. Colonel McHenry had said we had done a good job; but if what he was hearing was correct, we would soon be going after the Confederates.

The one thing I could see from our position was a small area where there were both blue and gray uniforms on the ground. Since I was looking through my field glasses and we were quite some distance from where the men had fought, some in hand-to-hand fighting, it was difficult to tell how many had died there, but I was sure there were hundreds.

I could see a few men walking around the battlefield. I wasn't sure if they were injured or not, but they seemed to be looking for any men who might still be alive. I did see one of them bend down and touch a man's neck, then get up and walk away leaving the man lying there.

I just got word we are to move out immediately. We are going after the Confederates. From what we were told, they are headed toward Sharpsburg, Maryland. I hope to finish this tonight.

We are now camped along a creek for the night. I have posted guards in case we should be attacked. It is rumored our fighting in the gaps was with General Robert E. Lee and his Army of the Northern Virginia, but we had heard that earlier. It has now been confirmed.

In our move toward Sharpsburg, we had been trailing most of the others. It has been a hard move for all. I'm very tired and it is getting late. I will close for now.

September 17, 1862

Yesterday had been a very busy and very deadly day. I have not had a chance to write about it as we were in a fight for our lives from daybreak to almost dark. Right now, I am lying on the ground leaning against a tree with my journal hoping I will be able to keep my leg. The pain is terrible, but the fighting is over, at least for now. It may be over for me for the rest of the war. I must write about what happened yesterday before I can no longer write at all.

Yesterday, September 16, 1862, we woke early to the sounds of cannon fire off in the distance. We were in a fight again with the Army of Northern Virginia. A messenger rode in and told us the II Corps was moving around and we were to join the fighting from the northeast. We were to give artillery support to Kimball's Brigade along the eastern side of the sunken road. We quickly formed up and started to move.

It was mid-morning by the time we got into position. We immediately got our orders with instructions on where they wanted us to concentrate our fire, and to begin firing as soon as possible. The fighting was fierce and the smoke hung thick along the slight rise where we were positioned. The smoke was almost too thick to see what was really going on.

We had only started firing our cannons when I had heard an explosion off to my right and saw one of our cannons had been destroyed. As the smoke and dust cleared, I saw several of the men assigned to the cannon lying on the ground. It was easy to see a couple of them were dead and a couple of them were wounded, one with his leg blown off. I immediately turned to run to the man in the hope of helping him. I had no more than turned when the cannon I had been standing near received a direct hit and exploded. The explosion caused me to fall to the ground. I felt sharp pains in my right leg and side. It was only seconds after feeling the pain that I lost consciousness.

I don't think I was unconscious for very long, not more than a minute or two. I found myself being taken off the field of battle to a place down off the hill from where my artillery battery was located. I was placed on the ground and was looked after by a couple of women. I never heard their names, but they cleaned and dressed my wounds and made me as comfortable as possible until a doctor could examine me.

I asked one of the women for my journal, but she didn't know where it might be. Another woman nearby told me it was in my bag. She said one of the soldiers who had brought me to them made sure I had it. She said the man was a sergeant and that he had returned to his unit.

Although I had been in only a small part of the fight, it was clear to me that this had been the worst fighting I had ever seen. As I looked around the area where I lay, there were so many wounded I could not see all of them. Some were crying out in pain while others were lying silently. I found I could not keep from crying for the dead and wounded. There were so many young men who would never be whole again.

I have to put up my journal for now. The doctor is coming to talk to me. He has an apron on that is covered with blood. His eyes look tired and the lines of his face show how much death he has seen this day.

* * * * *

It was clear Isaac had no idea at the time how bloody the Battle of Antietam had been. Over 3600 men had lost their lives in that battle with a total of 22,717 casualties. It would turn out to be the bloodiest single-day battle in American history.

As I thought about what Isaac wrote, I remembered the photo of his skeleton and the old fracture of his right leg. I now knew how he got the broken leg. I was surprised that he had been able to keep his leg. Most often an injury like Isaac sustained on the battlefield during the Civil War would have resulted in the amputation of the limb almost immediately. The doctors were too busy trying to save lives to take the time to set and splint a leg. There was also the fact that those kinds of injuries would often get infected due to the small pieces of shrapnel being left in the wound, and dirt and the lack of clean water to wash out the wound adequately. An infection often meant gangrene would set in and the limb would have to be amputated anyway. I had to wonder how Isaac had avoided that fate.

If Isaac had lost his leg, he would most likely have been discharged and sent home. But if he healed without any difficulty, he would have been returned to service. I had to wonder if he was out of action for a few months and then returned to duty to fight again. It was still early in the war.

I went to the kitchen and made myself a cup of coffee. I took the cup into the den and sat down at my desk. I just looked at the journal for several minutes before I began reading again.

September 19, 1862

I was in too much pain yesterday to write. When the doctor got to me the other day, he explained the injury and that he wanted to take my leg. I refused to let him cut my leg off. I had to beg him to let me keep it. He told me that he didn't have time to argue with me. He called over a couple of men to hold me down while he reset my leg and splinted it. I passed out from the pain.

When I woke the morning of the next day, the eighteenth, there was a woman sitting on the ground beside me. She was in her mid-to-late fifties. She looked tired. She asked me how I was feeling and I told her that I was in a lot of pain. I asked her if I still had my leg as I couldn't remember what had happened and I could not force myself to look. She smiled and said I did. She told me that she had done the best she could to clean my wounds. I spent the rest of the day going in and out of sleep. She was always beside me when I woke.

To-day, I was put in a wagon and taken to an old schoolhouse where I was put on a blanket on the floor. I was again looked at by a doctor who examined my wounds. I asked him about Colonel McHenry and the rest of my artillery battery, but he couldn't tell me anything. He knew that Kimball's Brigade had taken a lot of casualties, but could not tell me anything about the colonel or my artillery battery. He did tell me my wounds looked good and that I might be able to keep my leg.

I am still having a good deal of pain, but at least I have been able to keep my leg. I would not like to return to Susan half a man.

It is getting dark outside and I am feeling very tired. I will put my journal down for tonight. I am sure I will think of Susan tonight. I have missed her and her letters.

September 20, 1862

To-day it rained almost the whole day. It is hot, and the humidity has caused the old schoolhouse to smell of dried blood, sweat, and of decaying flesh. A number of the wounded died during the night and were waiting for the wagon that would take them to be buried. The stench has become overwhelming. I asked if I could be moved outside onto the porch. Two of the women who were looking after us, helped move me onto the porch. Even with the heat and humidity, it was better than the confines of the schoolhouse.

I had talked to the doctor who had stopped by this morning to talk about my leg. He told me that I would probably continue to have some discomfort from my injury for a long time. Running and hard use of my leg would most likely continue to be a problem for the rest of my life, but I could get by if I didn't "overdo it". He also said that I would most likely be discharged as I would not be considered "physically fit for service", and that he was going to recommend I be released from service as soon as I was able to walk on it.

I don't know why, but I was disappointed by the news. Even with all the death and destruction, I thought I had been doing something important, that I was a part of what it was going to take to keep our country whole. I knew there was nothing I could do about it, but I still felt a bit depressed.

One of the officers from McHenry's Artillery Brigade stopped by to see how I was doing. He told me Colonel McHenry was concerned about me. I could only report to him what I had been told about my wound. I asked the officer if I could send a message to Colonel McHenry. He said he would be glad to deliver a message for me. He was nice enough to provide me with an envelope and paper, then waited while I wrote out my message.

In the message, I told the colonel that since I was to be released from duty, I would like his permission to go to his farm, and ask Susan to marry me. If Susan would have me, I would stay on and do what I could to keep the farm going until his return.

I gave the message in the envelope to the officer and thanked him. I then watched as he rode off.

As the officer rode out of sight, I couldn't help but feel a little down at the moment. I felt I should have been riding off to battle with him, but my wound would not let me continue to serve my country. I leaned back against the wall of the schoolhouse and thought about my future. Right now, it didn't look all that good.

I sat on the porch until dark, often with tears in my eyes. I had come to believe that I belonged in the Army, and now it was over.

Toward the end of the day, I began to think about Susan. I had not received a letter from her in over a week. I began to wonder if it was because she had lost interest in writing to me, or if it was because mail for everyone was taking longer to reach us. I guess I am feeling a little sorry for myself.

It is getting dark. It is time to put up my journal. Maybe things will look better tomorrow.

* * * * *

I took a minute to think about what Isaac had written before I very carefully turned to the next page.

September 21, 1862

It was about ten in the morning when a wagon pulled up in front of the schoolhouse. There were three men in the wagon. I watched them as they talked to the doctor in charge. I had no idea what was going on, but the doctor kept looking over at me. I have to admit, I was a little nervous. It came to mind they were going to take me to a hospital and take my leg off. I had been told how fragile my leg was, and any downward pressure on it could cause it to break.

After they had talked for a few minutes, the doctor walked toward me with the three soldiers following along behind. When the doctor got close to me, he took a deep breath and looked me right in the eye.

He said, "Son, I'm having you taken to a real hospital. I want them to look at you and see if there is some way, they can fix that leg of yours so you can walk on it without having to worry about it breaking under you own weight. What do you think about that?"

I said, "Will they take my leg off?"

He said, "No, but you will have to have surgery on it if you want to keep it."

I asked, "What happens if it doesn't work?"

"You would be better off having it cut off and having a wooden leg. If it doesn't work, it is going to break again. It's just a matter of time," he said.

I had to think about what he was saying. It didn't look like I had much of a choice. I had not been allowed to stand on it yet anyway. The more I thought about it, the more it sounded like it was the only thing I could do if I wanted to walk without fear of breaking my leg again.

I told him I would go to the hospital and let them look at it to see what they could do. The doctor smiled and said that if *the surgery worked, I would have full use of my leg with minimal difficulty.*

The three soldiers picked me up and carried me to the wagon. I was laid in the back on several blankets. We left for a hospital. They said it would take several days to get there. I was told the hospital was located in New York City.

September 22, 1862

It is my second day on the road to New York City. The three men who are taking me to New York City are very nice to me. I am not sure if it is because I am an officer, or if it is just how they treat all their patients. There is the driver of the wagon and the two men to attend to my needs, and they do it without complaint. I try not to be a nuisance and make things difficult for them, but I find it very uncomfortable in the wagon while lying on my back.

I do know that when it came time to stop for the night, I was aching all over and wanted nothing more than to get out of the wagon. I found it much more comfortable lying on the ground near the campfire, than in the wagon.

September 23, 1862

Another day of travel and my body aches all over. I'm beginning to wonder if the trip to New York City is worth it. They have tried to make me as comfortable as possible, but nothing seems to help.

They were nice enough to lift me out of the wagon at night so I could sleep on the ground. It was strange, but I feel more comfortable on the ground.

September 27, 1862

It took longer than I had expected to arrive in New York City. Riding all the way lying on my back left me exhausted and aching all over, too exhausted and uncomfortable to write the last couple of days. I am currently lying in a nice clean bed at a hospital in New York City. We arrived just shortly before dinner time. I was given a bath and was shaved before my evening meal. The meal was good and served to me while lying in bed. It had been a long time since I had been served a meal in bed, to say nothing of having a chance to bathe with soap and clean water.

After I had finished eating my dinner, two doctors came in to see me. They removed the dressing from my leg, but left the splint in place while they poked around at the wound. It was not a very pleasant experience, but I was sure it was necessary in order for them to decide if they could do anything for me. When they were finished, one of the doctors looked at me and smiled.

He said, "We won't know for sure until we get in and get a good look at the bone, but I think we might be able to fix your leg so you can at least walk on it. But I have to warn you, it will take three to four months before you will be able to walk on it, and another three months before you will be able to move around pretty much normally."

I asked, "Why so long?"

He replied, "Because the bone is broken diagonally."

He then went on to explain that the bone had to heal enough so it could bear my weight. Too much weight on it before it was properly healed and the break in the bone would give way and the upper part of the bone would slide down along the bottom part of the bone most likely causing the bone to break through the skin. If that happened, then the leg would have to be removed.

The doctors had made it clear I would have to be very careful with my leg for some time if I wanted to keep it. They said they would take me to surgery in the morning. There was nothing else for me to do, but to wait for morning.

It had been a long and very uncomfortable trip for me to get here. Now it was going to be a long period of recovery if I was to keep my leg. It seemed my journey to recovery had just begun.

My thoughts turned to Susan. I had thought about writing to her to let her know I was still alive, but I couldn't bring myself to do it. If I could not return to her a whole man, I would let her think I had been one of the many unknown soldiers who had died on the battlefield. I knew her father would tell her that I had survived, but I just couldn't return and be a burden to her. Maybe I would write to her after I knew if the surgery was successful.

The nurse came in to see me. She suggested I put up my journal and get some rest. I couldn't argue with her. The long trip here and tension has made me tired. It is time to put up my journal. With surgery in the morning, I have no idea when I will be able to write in it again.

October 22, 1862

I haven't written for almost a month. I was in pain most of the time, and there was nothing for me to do except lay there and hope my leg healed so I could once again use it.

To-day, the doctor came in and unwrapped my leg, but left the splint on that was holding the leg solid so it didn't move. I was a little surprised until he said they were taking it off to check and see how well I was healing. I was told they would be putting a new wrap on my leg as soon as they were sure things were healing like they should. From what the doctor said, he was pretty pleased with my progress.

I asked him if there was some way I could get out of this bed and maybe go outside to get some fresh air. From the look on the doctor's face, he apparently didn't think it was a good idea, but relented when I told him that I was going crazy confined to the bed. He said he would have a couple of men lift me up and set me in a wheelchair with a support for my leg.

I was beginning to think the doctor had forgotten all about me. It had been over an hour before two rather large men came into my room. They brought with them a wheelchair that had a board attached to it that would support my leg. It didn't look very comfortable, but if it got me out of my room, I could stand it.

The two men picked me up, then carefully set me down on the wheelchair after they put pillows on the board. Once I was on the wheelchair, they adjusted the back. It wasn't all that uncomfortable once they had the pillows arranged. They would not let me wheel myself around. One of the men wheeled me outside for some fresh air. The man wheeled me to a nice spot under a large oak tree, and gave me my journal.

He didn't leave me alone. In fact, he sat under the tree beside me, I guess to keep me from trying to get out of the wheelchair. It was a rather pleasant day as I was able to sit under a tree and write in my journal.

When my time outside was over, he just said it was time to go back inside. Will write again later.

* * * * *

The next few entries in his journal showed how slow and long the days were for him. He was not spending as much time going outside as the weather had turned colder with winter coming on.

I had covered several weeks in his journal with little additional information on how things were going for him when I came upon one entry that piqued my interest. It had some real news in it.

December 5, 1862

It is late in the evening, and the hospital is quiet. About the only thing I can hear are the sounds of nurses going from one place to another. I can see out the window. It is still snowing and it has been all day. I watched the snow as it fell and landed on my windowsill. It has been a long day for me. It has been a day when I have spent most of it looking out the window and thinking, for I have much to think about.

It was the first day that they let me walk. I had only walked for a short time, and only with the use of a cane to help me support my weight on my injured leg. The doctors felt my leg had healed nicely, but still had some reservation about it. It will be a while before they will release me and allow me to go home. They have cautioned me about putting too much stress on the leg for fear it still might break. However, they didn't give me any restrictions except to be careful.

December 6, 1862

I was told today that I should start walking around the hospital without the cane for a couple of days, but use care in going up or down stairs. If I didn't have any problems, I would be discharged to go home. I was also told I could not return to duty as my leg would not withstand the rigors of military life, especially on the battlefield.

My biggest problem with going home was that my home, the place where my family lived, was in the South. Since I had fought for the North, I was sure I would not be very welcome there, even by my own family. The closest thing I had to a home was with Susan on the McHenry farm.

With the lateness of the hour, my mind is filled with thoughts of Susan McHenry, the beautiful young woman who had saved my life. Earlier to-day I received a letter from her. The letter was dated about a week before I was wounded which was several months ago. The letter had gotten lost somewhere along the way, but finally caught up with me in the New York City hospital.

In the letter, Susan wrote about how much she missed me, and how much she hoped the war would be over soon so I could return to her. She wrote about the farm and how difficult it was for her to manage it alone. She was worried about me because she had heard about the fighting and she had not heard from me. She was certain I would have been involved in it. She had not heard from her father, either, which caused me to wonder if he might have been wounded or killed.

As I read the letter from Susan, I began to realize just how much she loved me. She would be able to deal with my injury, and the limits it put on me. I also began to realize just how much I love her, not because it was the closest thing I had to a home, but because I really did love her and wanted to be with her.

I had to make a decision about how I felt about Susan. The more I thought about it, the more I realized there was nothing else for me to do, but to return to her and hope she still loved me enough to make a life with me. When I am discharged, I will return to the McHenry farm and help her keep it going, and hope she will still want to marry me.

I had not heard anything about her father and had no idea where he might be. I couldn't tell her if he was alive or dead. News of the battles was not hard to come by, but news of who died in the battles was not easy to get. The number of deaths was very high, with many of the dead unknown.

It is getting late and I need my rest. I will close for now, but I will write to Susan in the morning to tell her that I am coming home.

* ** * *

It appears that Isaac had finally dealt with his feelings for Susan.

December 7, 1862

I wrote a letter to Susan this morning, and asked one of the nurses to mail it for me. I wasn't able to tell her when I would be released and when I would arrive home, but I did tell her I would write to her again when I was about to leave.

To-day, I took my first walk without the use of a cane. I was rather nervous knowing what it meant if my leg could not support my weight. I had walked down the hall, moving rather slowly for fear my leg might not support me. By the time I got to the end of the hall, I was feeling a little more confident that I was going to be able to walk on it. I remembered what the doctors had told me about taking it easy.

I returned to my room and sat down in a chair. I had been able to walk some distance, but it had tired me out. Having not walked for several months, I soon found I tired rather quickly. I would have to spend some time getting back into shape. I quickly decided I would spend this day walking up and down the halls, once after each meal. Tomorrow I would try for twice after each meal. Once I got feeling comfortable with that, I would ask to be released so I could return to Susan. I knew it would take several months to build up my strength, but I would have most of the winter to do it. I had to build up my strength in order to help with the planting at the McHenry farm in the spring.

I made the three trips to the end of the hall to-day, each time feeling a little less afraid to walk. It is already dark and the place has grown quiet. It is time to put up my journal and get some rest. For the first time in a long time, I am beginning to feel I will be able to keep my leg.

* * * * *

The next few entries in his journal were about how good it felt to walk.

December 10, 1862

To-day was my big day. I was released from the hospital and from the military. I had mixed feelings about it. I was glad to be out of the hospital where I had spent most of the past five months, but I cannot explain how I feel about being discharged from the Army.

I also had mixed feeling about returning to the McHenry farm. I was looking forward to seeing Susan again, but I wasn't so sure how she would feel about me returning with a leg that I had to be careful not to overstress.

It was shortly after breakfast when I was released from the hospital and handed my discharge papers. I didn't have time to write to Susan to tell her when I would be arriving. I was given a ride to the train station where I got my ticket that routed me to Pittsburg with a number of changes at different stations and to different trains. I was unable to take any of the trains that would have made my trip much shorter due to the attacks on trains in Maryland and northern Virginia.

There was little doubt in my mind it was going to be a long trip, but it would be well worth it if Susan said she would marry me. I was sure that thought was enough to carry me all the way to her.

I was well aware that I would have to be very careful getting on and off the trains due to the high steps into the trains without the aid of a railing. I got on the train and found a seat where I could watch out the window. There were only a few people on the train so it was easy to find a place where I could write in my journal. I found the ride to be more pleasant than in the back of a wagon, but it was still not as smooth a ride as I would have liked.

To-day has been rather exhausting for me, so I think I will close my journal for now and try to rest a little.

* * * * *

I read through several more entries in his journal, but found nothing of any real interest. It mostly covered his changes from one train to another and the stagecoach ride from Pittsburg railroad station to the station at Uniontown where he picked up the train that would take him to Summerville.

December 14, 1862

The train had a short stop while they made sure the track ahead was clear and took on water and fuel. The stop gave me a chance to write in my journal. It is hard to write when the train is moving because of the movements of the coaches. The days have been pretty much the same. There has been pretty much nothing for me to do but sit here when the train is moving. The long hours of just sitting and looking out the window of the coaches and the stagecoaches is very boring.

My leg gets to aching from a lack of movement and the discomfort of sitting so long without being able to walk around. It is difficult to walk on a moving train as the cars tend to roll from side to side. It is pretty easy to lose one's balance.

I have seen military guards placed around several of the stations, with especially large numbers of guards at the stations in the norther part of western Virginia. It brought back memories of when I was assigned to guard duty at railroad stations when I first joined the Union Army

* * * * *

I found the next several days where pretty much the same. It was when I came to the December 18th, 1862 entry that I found it interesting.

December 18, 1862

I am only about two days from Summerville when we stopped for fuel and water for the engine. The conductor told me that I could get off the train for a few minutes to stretch my legs. I got off and discovered there was a telegraph office at the station. I walked over to the office and requested the agent send a message on ahead for me, but the agent refused saying it was for military use only because of the war. I looked at him for a minute before I returned to the train and put my uniform on. I then returned to the telegraph office. I almost laughed when the agent looked at me. He was very surprised. I told him that I was Colonel McHenry's adjutant and I wished to send a message to his home in Summerville.

The Telegraph agent immediately complied with my request, but he looked at me a little strange when he saw what I wrote down for him to send. The message I wrote said,

Please meet Lieutenant Isaac Madison at the Summerville station about noon on December 20th. He has important information for you.

The Telegraph agent really got confused when he asked who he should put down as the sender. I told him just use my name. I didn't want it to come from the colonel as I had no idea if he was alive or dead. If he was dead, it could be a shock for her to get a telegraph message from him. I would never want to upset her like that.

After making sure he sent the message, I returned to the railroad coach I had been riding in and sat down. I got a couple of strange looks from people on the train. They had not seen me in uniform before. I even had a couple of young women smile at me. I guess the uniform makes a difference to some women. The train is about ready to leave the station. I will put up my journal for now.

* * * * *

His telegraph message to Susan seemed like a good idea. It would give her at least a couple of days to get ready for his return. I had no idea how far the McHenry farm was from the town, but if it was a long way to the farm from the railroad station, it would save him a long walk which I doubted would be good for his leg. I turned the page of the journal.

December 19, 1862

It's dark outside the train. We have stopped at a station for the night. The conductor said that there were rebels in the area and the Army has suggested, rather strongly, that we don't continue on until morning. The only light I have to write by is a small lantern at the end of the coach. All the curtains on the windows of the coach have been drawn so no one can see inside and the light from the lantern cannot be seen outside the coach.

To-day has been a long day. We had several stops because of rebels attacking railroad stations up and down the line. According to the conductor, there had been a number of attacks by small groups of rebels using hit and run tactics.

The conductor has let me walk up and down the aisle of the coach when the train is stopped to help me get the stiffness out of my leg. I think he has been a little more informative of the situation to me than to the other passengers. I'm sure it's due to the fact that he knows I was an army officer. As far as he knows, I'm still an officer. I didn't change out of my uniform after my encounter with the telegraph operate yesterday.

The only thing that I'm worried about is my arrival at Summerville. If we continue to get delayed, I might not arrive on the date I put in my telegram. The only thought that made me feel a little better was that I was sure the station master at Summerville would tell Susan of the delays, and the reason for them.

I'm getting tired. I will put up my journal for now and hopefully get some rest.

December 20, 1862

It is about ten in the morning and I'm sitting on a bench at the railroad station to write this. We have just received word that the train will be pulling out of the station in about fifteen minutes. Apparently, the tracks have been cleared. I spent the last hour or so walking around the railroad station. It feels good to get some exercise. The long hours of sitting in the coach makes my leg get stiff.

I'll have to put this up as the conductor has called for everyone to get on board. If all goes well, I should get to Summerville by about seven this evening.

* * * * *

When I turned the page in Isaac's journal, I quickly discovered he had skipped three days.

December 23, 1862

I have not entered anything into my journal for the past three days, mostly because it has been the best three days of my life. I will back up a little.

I arrived at the Summerville railroad station at about seven-thirty on the evening of December 20th. As the train pulled into the station, I began to wonder if Susan would come to get me. I didn't see her on the platform. I hoped it was a case of her not getting my telegram, but I couldn't help but think that maybe she hadn't come because she no longer wanted to see me.

Just as I stepped off the train, I saw her come out of the train station. I dropped my carpet bag as she ran toward me. She threw her arms around me, almost knocking me over. I stumbled briefly to protect my leg, but regained my footing quickly.

She said she was sorry, but she was so glad to see me. She kissed me several times. I had never had a homecoming like that before.

After my warm greeting, she took my arm and we walked around to the back of the railroad station where there was a buckboard with the horse tied to the hitching rail. Susan noticed my slight limp and asked me about it. She seemed worried to me. I told her I was tired from the long trip from New York and we would talk about it later.

When we arrived at her home almost an hour later, she showed me to the room I had when I first stayed at the McHenry farm. She left me while I changed out of my uniform. As soon as I changed, I went downstairs to the parlor. She was waiting for me. We sat down on the sofa. We talked well into the night. It was about two in the morning when we finally said goodnight.

The next day, December 21, we spent just being together. She asked me about my injury, and I told her about my limitations, but that my leg should get stronger with time. She *cooked meals like I had not had for several years. When evening came around and we were sitting in the parlor, I asked her to marry me. She immediately said "yes". Up to this point I had not mentioned her father. I didn't know if he was alive or dead. Again, we turned in late.*

On the morning of December 22, we were sitting at the table over breakfast. I couldn't wait any longer to talk about her father. I asked her if she knew anything about her father. I told her I had not heard from him since I was taken to New York for the operation on my leg.

Susan told me that her father had written to her and told her that the last word he had from me was when I asked him for her hand in marriage. He said in his letter that he would be proud to have me as his son-in-law.

* * * * *

As I turned the page, I noticed that there were several days missing. I was sure that they had been spent helping around the farm and spending Christmas together.

December 27, 1862

I didn't write over Christmas as we were very busy. Colonel McHenry arrived on the evening of Christmas Eve. On Christmas day, about four in the afternoon, the local preacher came by the house at the colonel's request. Susan and I were married in the parlor. We were up pretty late celebrating our marriage and opening gifts. We were happy that the colonel could be there and that he was safe.

Early this morning, Susan and I took the colonel to the railroad station. We had hoped he would be able to stay a few more days, but he had to return to his artillery battalion. We waited at the station until the train left. As soon as it left, we returned to the farm.

Once we arrived back at the farm, I took care of the horses and did a few things that needed to be done in the barn. It wasn't long before my leg started to ache. I was told by the doctors not to overdo it for at least six months. It was time for me to go into the house and rest my leg.

It is getting late, so I will put up my journal.

* * * * *

I got the impression that Isaac was trying to do more than he was really ready to do. I'm sure he wanted to do his share of the work, but his leg was not ready to do it.

I turned the page and read on. All it showed me was that he had settled into a routine. He would work a few hours in the morning and a few hours in the afternoon. He had avoided any heavy lifting or anything that might cause his leg to ache. From the writing in the journal, Susan had accepted Isaac's limitations very well.

He seemed to have gotten back into the routine of writing almost everyday. His days were what I would have expected of a person working on a farm during the winter months. The next entry that gave me a clue as to how things were going with him came several months later.

April 6, 1863

It is about nine o'clock in the evening. I worked in the field planting corn to-day. For the first several hours things went well. It was about an hour before the noon meal when the plow suddenly struck a rock. The plow suddenly twisted and threw me to the ground. I hit my leg on the edge of the plow causing a deep cut in my leg just about where the surgery had been done to fix my leg.

I was afraid to try to stand up and hobble to the house, and it hurt to move. I called for Susan, but she couldn't hear me. I laid there in the field, not sure what I should do. I could see that I was not bleeding very much, which was a good sign. I was worried more about reinjuring my leg. I don't know how long I laid there, before Susan came running out into field.

Susan looked at my leg, then at me. After looking at my leg, she said that she didn't think I had reinjured my leg, but she didn't want me to try to walk back to the house. She went to the barn and got the horse, hooked him to the wagon then came and got me.

Once I was back in the house, she cleaned and bandaged the cut in my leg. I rested the rest of the day. Just before it was bedtime, I looked at it, then tried to stand up. I was able to put my full weight on the leg, which was a big relief for both of us.

* * * * *

The next several entries showed that things had returned to pretty much the routine for anyone who farmed. His leg injury healed and he returned to doing the normal daily chores on any farm of the day.

It wasn't until I got to the month of June that I got a surprise.

June 14, 1863

To-day I got a big surprise. When I came in from the garden with some vegetables, I noticed that Susan was smiling at me. I set the vegetables on the counter, turned around and looked at her. I asked her what was so funny. She said very softly, "We're going to have a baby". I guess it took a minute to sink into my head what she had said.
"A baby?" I asked.
She said "Yes. A baby."
I couldn't think of anything to say. I grabbed her and swung her around. She held me tight. It was the happiest day of my life. I'm going to be a father.
While we ate our dinner, I talked about all the things we would need to get for the baby. She kept saying, "We have time to get them." "We don't need to get them to-day."
She told me the baby would be due about mid-February or early March.
After I settled down and we had finished our dinner, I went out to the barn to finish my chores. We spent a good part of the evening sitting on the sofa and being close.
That night I held her close most of the night. We were so happy with the thought that we would be a family.
It was late as I watched Susan sleeping in our bed. I got up and sat down to write in my journal.

* * * * *

I couldn't help it, I was very happy for them.

The next several entries in the Isaac's journal were filled with the joy of the pending birth of a child.

After a short time, about a couple of weeks, the entries became rather brief, usually only a couple of sentences. They no longer provided any real insight into Isaac's thoughts. They were mostly what they were doing each day. As time went on, Isaac seemed to skip a couple of days here and there. I could only assume that it was pretty routine working around the farm. In fact, his entries became only once a week and with very little information. They were still about the routine of working on the farm, and the anticipation of the coming child. It wasn't until the July of 1863 entry that I found anything of real interest.

July 8, 1863

To-day we received a newspaper that had news about the war that caused both Susan and myself a great deal of concern. The newspaper was a few days old, July 3, 1863. The news told of a big battle that was shaping up at the town of Gettysburg, Pennsylvania. The Union troops had made contact with some of Robert E. Lee's Army of Northern Virginia in the town of Gettysburg.

The article in the paper said that it was forming up to be a very important battle in the fight to save the Union. In the listings of some of the union troops that would be at the battle, Colonel McHenry's Artillery Battalion was very briefly mentioned among others. This news gave us great concern for his safety.

July 10, 1863

Yesterday, we received a telegraph message that the colonel had survived some of the heaviest fighting near Cemetery Ridge. The center of the Union line had been attacked by General Picket of the Confederate Army, but although several Confederates pushed the line back a few feet, the line held with the help of artillery.

For the first time, I felt that I should have been there. I knew I would not be able to stand the riggers of combat, but that didn't matter. I had a feeling of sadness that I was no longer able to fight for the Union.

Needless to say, Susan was very happy with the news that her father was safe, as was I.

* * * * *

I was glad to hear that Colonel McHenry had come through the battle without injury.

Over the next few weeks, Isaac's entries in the journal were once again rather brief. The entries had returned to what was going on at the farm. I managed to cover almost six months of time in his journal. There was an occasional mention of the war, but it was only when it involved Colonel McHenry; and those were rather brief probably because there was little communication about him. There were often periods of time when Isaac didn't write anything.

It was after the last period of time that his entry caught me by surprise. It was his entry dated January 30, 1864.

January 30, 1864

 Just seven months ago I experienced the best day of my life, the coming of a child that would make our life as a family complete. Five days ago, I experienced the worst day of my life. On January 24, 1864, Susan became very ill. I called for the doctor to come out to see what was wrong with her. He didn't arrive until January 25, 1864, and it was too late.
 On the afternoon of January 25, 1864, my world came to an end. On that day, I lost my beautiful Susan and our baby boy. The doctor said there was nothing he could have done to save them. "It was God's will".
 I find it hard to believe that it was God's will to take such a loving woman and a son from me. I guess there is no explanation other than to say "it was God's will".
 My love and my child were laid to rest on January 27, 1864.

* * * * *

 I was not prepared to see Isaac's last entry. I just stared at his journal. I could not imagine how it would feel to lose a wife and child. I simply closed his journal and sat back in my chair.
 I needed to know more about Isaac. I needed to know how he was going to cope with the death of his wife and child, and how it would affect the rest of his life. I had to read on.
 I opened Isaac's journal to where I had left off. He had not written in his journal for over two weeks.

February 16, 1864

To-day it is snowing very hard. I have taken care of the animals, then returned to the house. I have not written in my journal for some time. The house seems so empty. I have not been able to sleep in the same room I shared with Susan. In the past couple of days, I have thought about leaving the farm and heading out West.

I no longer have the desire to continue to be a farmer, at least not here. There are just two many sad memories on this farm for me. I know that I can't simply leave the farm. It would not be fair to Colonel McHenry since it is really his farm and he has been so nice to me. He also took me into his confidence and trusted me to do what is right, and it is right to stay here until he returns.

I got a letter from him yesterday. He seemed to think that the war would not last much longer. I hope he is right. I wrote back and told him that I would keep the farm going until he returned, and that is what I will do.

It has been a long day. I'll close for now.

* * * * *

I sat back and looked at the picture in the silver frame. It was a picture of Susan. After a few minutes, I turned the page and found the next page blank. It surprised me that he had stopped writing in his journal.

The next entry in his journal had been over a year since he had written anything. I was curious why he had left four pages blank. He had not done that before when he didn't write for several days. Maybe it was his way of shutting out a painful part of his past and somehow starting a new life.

When I came to the next page with writing on it, I hesitated to read it. I needed to let my mind clear a little before I returned to the journal.

When I returned from a walk, I opened the journal to where I had left it.

April 12, 1865

I just received word that the war between the states is over. General Lee surrendered on April 9th at a court house at Appomattox, Virginia. I'm not sure how I felt. Of course, I'm glad the war is over and that Colonel McHenry will be returning to the farm, but I wish I could have been there at the end.

I will get everything ready for the colonel. I will also get myself ready to head west into the Frontier west of the Mississippi River. I have been thinking about it for some time, now. As soon as the colonel returns, I will have no reason to stay here.

My dream of going west has filled my thoughts ever since I lost my beautiful Susan and our baby. I'm sure Susan would understand.

I will close for now and get the farm ready for Colonel McHenry to take over. I do not want him to think that I didn't take good care of his farm while he was gone.

* * * * *

It looked like Isaac is finally going to go west. I get the impression from his writings in his journal that he was looking forward to the day when he could leave the farm and head for the Frontier. I had to wonder if his desire to go to the Frontier was more due to a desire to get away from the farm with its memories, than a real desire to see the Frontier.

I was looking forward to finding out how his travels into the Frontier would go for him. He was still a long way from the Black Hills where his body had rested for over a hundred years. I had to turn several pages of short notes on what he was doing around the farm. I was wondering how he was going to explain what he was planning to the colonel.

April 21, 1865

Colonel McHenry returned late this afternoon. I picked him up at the Summerville train station. We had a nice talk on the way from the train station to the farm.

The colonel asked me if I would stay on for a year and a half to keep the farm going. He had agreed to take a position in Washington DC to oversee the rebuilding of the union. He explained how important this position was for the country. As much as I wanted to move on, I told him that I would stay on. After all, it was only for a year and a half. The Frontier had waited for me this long, a year and a half longer would not be too much.

I couldn't refuse him. He and his daughter had saved my life, and he had been more like a father to me than my own father. I felt I owed him that much.

I explained to him that I wanted to continue what I started, but I would delay my dream of seeing the Fronter for a year and a half.

We had a pleasant meal together. Shortly after dinner, a widow lady who lived on the farm just east of the McHenry farm stopped by to welcome the colonel home. I got the impression that she liked the colonel and that they knew each other fairly well. I also thought that they would make a good couple. I sat in the parlor for a while just listening to them. I got to feeling that they would like to be alone.

I excused myself by saying that I needed to get up early so I could take care of the animals. They said goodnight and I left them alone.

I returned to my room and wrote this. I think I heard the woman and the colonel go out of the house. It was not long before I heard the sound of a horse as it left the farm.

I will close for now and get some rest.

*****
I was a little surprised that Isaac was willing to delay his travels into the Frontier. However, I could understand his reason for delaying his travels.

There were no further entries in his journal until September 30, 1866

September 30, 1866

Yesterday, Colonel McHenry returned from Washington having completed his agreed service to the Union.

To-day, I stood up for Colonel McHenry for his wedding to Mable Sutton. She was the widow lady that owned the farm right next to the colonel's farm. They had known each other for a good number of years.

After the wedding and the reception, I gathered my belongings and got everything ready for my departure. I was finally going to see the Frontier.

October 1, 1866

The sun was just starting to come up over the hills to the east. I had my packhorse ready and my riding horse saddled. I had taken time to have breakfast with the colonel and his new bride before leaving.

I had no more than gotten to the end of the lane to the road when I heard Mable scream. I quickly turned around and rode back to the house. Mable came out of the barn. She was almost hysterical. When I got to the barn, I found the colonel lying on the floor of the barn. From what I could see, he had fallen from the loft and injured his leg.

I got up in the wagon and took him to the doctor. The doctor put his leg in a cast and told him not to walk on it for at least two months.

He told me that I should go and not worry about him. He could probably hire someone to help around the farm.

Since it was already late in the fall for me to start my journey into the Frontier, I told him I would stay around until spring and help out. He was truly disappointed for me, but he knew he needed the help.

I was disappointed, too. When I got back to the farm, I unpacked my horse and stored my gear. I then settled in to work for a few more months.

* * * * *

It was apparent that he was disappointed he was being delayed again. His journal showed his disappointment very clearly in all his entries written during the time he stayed on.

The colonel improved and was eventually able to take over the farm. When spring came around, Isaac was once again ready to continue on his dream.

April 22, 1867

I once again packed up my supplies on my packhorse and saddled my riding horse. I got in the saddle and said my goodbyes to the colonel and his wife.

The colonel wished me well just before I rode down the lane to the road. As I turned west on the road and headed toward Charleston, I looked back and saw the colonel and his bride watching me as I left. I gave them a wave before I could no longer see them or the farm house. They waved back.

The day was pleasant as I rode on toward the west. I had mixed feeling about leaving, but this was probably the last chance I would have to see the Frontier, something I had wanted to do for a good number of years.

I think I made about thirty miles to-day. The horses do not seem stressed too much, but I might slow down a bit to-morrow. They seem to be content with the thick grass next to the stream where I stopped for the night. To-morrow I will continue on.

It feels good to be writing in my journal again. I have written this by the light of my fire. It is burning down and I'm tired, so I will close my journal for now.

April 23, 1867

This morning the sun was up before I rolled out of my bedroll. After a breakfast of biscuits, bacon and coffee, I broke camp. I got in the saddle and headed out. It was a pleasant day. I traveled about twenty-five miles to-day. The ground I had been traveling was fairly flat up until late in the day when I began to get into some hilly country. I think I'm getting close to a river.

When I picked out a place to rest for the night, I couldn't help but think about Susan. I was sure she would understand why I left.

I guess I'll close my journal for tonight. I have a long way to go to get to the Mississippi River.

* * * * *

Isaac was once again on his way toward fulfilling his dream of seeing the Frontier. I doubt that he had any idea what the future had in store for him. He still had a long way to go just to get to the Mississippi River.

I turned the page and discovered that he had not written for over two weeks. I was curious to find out why he had not written so I began to read.

May 13, 1867

The past few weeks have been rather boring. I need to get back into the routine of writing every day or so. At least more often.

I was beginning to think that I had lost my way. It was fairly hilly country, but there had been very little to see. I think that twenty miles a day in this hilly country was enough for my horses. I didn't want to work them too hard. We have a long way to go. I think that was about the average miles per day for the past sixteen days.

I was able to kill a rabbit for my dinner yesterday. I had the rest of it to-day. It was good to have some meat. I am camped next to a small creek. It flows close to the side of the road in a generally westerly direction. It is a pretty spot.

I took a little time after dinner to climb a hill behind my campsite to take a look around. Off in the distance I could see what looked like a rather large town. I cannot express my feelings of joy when I saw the town. It had to be Charleston. My first thought was maybe I could get a riverboat on the Kanawha River that would take me north and west to the Ohio River, then along the Ohio River to Fort Mitchell near the town of Cincinnati.

The thought of being able to take a riverboat on the next leg of my trip to the Frontier was exciting to me. It would give me a chance to rest my horses as well as myself for several weeks. Even though the river twists and turns a lot, the boat continues to move along day and night, with only a few stops along the way.

I figure it will take a couple of months to get to the Mississippi River. If everything goes well, I could get to the Missouri River before winter. I hope to find a place where I can hole up for the winter.

It was almost dark when I returned to my campsite from the hill. I laid down, but sleep didn't come. I guess I was too *excited. I wrote this by the light of my fire. I will close now and try to get some sleep.*

* * * * *

I could almost feel Isaac's excitement. Traveling on a riverboat would not only give him a chance to rest, but would allow him to make progress on his way to the Black Hills, which was his goal. As I thought about it, I was beginning to realize that Isaac had at least some idea how much further he had to go to get to the Black Hills in the Dakota Territory.

However. there was something else that he might not realize, and that was the dangers he would face just getting across the Great Plains. But that was some distance away, as was the Mississippi River. He would probably learn a lot about the dangers of crossing the Great Plains before he got to it.

I continued to read his Journal.

May 15, 1867

I arrived in Charleston at the dock where a small riverboat was loading fright for a trip up the Kenawha River. I found the captain of the riverboat and asked him to take me and my horses to the Ohio River. The captain of the riverboat told me that he could take me to the Ohio River, but if I was planning on going downstream on the Ohio River it would be quicker to ride my horses straight west to the Ohio River. He said it was only about fifty miles or so and would take me only about three days to get to the Ohio River. He also said it would take him nine days by river to get back to where I could get on the Ohio by going straight west from where I was now.

After taking a good look at my horses, and seeing that they were in good shape, I decided that I would go west to the Ohio River, and take the riverboat from there. The fact that it would save me about five to six days, and I would not have the additional expense of paying for the riverboat ride, made it a good deal for me.

I thanked the captain, then asked him where I might find a place to camp for the night. He suggested that since I had horses, I might like to stay at the landing. There was a small grove of trees next to a small building where there was some good grass and water for my horses. I thanked him then went over to the small grove of trees and set up camp for the night.

* * * * *

It was good to see that the captain of the riverboat was helpful. Saving almost a week may not seem like much when considering the whole trip, I'm sure Isaac seemed pleased with the captain. A look at the map of the area, I could see where it would be better for him to ride west to the Ohio River.

May 19, 1867

I found it took a little longer than the captain had said it would, but it was still a lot less time than it would have taken by riverboat.

I arrived at the docks in Burlington, West Virginia, about noon this date. It had taken me an hour or so to find the docks on the Ohio River where the riverboats would tie up. I was about to purchase passage for myself and my horses on the next riverboat when a soldier from the Union Army walked up to me.

As soon as I saw him, I couldn't help but think that he looked familiar. He walked up close to me and smiled. He asked me if I was Lieutenant Isaac Madison. I told him I was, but I had been discharged from the service due to a leg injury. He said he knew about my injury.

We got to talking and I found out he had been one of the privates in my unit. His name was Josh Savoy. He was now a sergeant and he was on his way to a new duty post at a fort on the Mississippi River down near the Louisiana border with Arkansas. We went to a little café and sat down to talk. We had dinner together.

I told him where I was going and that we could ride on the riverboat together for several days. He looked at me for a minute before he spoke. He told me that since I had horses, I would probably make a lot better time if I traveled by land almost straight west from here until I got to the Mississippi River. I should then cross the Mississippi River and keep going west to the Missouri River. Once I got to the Missouri River, I should follow the river north and west to Fort Randall or Fort Pierre Trading Post. From there I could head straight west to the Black Hills.

Since I didn't have a map that was much help, he took the time to draw out a map of the rivers. It was easy to see that *the rivers wound and twisted making long loops in the river that made it much further to go. It was quite a distance south to the Missouri River. Looking at his map, it would add a good number of miles because I would have to travel back up the Missouri River to get to where I would be if I went straight west to the Missouri River.*

After talking with him for several hours, he agreed that the riverboats would make the trip easier, but riverboats didn't move very fast and the rivers would wind and twist around just to get a few miles. He also pointed out that the riverboats would be going upstream, making it move slower yet, and there were a lot of stops along the way.

It was clear that it was much shorter by land. He also pointed out, that after a couple of days on a riverboat, I might find it rather boring. I had to agree with him.

It was getting late when we went our separate ways. I figured I might never see him again, but it was nice to have someone to talk to for awhile, especially someone who knew the way.

I crossed the Ohio River and found a place to set up camp. I spent some time looking over the map I had been given, then finished writing this by the light of my campfire.

* * * * *

It was nice that Isaac found someone who could help him find his way to the Black Hills. I'm sure it had been a pleasant evening, as well. I got the feeling that Isaac trusted the young sergeant.

Looking at my map, I could see what the sergeant had told him was correct. My map also showed me that Isaac would also pass by several Military Posts along the Missouri River when he got to the Dakota Territory.

May 20, 1867

I broke camp just shortly after the sun was up. I followed along the Ohio River up to Wheelersburg, about twenty miles. I spent the night just out of the north side of the town, close to the river. It was a pleasant night. I did a little fishing, which proved to supply me with my dinner. Other than the fishing, it was a rather uneventful night. My horses enjoyed the stop as there was plenty of grass and water for them.

I saw a riverboat go by just before dark. It was moving rather slow. I couldn't help but think that I could have been on a riverboat like it.

By late morning, I should be far enough along that I would be well away from the river. It will be a long while before I will have another major river to cross.

I can see my horses have already eaten their fill as they are sleeping. It would be a good idea if I do the same.

* * * * *

It looks like Isaac is going to take the advice of Sergeant Savoy's suggestion and leave the river behind. He has a long way to go just to get across Ohio.

May 21, 1867

I got a good early morning start to-day. The horses seemed pretty rested and were ready to go. I left Wheelersburg and followed the river just around a big bend. From there, I headed northwest on the first road I found heading in that general direction.

This morning started out with the sun shining, but as the day went on, clouds began to form and the winds started to blow a bit. By mid-day, it looked like it might rain before long. I had just gone past a little settlement, I think was called Sugar Grove, when I came upon a lake. There were a lot of good sized trees making the perfect place for me to build a shelter. I had no more than finished my shelter when it started to rain.

I quickly gathered up some branches and twigs before they got too wet to burn. I built a fire where it was sheltered from the wind and rain. I fixed my dinner from the supplies I bought in Wheelersburg.

I am sitting in my shelter with a small fire in front of me while I write to-day's happenings. It is starting to get dark. The rain and winds have settled down. It is time for me to get some rest.

*****

I got a cup of coffee and took it into the den and sat down to read some more from the journal. I was surprised to see that he had not written over the past few days. I hoped to find out why. I began reading.

May 26, 1867

It has been pretty much the same thing every day for the past five days. The weather has been sunny in the morning then rain in the evening. The land didn't change much either. It was dotted with small farms, small groves of trees and some open fields. After awhile, they all seem the same. It is gently rolling farmland. From the look of the crops, the land is very good farmland.

I passed through Russellville only stopping to add to my supplies. I'm about two miles west of the town. I found a nice place to rest myself and my horses for the night. There is a creek that has fish in it, I was told. I did a little fishing and found the fishing good. I only kept what I could eat.

About eight this evening, it clouded up and began to rain, again. I put my shelter up in among the trees. The horses have gotten accustomed to the rain and don't seem to mind it.

My fire is about to go out, so I will close for to-night.

* * * * *

Spring rains can get pretty nasty in this region, but it appears from what he writes, there had been just showers, not the storms often seen in the midwest in the spring.

May 27, 1867

I only got as far as Hamersville to-day, about twelve miles. I spent most of the day standing in the door of the Blacksmith's shop watching the rain come down in sheets and run off toward a creek. There was a lot of lightening and wind with the rain. This little settlement has very little in the way of businesses. The Blacksmith, Mr. Atwood, offered to let me sleep in the loft of his stable as long as I don't smoke. He was also kind enough to let me put my horses up in his stable.

We spent most of the time talking. It turned out that he had been in the Union Army during the war. Mr. Atwood helped train horses for one of the Ohio regiments. He said he trained the horses for several artillery units, too. It seems we had a lot to talk about while it rained.

Mr. Atwood invited me into his house for dinner with his wife and daughter. I had a very nice home cooked meal and pleasant conversation with him and his family. We talked well into the night before I went out to the stable. I write this by the light of a lantern. I hope the roads are not too muddy tomorrow when I leave.

May 28, 1867

I didn't get a very early start this morning. Mr. Atwood insisted that I have a good breakfast before I headed out.

I found the roads to be a little muddy, but if I kept the horses just off the dirt part of the rode and in the grassy edge of the road, they could move along pretty well, and make good time. It was getting late in the afternoon when I reached Norwood, just a short distance from Cincinnati.

It was evening when I rode into Cincinnati. I found a small boarding house that had a barn out back where I could put my horses up for the night. I had to take care of my horses myself, which was alright with me.

The lady that ran the place was rather cold toward me at first. I wasn't sure why until her son came in the house. I noticed that he was missing an arm. After asking him about the loss of his arm, I found out he had been a Confederate soldier. Even though he had lived in the north, he fought for the south. He had been injured at the Battle of Antietam in 1862. I avoided talking to him about my part in the war, mostly because that was where I fought and was also injured, and I had fought on the Union side.

He was still very bitter about the outcome of the war. I was sure it was partly because he had lost his arm due to an artillery explosion. I'm sure there would have been problems if I brought up the subject of the war, especially if I told him that I had been an Artillery Officer at the Battle of Antietam. I had no desire to get into our differences with him. I made it a point not to mention that I was also in the war and what I did.

Later that evening, after her son left the room, the young man's mother thanked me for not bringing up the war. She somehow knew that I had been in the war. It might have been the fact that I avoided talking about it, and she caught on.

I went to my room and wrote this. I'll try to get a good night's sleep. I hope to get a good start to-morrow.

June 1, 1867

In the early morning of May 29, the barn of the boarding house was struck by lightning. The barn was burned to the ground, but I was lucky. We were able to get the horses out of the barn, but most of my camping supplies were destroyed in the fire.

After the fire was out, I went and looked over the damage. What I found surprised me a little. I found evidence that the lighting did not start the fire. It was started inside the barn in a bin for hay.

I called the sheriff to come out and take a look. He agreed. After the sheriff got to questioning everyone who was at or near the barn, he found out that the son of the owner had started the fire. The sheriff took him to jail.

Later that afternoon, the sheriff came to me and told me that the owner's son set the fire in the hope of killing my horses. He wanted to get back at you for the loss of his arm. He figured I was in the war and fought for the north.

I told the sheriff that I had been in the war, and I had been an Atillery Officer. I also told the sheriff I did not mention that I was even in the war or that I had been an Artillery Officer. I didn't say anything about it because he was so bitter about it.

The mother told the sheriff that what I told him was the truth.

The mother of the young man asked me if I would not charge her son for starting the fire, she would pay for all my supplies. She would send a rider into Cincinnati the next day to get everything I had lost in the fire. She also said she would give me free room and board while I waited. I agreed as long as her son was kept in jail until I had my supplies and was gone. She reluctantly agreed.

The sheriff said he would keep the young man in jail until I was gone for at least two days. He also said he heard the agreement and would see that it was carried out.

I gave her a list of the supplies and equipment I lost in the fire. It took her several days to get my supplies. I used that time to work with my horses. The fire had scared them. I needed to get them back in shape before we continued on our way.

* * * * *

The next several entries showed that the woman kept her word. He had little else to comment on except for the fact it had delayed him for several weeks.

Once he was on his way, again. I was surprised to see he had not made any entries in the journal for four days.

June 23, 1867

I made it almost as far as Harrison when my packhorse stumbled in a hole near the edge of the road about a half mile from the settlement of Harrison. I was able to get him to the blacksmith's shop and stable in Harrison. The blacksmith took one look at the injury and shook his head. He suggested that I leave the horse with him for at least a week to see how he responds to the treatments the blacksmith would use. Since he felt the horse might be ready to travel in about ten or eleven days, I decided to stay in the hope of being able to move on with my pack horse.

July 2, 1867

I have been camping in a grove of trees at the west side of the town. My riding horse didn't seem to mind hanging around and eating the grass. I did purchase some oats for him. I walked into town every day to help with the treatment of my packhorse.

By the second week, my packhorse seemed to be doing only a little better. By the end of the third week the blacksmith said he thought the horse was ready to travel, but only if he did not carry any extra weight for at least a week, but more like ten days.

I wasn't sure what I was going to do. It seemed that everything that happened to me over the past few weeks or so was to prevent me from getting to the Black Hills.

I had to have a packhorse if I was to move on. My travels had been delayed by three weeks already. I told the blacksmith that I needed a packhorse.

A local man, a friend of the blacksmith, stopped by the blacksmith's shop. The blacksmith suggested that I talk to the man because he raised mules. I took his advice.

The man suggested that I trade my packhorse to him for a mule. He said he was looking for a riding horse for his young son. He seemed to think that my horse would recover completely in time, and would make a good horse for his son. He also said that a mule was a better animal as a pack animal. I was sure he was right. I took the rest of the day to think about it.

I decided that the man was right. The man brought three mules into town for me to look over and hopefully pick out one to help me get on my way.

I looked over the animals. Since I had dealt with mules in the past, I had a pretty good idea of what to look for in a good animal. The animals were good strong animals and in very good shape. I picked out one that was not a real young mule, but not very old either. He was almost as big as my saddle horse, and would have a gait that was about the same as my horse. I could not see anything that would cause me not to make the trade.

Since I was not all that attached to the horse. I was sure that the horse would make a good riding horse for the man's son, once his injury healed. I also knew that I would be getting into some rough country. I made the trade and will get on my way in the morning.

I'm writing this while watching my new mule. My horse and the mule seem to get along well. I'm hopeful that they will work together on the trail. It's getting late so I will close my journal and get some rest.

I might note here that the past few weeks have given me and my saddle horse some time to get rested up. Traveling everyday can be taxing on a person and on a horse. I was able to fill my time helping the blacksmith from time to time as well as doing a little fishing and hunting. I sold some of my meat from a deer I shot to the blacksmith and his family.

* * * * *

Isaac must have had a great deal of concern when his packhorse came up lame. He was lucky to find someone who could help him without taking advantage of him. I'm sure the rest was well needed as Isaac had been pushing pretty hard for several months to get as far as he had.

July 4, 1867

I had lost almost a month of travel time. I got up early, had breakfast then packed up my things. The mule had no objections to being used as a pack animal. As soon as I was ready, I started out. The day was warm, but not too hot, and the sky was clear all day. The road I was taking was a pretty solid road. The rain over the past couple of days had not made it muddy. The land was fairly flat with a number of farms along the way. The end result was I made good time.

I figure I made about twenty-nine to thirty miles to-day. I got as far as Greensburg. I found a place to camp near a creek just outside of town. I managed to kill a rabbit for dinner.

I checked over my horse and mule to see how well they handled the long day. Both of them look to be in good shape. They did seem to like where I was camping. There was plenty of grass and water. I also gave them each a handful of oats.

I just looked over at them. It looks like they are sleeping. I should do the same.

I had just laid down when I heard what sounded like someone shooting in the town. I soon heard the sound of people cheering.

It suddenly came to me. The people of Greensburg were celebrating the fourth of July, our nations anniversary. It was a sad moment for me when I thought of all the July 4ths that didn't get celebrated during the war. But by the same token, I was glad that people were celebrating the fact our Union was still one country. I laid down in my bedroll and listened to those celebrating while I wrote this.

As soon as things settle down for the night, I will put my journal down and get some rest.

July 5, 1867

I woke to a nice bright morning. My horse and mule were looking at me as if to say, 'it's time to get up and get moving". It didn't take me long to have my breakfast and get the animals ready to travel. There was a slight breeze out of the south, and the day looked like it was a good day to travel. I went into Greensburg for a few supplies, then moved on. The road I was on took me west and a little South to Columbus on the Driftwood River. I made about twenty-four miles today. I camped along the river after crossing it. To-morrow, it looks like I will be getting into some hilly country. I doubt I will make very many miles, but I will still be moving toward my goal.

July 6, 1867

I left the Columbus area and continued west. The road was not very straight as it meanders around some hills and around a few lakes. The one good thing was that there seemed to be a variety of small animals that would provide me with meat. I killed a couple of rabbits which would last me about two days, maybe three.

The fact that it was pretty hilly in this region caused me not to make as much progress as I hoped. Although my horse and mule didn't seem to mind, I felt it was better not to make as many miles as I had been making. I didn't know how many miles of this type of terrain I would have before it leveled out.

I stopped at a little settlement called Belmont. There was not much there, just a small general store and a blacksmith's shop. I camped in a grove of trees only about fifty yards from the general store. After I took care of my horse and mule, I walked over to the general store.

The gentleman that ran the general store was very talkative. He seemed very much interested in where I was from and where I was going. We must have talked for an hour.

As soon as I left the general store, I noticed that my horse and mule were not where I left them. I knew I had secured them before I left. It didn't take but a minute for it to became clear why the owner of the general store wanted to talk so long.

I immediately turned around and went back in the general store. I walked up to the owner of the store, quickly drew my gun and stuck it under his chin. I quietly said, "You will return my animals within the next two minutes, or I will blow your head off."

"I don't have them," he said, obviously scared that I might just kill him.

I looked around the general store. I grabbed the man by his shirt and moved him in front of the counter. It didn't take me long to see three cans of coal oil. I picked up a rope that was close to the cans. I made a loop in it and put the loop around the owner's neck. I pulled it up tight making it easy for me to control him. I walked him over to a ceiling beam and tossed the end of the rope over the heavy beam and tied it so he could just barely have his feet on the floor. I took one of the cans of coal oil and poured it on the floor. I could see the fear on his face.

"Now, I want my animals back in as good a condition as when they were taken, or I will light the coal oil. How long do you think it will take to burn this store to the ground?" I asked, not really interested in an answer.

I also told him if anyone tried to stop me from getting my animals and leaving this place, I would do a lot more than burn his store down. With the owner under control, I started looking for anything that I could use to make sure I could get away. I found a box of dynamite and fuses. I showed it to the owner of the store as I took a half a dozen sticks.

He became very cooperative when I took six sticks and put fuses on them. I also took a couple of cigars off the counter. I put one in my mouth and lit it. I didn't have to tell him what I was prepared to do to get my animals back.

The owner of the store started yelling for someone named Buck to return the animals immediately or I would burn down his store. He also told this guy called Buck that I had explosives and wouldn't hesitate to use them to destroy the town.

It wasn't but a couple of minutes when I saw someone come out of the woods near the side of the store. He was leading my horse and mule. I told him to drop his guns, and if I saw anyone with a gun, this little town would no longer exist. It was only a minute or so before three other young men came out of the woods, drop their guns on the ground, then stood in front of the general store. All the young men looked a lot like the man I had inside the general store.

I had the four men move over to the porch of the general store. *While keeping a close eye on them, I picked up their guns and dropped them in the rain barrel at the corner of the store.*

I moved across the road to where I had my camp. While still smoking a cigar, and with a couple of sticks of dynamite in my belt, I packed up my horse and mule. None of them made a move.

I swung into the saddle and looked over at those standing there watching me. I took one stick of dynamite and touched the fuse to the end of the cigar. As soon as the fuse started to burn, I tossed to toward those standing in front of the general store. They started to scatter while I got the hell out of there. I hadn't gone very far when the dynamite exploded.

I went down the road about four miles then turned off and set up camp where I could not be seen from the road. I didn't build a fire that might give my location away. I found a place where I could get some sleep.

* * * * *

WOW! I knew that there was a possibility that Isaac might run into some trouble during his travels, but I never thought it would be anything like that. It was probably the only way he could handle the situation by himself and still get his animals back, and get away. I felt that I was getting my first real look at Isaac, and the man he had become.

July 7, 1867

I woke rather early. I wanted to get as far down the road as possible. The last thing I wanted was to have those men from the settlement of Belmont find me. I packed up and headed out without having breakfast. I moved along at a pretty good pace until about noon when I got to Clear Creek, Indiana.

I stopped in at the Sheriff's Office and told him about the confrontation in Belmont. He started to laugh. I didn't know what was so funny. I certainly didn't think it was funny or even fun at the time. I was scared. It was me against five.

The sheriff said he didn't think what they had tried to do was funny, but he would have liked to have seen those men's faces when I tossed that stick of dynamite at them. He did say that the only disappointment he had with it was that I didn't blow up the general store.

I went to a little café in Clear Creek and had a good meal. It was run by the sheriff's wife. The sheriff and I talked while we ate together. He bought my meal. After saying goodbye to the sheriff and his wife, I got on my way again.

I continued on down the road as far Bloomfield where I picked up some supplies, then went on about another mile and a half to the White River. I took my horse and mule off the road and down by the river to a small grove of trees. I set up camp there for the night. It was quiet there.

It is getting dark so I think I will put my journal away and get some sleep.

July 8, 1867

To-day, I had a good day. My horse and mule seemed to want to move along. It was mostly gently rolling hills, without many steep hills. Where I grew up, we would have called it farmland. We made about thirty miles to the little town of Sullivan. I talked to the blacksmith. He told me that it was about eleven miles to a ferry that would take me across the Wabash River and into Illinois. He suggested that I camp in a little grove of trees out behind his shop after I purchased some hay and a small bag of oats for my horse and mule. He said no one would bother me there.

After I set up my camp, he came over and sat down with me at my campfire. He was an interesting man. We had a lot to talk about as he was a blacksmith for the U.S. Army during the war.

When it was getting dark, he said good night and left. I sat back against a tree and wrote this entry into my journal.

July 9, 1867

The blacksmith's wife fixed me a plate of eggs and ham, and a cup of coffee. Needless to say, I didn't get a real early start, but my horse and mule didn't mind. It was mid-morning, a little after ten when I arrived at the ferry. It cost me 25 cents for each of my animals and 25 cents for me to get across the Wabash River. The horse didn't like the movement of the raft, but he settled down when I stood by him and rubbed his neck and talked to him softly. The mule didn't seem to care. It took about thirty minutes to get across the river.

After we got across the river, it was pretty easy going. It was a lot like Indiana, mostly farmland with fairly large groves of trees between the farms. We got to Newton before we stopped for the night. There was a small lake just outside of the town. Since the day had been pretty hot, I took a swim in the lake. The cool water felt good. I set up camp there and built a fire. I'm sitting next to a big oak tree while I write this in my journal. The sun has set, so I will close for now.

* * * * *

I had to smile at the cost of using the ferry raft to get across the Wabash River.

I turned the page.

July 10, 1867

To-day I only made it as far as Wheeler, Illinois, about fourteen miles. The day was hot and sunny. At Wheeler, there was a small creek where I was able to get water for my horse and mule. The Creek was only about two and a half feet across and about six to eight inches deep. There was a big oak tree only a few yards from the creek. I set up camp there.

It was just a short time after I set up camp when a boy about ten or eleven years old came by with a fishing pole. He sat down on the bank of the creek and dropped his line in the water about fifteen feet from me. I walked over to him and asked him if there were any fish in this creek. He told me there were, but I would have to be very quiet if I wanted to catch one.

I got my fishing pole out, dropped my line in the water, and sat down beside the boy. I started to talk to him, but he told me if we talked the fish would go way upstream because they don't like noise. We sat quietly for close to an hour before he caught a fish. It was about ten inches long. He looked at me and smiled. I didn't say anything, but I nodded an approval. Suddenly, I had a fish on my line. My fish was about 9 inches long, just right for my dinner.

It was just at that moment I heard a woman call for the boy to come home. The boy looked at me, then said he had to go home for dinner. He took his fish and left without another word.

As I watched him leave, I wondered if my son had lived if we would go down to the creek near the farm to fish together. It was a moment of sadness for me, but at the same time it had been a pleasant time, too.

I got up, built a small fire and had the fish for dinner. It tasted good.

After dinner, I laid out my bedroll. I sat there and wrote this while it was still fresh in my mind.

I think I will put up my Journal and go to sleep with pleasant thoughts of a little boy who kept me company for a little while without doing a lot of talking.

* * * * *

I'm sure it was a pleasant time for Isaac, but at the same time it was a sad time. I recalled a few times when I went fishing with my son. I turned the page. The date on the next page immediately caught my attention. I wondered why there were so many days between his last entry and his next one. I would only find out by reading on.

July 16, 1867

The past few days I have not felt much like writing. During the thunder storm on the morning of the eleventh, lightening hit a tree near me. It spit the tree, knocking it down. One of the large branches hit me in the head knocking me out. It also hit my shoulder.

The woman whose little boy I had fished with came to my aid. She took me into her small cabin and dressed my wounds. She also brought my horse and mule to her place and put them in her barn where she took care of them.

She said that I was out for two days. When I came around, I was a little confused. She nursed me until I was able to get up and move around without help.

Today, I was able to walk around outside for a little while. I spent some time in the barn taking care of my horse and mule. The woman had also taken good care of them. I found my belongings in the barn. She had carefully stacked them on a bench so they would not get dirty. I searched through my pack and found my journal.

I spent a good part of the day with the little boy. I found out his name was Billy. Of course, we had to go fishing, so we didn't talk much. However, he did tell me his mother's name was Emma Saxton, and his father had died in the war. He said his father was in the U.S. Army and that he was a cavalry officer.

Emma works in a small shop in Wheeler. It was owned by one of her three brothers. She did have a young man come to call and sit with her for awhile. I don't think he liked the idea that she had taken me in, but he was still very polite, though rather cool toward me when I was around.

I am feeling pretty good today. I told Emma that I would be leaving in the morning and asked her if there was anything I could do for her. She told me to be careful in my travels and to have a safe journey. I decided to leave her a few dollars for taking care of my horse and mule, and for the cost of taking *care of me. It is time for me to get some rest, so I will close for now.*

* * * * *

It was good that there was someone to help Isaac. I am pretty sure he will probably be moving rather slowly over the next couple of days. Some of his juries would still bother him for a little while. If nothing else, he would have some bruises that would cause some discomfort and stiffness. He might even get a headache if he does too much.

I found it interesting that he didn't say much about Emma other than she was Billy's mother, and that she had taken care of him.

It was time to turn the page and read on.

July 17, 1867

I was up pretty early this morning. Emma was also up early. She insisted that I have a good meal before I left. She fixed me breakfast of pancakes, eggs and venison steak. I have to admit it was very good and very filling.

After breakfast, Billy and his mother saw me off. Just before I went out of sight, I waved them goodbye. I don't know what it was, but I thought about the little boy and his mother all day.

I only made it about ten miles today. After having breakfast with Emma and Billy, I didn't get as early a start as I would have liked. There was also the fact that by mid-afternoon, I was not feeling like I wanted to travel much longer. I found a place where I could settle in for the night in a small grove of trees at the edge of a farm. It was just a few yards off the road. I guess my head was not completely ready for any hard traveling. It was better to stop early and get some rest.

July 18, 1867

To-day, I passed through the town of Effingham. I stopped at a general store and talked to the owner for a few minutes after I purchased some supplies. He told me of a lake not very far down the road where I could camp out for the night. He seemed like a nice enough fellow, so I took his advice. He also told me that the fishing in the lake was good.

I spent about an hour fishing and had two nice sized fish for dinner. I also had a few vegetables I got at the general store.

It was nice to get a chance to swim and wash the dust off from my travels, and wash some clothes. By the time it was getting dark, I had a full stomach and I had clean clothes to wear the next day.

My fire is about to go out, so I will close for now and get some rest.

* * * * *

It appears that Isaac had a pretty good day. He didn't get very far, but it seems that he was feeling good after his bout with the storm. I'm sure the chance to get a bath in the lake, and to get clean clothes on did a lot for how he was feeling.

July 19, 1867

This morning, I got a good start to my day. I had a good breakfast, then left the lake. I continued heading west. The area was mostly farmland. It had slightly rolling hills, but for the most part it was reasonably flat. My horse and mule didn't seem to object to flatter land with a lot of farms. It was an easy walk for them. There was also plenty of grass to graze on when we stopped for a short rest.

I'm not sure how far we went to-day, but I do know we made very good progress. I'm camping along a river. I don't know what the river is called, but it has a pretty good current. I checked it out because I have to cross it. It looks like there is a place about a half a mile upstream from where I am camping where I can get across. I'll check it out in the morning.

It is starting to get dark. I'll put up my journal for now and get some rest. My horse and mule have already gone to sleep.

* * * * *

The next few entries were rather short. He had gotten across the river without difficulty. He never mentioned the name of the river, but looking it up on a current map, it appears that it might have been the Kaskaskia River. The next few entries were just short descriptions of mostly open farmland and of the few small settlements he passed through. They also showed that he was making good progress toward his goal of getting to the Black Hills.

July 28, 1867

Over the past few days, it began to become rather hilly. Every day was the same. By the end of the day, I was tired and my horse and mule were feeling the strain. I didn't feel much like writing. I was hoping that it would not be much longer before I would reach the Mississippi River. The hilly country was beginning to wear on my horse and mule.

About mid-day, to-day, we came over a hill and stopped. Laying out before me was a rather large river. It went north and south as far as the eye could see. It was also very wide. I was able to tell that it flowed in generally a southern direction. It had to be the Mississippi River.

From the road I was on, I could see off in the distance what looked like a ferryboat that I might use to get across the river. It was still some distance away, but we would get there by some time to-morrow.

Since I had put in a full day, I decided it might be a good idea if I set up camp in a small grove of trees. It would give my horse and mule a chance to rest a little before we headed down the hills to the river. They were showing the signs of being tired, but then so was I.

There is a clear sky to-night and a gentle breeze. It should be a good night to get some rest. I will close my journal for to-night.

* * * * *

It looks like Isaac has finally reached the Mississippi River. It had taken him only a few days short of four months to do it. He still has a long way to go to get to the Black Hills.

July 29, 1867

I got up this morning with high spirits. The only thing I could think of was I had made it to my first goal, the Mississippi River. I knew it was still a long way to the area called the Black Hills. I was sure that as soon as I was across the river, I would finally be in the Frontier.

As I looked at my horse and mule and saw that they were both still sleeping, I thought it might be a good idea if I took my time to get to the river. We still had a long way to go. I needed to make sure they had enough rest and grazing time, or I might not get to my goal.

After my horse and mule had time to graze on the nice green grass, I packed the mule, saddled my horse, then started down the road to the river. I made it a point not to push them too hard.

When we finally reached the river, I turned north and rode along on a trail toward where the ferryboat was tied that I had seen last evening. It was mid-afternoon when I arrived at the ferry landing.

The attendant of the ferryboat told me that the ferryboat had just left for the other side. It would return about supper time. He told me that there would not be another crossing until morning. He also said that it would be one dollar for me, and one dollar for each animal. I thought that was very expensive, but I had little choice but to pay it.

Since I couldn't cross until morning, I found a place just off the trail along the bank of the river where I could camp for the night. I took the pack off my mule and unsaddled my horse.

It was a nice clear night, and there was almost a full moon, so I just laid out my bedroll under a tree for a place to sleep. I had my horse and mule tied fairly close.

It was a good thing that I am a light sleeper. Sometime during the night, I heard a twig snap. I quickly rolled off my bedroll to a place behind a tree close to my horse and mule. I saw two men. It was really only the shadow of two men. They were sneaking up to my horse. *I drew my pistol and pulled the hammer back. The loud clicking of the hammer of my Navy Colt setting seemed to get their attention.*

"Taking a man's horse can get you killed," I said quietly. The shadows disappeared rather quickly. I could hear them run off, well away from my horse and mule.

I moved my bedroll, as well as my horse and mule, to a different location just in case they decided to try again. They would not find me very easily, if they did, I would be ready for them.

* * * * *

It seems that Isaac drew a bit of attention from local ruffians who had it in mind to steal his horse and mule. It was good to see that he was aware of the dangers he would face traveling alone.

July 30, 1867

I got up early this morning. I had a breakfast of biscuits, salt pork and coffee. As soon as I was done, I put out my fire, then packed up and put the packs on my mule. As soon as my mule was ready, I saddled my horse and headed toward the ferry landing.

When I arrived, the attendant seemed surprised to see me. I stepped out of the saddle and walked up to him. From the way he looked and acted toward me, I was sure he knew what had happened last night.

"You didn't expect to see me, did you?" I said to him.

He didn't comment. He looked at me as if he was angry with me. He also looked a little disgusted, but it was probably not with me. I figured he was disgusted with his two boys because they didn't get my horse and mule, and I was still alive.

"You are going to take me across the river for free," I told him as I drew my pistol and pointed at his stomach. "In fact, you are going to ride the ferryboat with me all the way to the other side."

"I don't go across", he said sharply. "My two sons will be on the ferryboat and take you across," he replied.

"Not this time. Your two sons are going to stay here. They tried to steal my horse and mule last night, but didn't get them. If they try anything, or even look like they might try something, you will be the first to die. I suggest you let them know that."

I had given him instructions on how it was going to be, and used my pistol to make sure he understood how things were going to be. With my pistol pointed at his gut, he decided that it was in his best interest to take me across alone.

With my gun on him, and walking close to him, he led my horse and mule onto the ferryboat. Once on the ferryboat, I tied the attendant to the rail.

With not so gentle a jab of my pistol in his gut, he told his sons to wait for him to come back, and not to do anything that might cause me to shoot him. I told them that if they did try to stop me, they could pick up their father's body downstream. Since the attendant didn't have a weapon and was secured to the ferryboat, the crossing of the river went without a hitch. I could see his two sons were standing on the landing. There wasn't much they could do except what I told them. The two sons were mad as hell, but knew better than to try anything if they wanted their father back alive.

I decided that it would not be a good idea to leave them with a way to get across the river and come after me before I had a chance to get some distance away from the landing.

Once I got across, I got my horse and mule off the ferryboat and tied them to a nearby tree. Since the attendant was secured to the ferryboat in a way that prevented him from having any control of the ferryboat, and I was sure he couldn't get loose, I cut the lines so the ferryboat would simply float free and would slowly drift down the river with the current.

It would probably go for several miles before it would hit land or something that would stop it. The boys would have to work their way down the river until they would be able to retrieve it. It would probably take them a couple of days to get the ferryboat back to the landing. The river was wide enough at this place that it would be very difficult for the boys to swim across or get their horses across without the ferryboat.

As soon as the ferryboat began to drift down stream, I got in the saddle and rode away with my mule trotting along behind. I figured it would take them the better part of three days, maybe four to get the ferryboat back to the landing and be able to come after me. In that time, I could be a long way from the river.

Just to make sure I was safely away from them, I rode until it was starting to get dark. I found a nice place to camp for the night. I make this entry by the light of my fire.

* * * * *

It seems that Isaac had things under control. It would be my guess that the ferryboat attendant and his two sons would have their hands full just trying to catch the ferryboat. And once they got the ferryboat, they would have to drag it up current to the landing before they could even use it.

August 2, 1867

I was up early this morning. I had traveled rather hard the last couple of days in order to get as far away from the Mississippi River as I could. I had traveled almost straight west.

To-day, I turned onto a road that seems to run in a northwesterly direction. It should take me to the state of Iowa. The road seems to have been well traveled which will make it harder for anyone to follow me.

I will not push my horse and mule as hard today, but I should still make a fair number of miles. The road is a little way away from the river. It is fairly flat with a lot fewer trees.

I will still have to keep my eyes open. I stung the ferryboat attendant and his two sons pretty good. I doubt they will follow me very far, not more than a couple of days from the ferry landing. However, the attendant just might be mad enough to tell his boys not to come back until they were sure that I was dead.

I found a place near a creek where there was a little grass and plenty of water for my animals. I moved well off the road where it would be hard for anyone to see me or my animals. There were several bushes and a couple of trees that made a good place to rest for the night.

I will close for now.

August 3, 1867

  I had been up for awhile and was just getting my horse saddled when I heard what sounded like a couple of horses running down the road. Since I was well off the road, I ducked down behind the bushes and watched to see who it was. It was no surprise that it was the ferryboat attendant's two sons. They apparently had not waited to get the ferryboat back to the landing, or it got tangled up and didn't go very far down river.
  Just as they passed by me, I stepped out onto the road and fired a shot in the air. They reined up and looked back to see who had fired the shot. The older son decided to try his luck and started to draw his pistol. I quickly shot him.
  He had broken the first rule of gunfighting. 'Never draw against a man who has a gun in his hand and it is already pointed at you'.
  The younger son looked like a kid. He looked at his brother as he fell out of the saddle onto the road. He then turned and looked at me. I could see the fear on his face.
  "Kid, you can either try to kill me, or you can take your brother's body back to the ferry landing and live to see another day," I told him. My gun still in my hand.
  "I don't want to go back and I don't want to try to kill you." He also said that his father was wrong to rob people.
  "If that is how you truly feel, then we can bury your brother here. After we bury him, you can go wherever you please. But you will not be going with me."
  "I understand. I've often thought that I would like to go to New Orleans."
  "You head south. You can avoid your father's ferry landing by staying away from the river until you are past it. After you get well past where your father has his ferry landing, you could turn and move close to the river. Then it's just following the river downstream." I also told him not to try to follow me, and if he did, I might have to kill him.

The kid didn't say anything. He simply nodded, swung his horse around, spurred his horse, then headed south on the road without looking back. I watched him until he was out of sight.

As soon as I was sure he was gone, I then buried his brother just off the road. I kept an eye out to make sure the kid didn't come back. The kid left the area, leaving me with an extra horse and saddle. I figured it was owed to me.

I continued along the road, looking back every once and awhile just to make sure he didn't come back. I didn't see the kid again.

I went as far as Frankford before I stopped for the night. I stopped in to talk to the blacksmith. I had him put new shoes on the new horse. I traded him the extra saddle for shoeing the horse and for putting my animals up for the night.

I went to a boarding house where I had a good meal and will spend the night in a real bed. I'm sitting on the bed writing this. It is really comfortable. I'll close for now and get some sleep.

August 4 1867

I got a good night's sleep and a good breakfast at the boarding house. My two horses and mule seemed to be well rested after a night in the blacksmith's stable.

I continued to move in a northwesterly direction. I made a point of staying away from the river where the land was flatter and my animals didn't have to work so hard. I figured that it would take at least a week just to get to Iowa.

I still kept an eye out for the kid. I wasn't sure if he would go south to New Orleans or try to sneak up on me. He sounded sincere about going south, but it wouldn't hurt to be watchful.

I got past the little town of New London to-day where I came upon a small river. I crossed the river and found a nice quiet-looking place where the grass was green and the trees provided me with a place to put my shelter. I set up camp, then spent a little time in the river. The cool water felt good after a hot day of travel. Even the animals went wading in the river.

After a meal of rabbit and a few vegetables, and an apple for dessert, I laid back against a tree to write this. It is time to get some rest.

August 7, 1867

To-day I arrived in Kirksville. The past few days have been pretty routine with a good number of farms along the road.

The area was fairly flat until to-day when it became more like rolling hills. The animals handled it well.

After getting some oats for my animals, I went to the local saloon for a beer. It might have been better if I had skipped the saloon. There were two men who had been drinking heavily, apparently for awhile. One of them was getting pretty nasty.

When I walked in the door, he shouted rather loudly something to the effect that there's a damn Yankee coming in the saloon, as he pointed at me. His voice was so slurred I could hardly make out what he said.

His partner tried to get him to shut up, but he was too drunk to listen. He went for his gun, but I was faster. He was so drunk that he almost missed his gun when he reached for it. He didn't clear leather before I had my gun right in his face, only a few inches from the end of his nose. He froze. It seemed a gun in his face sobered him up enough that he realized I could kill him.

I told his friend to get him out of there, and that if I saw him again, I would not wait for him to draw on me. I would simply shoot him.

I watched as his friend took him out of the saloon. As soon as he was gone, I got my beer and sat down at a table in a corner to drink it. Things quickly settled down. The bartender came over to where I was sitting and sat down.

"I'm glad you didn't kill him," the bartender said. "He only gets like that when he drinks too much."

I asked the bartender "why do you let him drink like that? Some one is going to kill him if he keeps up that way."

"I'm not sure that isn't what he wants," the bartender said.

He didn't say anything more, he just nodded that he agreed with what I had said, then returned to the bar. I finished my beer and went back to the blacksmith's shop and got my animals.

I decided it might be best if I left town, so I moved on. There was a creek about two miles out of town with several trees along the bank. I settled down for the night there. I am sitting against a tree while I write this.

* * * * *

I guess it takes all kinds of people, but I'm not surprised. Shortly after the war between the States, there were a good number of men who were angry about the outcome of the war, or about the futility of it, I'm not sure which. There were a number of reasons for their anger. For some it was the injuries they sustained, and for others it was the loss of friends. It has been that way all through time.

August 9, 1867

Yesterday was rather uneventful. The weather was pleasant and the animals seemed to do well.

To-day, I crossed into Iowa. I made a brief stop in the little settlement of Centerville and picked up a few supplies.

I continued to a lake where I found a place to camp. The water was cool and felt good after a hot day in the sun. The animals enjoyed some time in the water as well. I washed a few things and even splashed some water on my horses and mule. I think the mule liked it more than the horses.

I got a rabbit for my dinner. All in all, a pretty good day. I'm sitting under a nice big cottonwood tree to write this. It is growing dark, so I will put my journal up for to-night.

August 12, 1867

The past few days have been pretty much the same. A lot of open spaces and farms. Not much to write about. The land has been pretty flat except for this afternoon. It has slowly turned into more rolling hills. And it had been hot every day. I stopped for the night in Attica.

I met a young lady at the general store. While talking to her, I told her I was heading for Lone Tree Crossing. I didn't tell her why.

According to the young lady, I was getting close to the Des Moines River. She told me that there was a place to cross the river about five or six miles from Attica. However, she said if I was headed for the Lone Tree Crossing, it would be easier if I headed straight west from there and didn't cross the Des Moines River. By going straight west, I would almost run into Lone Tree Crossing at the Missouri River, and I would not have to cross the Des Moines River at all.

I asked her how she knew the way to Lone Tree Crossing. She said her uncle had been there, and he had told her about it. She also said that her uncle had been a wagon master on two trips to the Promised Land a few years ago. Omaha was only one of several starting points for those going to the Promised Land or just moving west.

I bought a few things at the general store, then went to the edge of town. I will spend the night in a small grove of trees at the edge of town. I will start west in the morning.

August 13, 1867

I only got as far as Sandyville to-day. It was rather hilly, and mostly uphill as I rode up out of the Des Moines River valley. Once out of the river valley, the ground seems to be much flatter. I will not push my animals very hard to-morrow as they worked pretty hard to-day. I traded off riding between the two horses just to make it easier on them. The mule didn't seem to mind, but he looked a bit tired when we got to Sandyville.

I found a place where there was some shade and a little creek nearby. I will spend the night there. Once my animals had grazed a bit, I gave them all a good helping of oats, and rubbed them down.

It seems they have settled in for the night. I think I will do the same.

* * * * *

I have some knowledge of Iowa. It has large areas where it is fairly flat with mostly gently rolling farmland except in areas where there are creeks and small rivers. Over the next few days, his journal entries confirmed that.

August 17, 1867

To-day I passed through the little town of Greenfield. I only stopped long enough to get a few supplies from the only store. The only other business was a blacksmith's shop and stable. I bought a bag of oats since I was running low on it.

When I arrived in the town, I saw a man sitting on the porch in front of the store. It made me a little nervous since he watched me very closely as I tied my animals to the hitching rail in front of the store. He never took his eyes off me from the time I arrived until I was in the store. As I came out of the store, he seemed to be taking a little more interest in my animals than I thought was reasonable. He never said a word, and he looked like he didn't want anyone to talk to him.

Although there was what looked like a nice place to camp for the night across the road from the store, I decided to continue on. I went on down the road about two miles when I came to a narrow river. I crossed the river and went about a hundred yards south along the river before I stopped for the night. I will keep my animals close so they will let me know if anyone comes around.

Nothing had happened while I sat under a tree to write in my journal.

* * * * *

After what has happened during this trip, it is easy to see why Isaac is being cautious. I hope nothing happened to delay his trip. I turned the page to find out.

August 18, 1867

Last night I didn't get a lot of sleep. I guess the man on the porch of the store made me a little nervous. I woke up every time any of my animals made any kind of sound. I got up early and couldn't go back to sleep. I fixed my breakfast, got my mule packed up and saddled my horse. I made about twenty-five miles to-day and camped along another shallow river.

It was another hot day with little breeze. I spent a little time in the river just to cool off a bit.

After last night, I will try to get some sleep to-night. It's just getting dark and my animals have already gone to sleep. I'll put up my journal.

August 19, 1867

To-day I got to a little river about two miles west of Carson. There was a rather large heavy covered Conestoga wagon just on the west side of the river. There was little doubt in my mind that it would take large, strong animals like they had to pull such a large wagon. Down at the river there were eight very large oxen. There was also a young girl knee deep in the water standing watch over the oxen. I crossed the river.

As I rode toward the wagon, a man stepped out from behind it. He had a rifle he held loosely in his hands. I stopped close to the wagon, but didn't get down off my horse. I introduced myself to him and told him that I was going to Lone Tree Crossing on the Missouri River, and asked him if they were also headed that way.

He asked me if I was planning to camp there. I told him that I was, but if it bothered him that I was there, I would find another place to camp. He suggested that I move on.

Just as I was about to "move on", a woman came around the wagon and called to the man. She told him that he should allow me to camp there.

The woman told me I would be welcome to have dinner with them, and I should feel free to camp any place I would like. I told her I would like to have dinner with them, and I would camp just down the river from them.

After I got my animals watered and hobbled for the night, I walked over to where they had their fire. I had a very good dinner with them, then sat around their fire and talked.

They were the Jenkins family from Atlanta, Georgia. The woman was the wife of Harold Jenkins. The young girl was their daughter. She was about seventeen and seemed very interested in me and where I was going.

We talked for some time. The girl even asked me why I had two horses. I explained how I came about having them. She was not sure how she felt about what I had done to end up with two horses, but she certainly understood about defending *myself. I found the girl to be very knowledgeable, and wise beyond her years. She was also very pretty. She reminded me of my wife in many ways. It was well after dark when I excused myself and went to where I was camped. I leaned back against a tree to write this while my fire burned itself out.*

* * * * *

It seemed that Isaac had met a young woman he found he liked. I wondered if he would travel with them for awhile, or if he would go on his way like he had planned.

August 20, 1867

I got up early and headed out. The Jenkins family was hitching up the oxen when I left. The young woman saw me as I was leaving. I waved to her. She looked as if she was disappointed that I didn't take the time to have breakfast with them, although I did say goodbye to all of them last night.

I arrived at Lone Tree Crossing in late afternoon. There were several wagons that were in line to be ferried across the Missouri River ahead of me. I had been waiting for my turn for over two hours to get across when a big man came up to me. He asked if I was with any of the wagons. I told him that I was not, and that it was just me and my three animals. He told me to follow him.

I followed him to the front of the line. I paid him the three and a half dollars for myself and my three animals. He then guided me onto the ferryboat. There was already a covered wagon and four horses on the ferryboat. As soon as I had my animals tied to the railing, they pushed off. I was told that there was room for me because the covered wagon was fairly small, but not for another wagon. He also said that it would be most of to-morrow if I had to wait for the big covered wagons ahead of me to cross.

I also got the impression that the more he could put on the ferryboat, the more money he would make. From a business stand-point, it only made sense to me.

Once I got across to Omaha in the Nebraska Territory, I found a very busy town. There were wagons of all different sizes and kinds. There were people trying to buy animals to pull their wagons or to ride. Everything was very expensive, and I mean everything was expensive.

I went to the blacksmith shop. The blacksmith was very busy. There was a woman sitting at a table in front of the shop. She seemed to be dealing with everyone. I walked up to her. She looked up and said "I don't have any wagons or horses or oxen to sell you."

I said, "I don't want to buy anything. I'm looking to sell this horse." It was the one I got awhile back.
She got up and looked at the horse that I was willing to sell. After looking it over, she called the blacksmith over to look at the horse. He seemed pleased.
"Is this here horse yours to sell?" he asked.
"Yes. It belonged to a man who tried to steal my horse and mule. He no longer has a need for it," I told him.
"What do you want for the horse?" he asked.
"What would it cost me for a room and a bath, and a place to put up my other horse and mule for the night? That would include feeding them." I asked.
He took another look at the horse, a very close look. He seemed very interested in the horse. With the prices of everything there, I was sure he could make a fair profit by selling it.
"We got a little cabin out back next to the barn. One night with dinner and breakfast. There's a tub in the cabin you can use for a bath. My daughter will heat up the water for you, and wash out one set of clothes. Your horse and mule will be put up in the barn out back and given a good rub-down and fed well. All that for the horse you want to sell. By the way, there ain't no place to get lodging in this town. All them places are full up," he told me.
I told him that he had a deal. Not having two horses, one I didn't really need, would cost me less in feed and a second horse would be hard to handle if I should be attacked out on the plains.
I got my dinner with a young woman serving it. She also heated water for my bath and washed a few of my clothes. I spent a good part of the evening at the blacksmith's shop. It was a pretty busy place, so I helped out a little by taking care of my own animals. When it started to get dark, I went to the cabin. It took awhile to get some sleep because it seemed that

the town was busy all night. However, I did get this entry in my journal finished.

* * * * *

It seems that Isaac had a pretty busy day. It turned out to be a good thing he had the extra horse. It sounded like he didn't have enough money to get a room and a meal in Omaha. If I remember my history, he described Omaha very well. It was one of several jumping off places for those heading for the Promised Land or out west. Everything was very expensive.

August 21, 1867

I didn't get a real early start, but I did have a very nice breakfast. The blacksmith tried to get me to stay around and work with him, but I told him I had plans and I needed to get on my way.
I told him where I was headed. He told me to be very careful. There were a lot of Indians who roamed the prairie, and they attacked people now and then, especially if the person was alone. He did say that there were several forts along the Missouri River that tried to keep the Indians settled down, but they couldn't watch every mile of the area with so few soldiers.
I thanked him for the advice, got on my horse and headed north along the Missouri River. I had to travel sometimes a mile or more away from the river in order to avoid deep gullies and ditches. There were a lot of gullies and ditches where water could run off the land into the river. Crossing all of them would make it hard for my horse and mule. It was easier on them if I stayed away from the river. I only made about fifteen miles to-day.
I'm camped in a large grove of trees north of Omaha and on a creek that runs into the Missouri River. My horse and mule have settled in for the night, and I think I will, too.

August 22, 1867

To-day I have decided that I will go west for a little while to get me away from the Missouri River to where it will be easier for my horse and mule. From what information I have been able to gather from a couple of people I talked to in Omaha, the land away from the river is much flatter and will make it easier on my animals.

If I go west for a day or two, then turn north toward the river, I should come back to the Missouri River pretty close to Fort Randall. I'm thinking that I might be able to stay there for the winter. I have no desire to be out on the open prairie during the winter.

Sometime ago I read that the prairie of the Dakota Territory, and Nebraska Territory, can be rather harsh in as early as mid-September. It said that many had died crossing the prairie in a mid-September blizzard. If things go as they have, I could be in the middle of the South Dakota plains about that time.

August 23, 1867

I made it as far as Waterloo in the Nebraska Territory today, only about sixteen miles from Omaha. I met a man who lived just outside Waterloo. He has a small farm there. He told me that I could spend the night in a grove of trees about fifty feet from his cabin. He seemed like a nice enough fellow, so I camped there. It looked like his farm was doing pretty well.

His wife came out of the small log cabin after awhile. I spent a good part of the evening talking with him and his wife. The man told me that I was just a few miles east of the trail they called the Oregon Trail that ran along the Platte River.

I told him that I was not going that way. I told him that I was headed for the Army outpost called Fort Randall. He reminded me that I still had a long way to go.

He asked if I was in the Army, I told him I wasn't. I didn't want to get into an argument if he had served in the Confederate Army. It turned out that he had been in the Union Army.

After that we seemed to have a lot to talk about. We talked almost 'til dark, before I said good-night and went to where I was camping. I write this by candle light.

August 24, 1867

To-day, I left Waterloo in the Nebraska Territory and followed the Elkhorn River upstream. It was one of those fairly flat rivers that sort of meandered in a generally south and east, mostly south direction. Some places I had to move well away from the river so I could be on more even ground. Even so, I was able to stay fairly close to the river.

By mid-day, I noticed that clouds were starting to build, and the wind seemed to be getting stronger. I could see a storm brewing.

By mid-afternoon the clouds were getting darker. It looked like it might rain, and rain pretty hard. I moved toward the river so I could put up my shelter in the trees along the river.

I found a place were there were a couple of trees that had fallen. I built my shelter there and tied my horse and mule to a fallen tree. I wanted them close in case I needed to settle them down or move away from the river.

By the time I had gathered some dry branches for a fire, it started to rain. It wasn't long and it was blowing and raining pretty hard. I was glad that I built my shelter among the trees.

It rained and the wind blew pretty hard for about an hour before it settled into a nice gentle rain. I had been able to keep my firewood dry. I built a fire and cooked my dinner. After dinner, I sat in my shelter and watched it rain. It was dark before it stopped raining. I write this by the light of my fire. I will turn in for the night.

* * * * *

It seems that Isaac had learned to watch the weather out on the plains. It certainly can be unpredictable.

August 25, 1867

I didn't get a very early start to-day. It was mid-morning when I got to Fremont Station, a stage stop. I stopped to pick up some supplies at a general store. It was run by a lady in her early fifties. She seemed interested in where I was going. She said that she didn't see too many travelers along this route.

I told her that I was going to an Army outpost in the Dakota Territory. She said I was headed in the right direction if I was headed for Fort Randall.

She told me that I should keep following the Elkhorn River upstream until I got to a little settlement called O'Neill. She said it wasn't much, just a blacksmith shop, a saloon and a small general store. All were run by a man and his wife. She wasn't even sure it was still there as they had been having some problems with the Indians in that area.

She also said that some of the information she got about the area west and north of them was not always very good. It wasn't something a person could count on as being accurate. I had been warned about the Indians before, but so far they had not been a problem. I picked up a couple of things from the woman, then headed on my way.

I passed through Winslow; I went a few miles further then stopped for the night on the bank of the Elkhorn River. It had been a long day, but we didn't have any problems. After grazing a bit and getting a good drink of water, my horse and mule settled in to get some sleep. I think I'll do the same.

* * * * *

This is not the first time Isaac had heard about the Indians that he might encounter. I turned the page to see what Isaac was going to do.

August 26, 1867

To-day I started moving north and west along the Elkhorn River. I stayed on the east side of the river so I would not have to cross it when it was time for me to head straight north to Fort Randall. It was a good size river, but nothing that would cause me problems. There were a few areas where I had to go a little way away from the river so my animals didn't have to work so hard.

I found a good place to camp about seventeen miles from where I started to-day. It was a pleasant spot with large cottonwood trees and green grass.

I settled down under one of the cottonwood trees to write.

*****

The next few entries were not very interesting. The country was much the same.

August 29, 1867

I got a good start to-day. I arrived at Norfolk about mid-afternoon. It was a fair size settlement with several stores and shops.

Although there were still several hours of daylight, I decided that I would spend the night here. I would get a room at the small hotel, and have my animals put up at the blacksmith's shop and stable. I had the blacksmith give them a good rub down and plenty of feed with a bit of oats.

I went to the hotel, which was really a saloon with rooms to rent upstairs. I was able to get a bath in a little cabin out back of the saloon. After my bath, I had a drink in the bar then went to my room. I have to say, the bed was much more comfortable than sleeping on the ground.

I might note here, that there was some talk of problems with a few Indians making trouble a few miles west of town. I heard one of the men in the saloon say that they had burned out a family just west of Meadow Crossing. The family got out before they burned the buildings down, but the Indians got a couple of their work horses.

I found out that Meadow Crossing was a day's ride from Norfolk, and on the route I had planned to take. I decided that instead of following the Elkhorn River that ran close to Meadow Crossing, I would head northwest out of Norfolk. That would keep me a good fifteen to twenty miles away from Meadow Crossing, but still get me headed toward Fort Randall.

I need to get some rest so I can get an early start, so I will put up my journal now.

August 30, 1867

I got a pretty good start this morning. My animals seemed to be ready to press on. I gave them a good rub down and some extra oats. It seemed to agree with them. The bath and a bed to sleep in was very refreshing for me.

I talked to the blacksmith to find out if he had heard anything more about Indians in the general area I was headed. He said he hadn't heard anything new. I believed my decision to take the road that went north and west out of Norfolk was a good one.

I kept a watch out for any Indians, but didn't see any. I passed through a little settlement of Pierce shortly after noon. I talked to a man who was sitting out in front of a cabin to see if he had seen or heard anything new with regard to Indian trouble. He said he hadn't seen or heard anything.

I continued on to the stage station at Foster Junction. I camped behind the stage station. I felt a little more secure knowing that if trouble came, I would be able to hole up in the stage station with the manager. The manager of the stage station told me he felt a little better having someone close by who could help if trouble came our way.

We had a nice meal together and spent a good deal of time talking. It seems he didn't get a lot of company.

I'm writing this while sitting at the table inside the stage station. The station manager invited me to spend the night inside. I will be spending the night in the stage station. I had put my horse and mule up in his barn with the horses for the stagecoach before I settled in for the night.

August 31, 1867

I left the stage station at Foster Junction after having a good breakfast with the station manager. He wished me well. I don't know if he thought I was crazy going across the plains of the Nebraska Territory alone, but he did give me a few suggestions.

He suggested that when I stopped for the night on the plains, that I don't build a fire that gives off smoke, or have a fire after dark. He also told me to try to find a place where I could hide if Indians came around. He reminded me that I should try to avoid them because you never know if they are friendly or not until it's too late. It was all good advice, but I already knew it. I think it made him feel better telling me.

I left him watching me as I rode on down the road. I waved back at him. I had enjoyed spending the time with the old gentleman. I wished him well before I left.

At Plainview I talked to the stage station manager there. He wasn't as friendly as the one at Foster Junction. He flat out told me that I was crazy to be riding across the plains by myself. He may be right, but I was headed for Fort Randall. I bought a few things then moved on.

About six or seven miles northwest of Plainview, I found a place where there was a dry ravine that was deep enough that my horse and mule could stand in the bottom and not be seen from out on the plains. I decided to make my camp there. I could make a shelter so a small fire could not be seen.

After a good meal of rabbit, I leaned back against the wall of the ravine to write this. My fire is about to go out so I will close for tonight.

September 1, 1867

When I got up this morning, it was overcast. It didn't look like it was going to rain soon, but it was cool enough for me to get my jacket out and put it on.

As soon as I had everything ready to go, I took a minute or so to climb up to the edge of the ravine and look around. About the only thing I could see moving around on the plain were a few antelope. They were grazing and didn't seem to be disturbed by anything. That was a good sign for me. If they were comfortable, then it was not likely to be anything out there that should be of concern to me.

I led my animals out of the ravine, then stepped into the saddle on my horse. I then continued my way northwest.

I had traveled about fifteen miles north and west of my last camp when I saw six to eight Indians. I quickly took cover in a shallow ravine and prepared for a fight. I watched the Indians for several minutes. It was clear to me that they had not seen me.

They were riding in a northeasterly direction. They cut across the narrow trail I had been following about three hundred yards ahead of me. I waited until I was sure they could no longer see me if I came out of the shallow ravine that I had hidden in.

As soon as they were out of sight, I looked around to make sure there were no more of them. They appeared to be a hunting party.

Since I could not see any more Indians, I continued on northwest. However, I did set a little faster pace.

I continued to move a little faster for about two hours before I slowed down to a steady walk. It gave my animals a chance to relax a little. A good look at my animals showed me that I needed to find a place where they could get some well-deserved rest. I think we went about a total of twenty miles today, and most of it in a fairly short time.

I found a small, rather narrow creek with a few trees along the bank. There were some bushes where it would be fairly easy to hide. I led my animals into the creek so they could get a drink. As soon as they had their drink, I hobbled them in the grass so they could graze.

I built a small almost smokeless fire and fixed myself a meal of salt pork I got from the station manager at Foster Corner, and had it with cornbread and coffee.

After I ate and cleaned up, I sat down to write this. The fire is almost out and my animals are sleeping, it is time for me to get some rest.

September 2, 1867

I was up early. There was a gentle breeze, and it looked like it was going to be a pretty nice day. After breakfast and getting my mule packed up and my horse saddled, I started out.

I had only gone about three miles when I came upon a small cabin. There was also a small barn with a corral along one side. In the corral were two horses. I could see just a hint of smoke from the chimney of the cabin.

I approached the cabin slowly and with my hands in full view of anyone who might be in the cabin. I had no idea what to expect.

When I got close to the cabin, I called out. It took a minute before I could see the door start to open. As soon as it was open, I saw a woman with a rifle with a little boy standing close behind her. The boy was about seven years old.

"Are you alone?" I asked.

The woman said they were. She looked as if there had been something wrong. It looked as if she had been crying. I could only guess that it might have something to do with her husband, although at the time I had nothing to base that thought on.

As soon as she put the rifle down, I got off my horse and walked to her.

She said that she had buried her husband yesterday morning. After talking with her for a few minutes, I found out her husband had died from an accident in the barn. It seems that while working with a horse, the horse had gotten excited about something and accidently kicked her husband in the head. He died two days later, that was three days ago.

I also found out her name was Martha Collins and her son was Joseph. Her husband had been Martin Collins.

I asked her what she was going to do. She said that she was planning to go to her sister's place in Niobrara. She would stay with her and her husband in town. She was sure she could get a job at the store her sister's husband owned.

She also said that she would talk to her sister's husband about selling her small farm as she could no longer live out on the prairie with just her son.

I walked my horse up to the corral and tied him and my mule to the corral fence. We went into the house to talk. I told her where I was going and that Niobrara was a little out of my way. I also told her about the Indians I had seen earlier to-day.

The more we talked, the more I believed that it would not be that far out of my way if I was to see them safely to her sister's home. She reminded me that Fort Randall was in the Dakota Territory but on this side of the Missouri River. I didn't have to cross the Missouri River to get to the fort. She also said that it was about two days ride, maybe a bit more, from Niobrara.

Since it was about twenty miles to Niobrara, I decided that I would help them get a few things packed up and put in the wagon. Early in the morning we would go to Niobrara.

We spent the rest of the day loading her belongings into the wagon. She fixed a good meal for the three of us. When I finish writing my journal entry, I will go out to barn to sleep.

* * * * *

It seems that Isaac felt sorry for the woman and her young son. I was not surprised because he had been helpful to strangers before. He was probably concerned about her staying there since there were Indians roaming the area. A woman alone would be an easy target for them. I was sure that Isaac had thought of that.

September 3, 1867

The three of us were up early. We had a good breakfast. Once everything was cleaned up and put away, and the fire in the fireplace was put out, I tied my horse and mule to the back of the wagon and we left for Niobrara.

It was slow going with a loaded wagon, but the ground was fairly flat. She didn't want to talk very much. I noticed that she looked back a couple of times until we were out of sight of her cabin and barn. I got the feeling that she didn't really want to leave, but she also knew it was not safe for her and her son to stay there.

Joseph was pretty quiet, too. I was sure that he was missing his father.

It was getting fairly late when we arrived in Niobrara. She directed me to where her sister lived. It was a very emotional greeting when Martha and Joseph met Martha's sister. I just stood back and watched.

It was only after a few tearful minutes before Martha introduced me to her sister and her husband. They seemed glad to see us. They invited me in, but I told them that I needed to find a place to spend the night. Mr. Reinhart, Martha's brother-in-law told me they had room for me. He said "It is the least we can do for helping Martha". I thanked him, and told him I would stay the night.

It was after I took care of my animals that I sat down with Mr. Reinhart. We talked for some time. He seemed interested in what I was doing and where I was going.

It was getting late. I was ready to turn in. He told me he would have breakfast for me before I left.

I thanked him, then went to my room. I write this before I turn in for the night.

September 4, 1867

I got up after a good night's sleep to the sound of someone in the kitchen. When I entered the kitchen, I found Martha and her sister making breakfast. It sure smelled good. It was the best breakfast I have had for a very long time.

As soon as I finished eating, I said goodbye to Martha and Joseph. I thanked Mr. Reinhart and his wife for allowing me to spend the night in their home and for feeding me and my animals while I was there.

As soon as I was packed up, I started northwest staying about a mile from the Missouri River where the land was a little flatter and easier for my horse and mule. There were fewer gullies and ravines than if I traveled close to the river. They were also not as deep as those close to the river.

I was told that it would take me about two days to get to the fort. I was hoping that they were right. I made it a point to keep an eye out for trouble.

It was shortly after noon when I was set upon by seven Indians. They came charging out of a shallow ravine to the south of where I was. I made a run for a ravine about two hundred yards ahead of me.

As soon as I was in the ravine, I jumped off my horse and drew my rifle from my saddle scabbard. I quickly laid down and took aim at the Indians. I was able to get two of them rather quickly. The others seemed confused and pulled up. While they took a few seconds to look for a place to take cover, I shot one more of them.

They found a place to take cover, but it was very shallow. They had to keep their heads down to be out of my sight. It wasn't deep enough to hide their horses. I took a couple of shots very close to their horses, and the horses broke free and ran off leaving the Indians on foot in a very shallow depression in the ground.

I waited to see what they were going to do. At first, they did nothing. I got the feeling that they had not expected me to stay and fight.

It was about two or three minutes before I saw any movement from the Indians. I could just barely make out one of them crawling on his belly toward one of their horses. I took careful aim at the Indian and slowly eased back on the trigger. When my rifle fired, I could see it kicked up dirt right where the Indian laid. I saw him roll over, but then he didn't move.

All of a sudden, the last three Indians stood up and began running away. I probably could have gotten one more of them, but it was clear they had had enough. They weren't even running toward their horses. They were just running for their lives.

I quickly decided it was time for me to get out of there, but I would make an effort to capture their horses. I got on my horse, leaving my mule in the ravine. I was able to capture four of their horses. Using the leather ropes around the Indians' horses' necks, I tied them together. I led them back to where I had left my mule. I grabbed the reins of my mule and headed away from there. I moved as fast as I could for some distance before I slowed down to a fast walk. Needless to say, I kept a watch out for Indians.

It was getting close to dark when I finally decided that it was time to find a place to hide and rest the horses and my mule. I found a place where there were some trees that would make a good place to spend the night, as well as a good place to fight from if I had to. I gave all the animals a chance to drink from a narrow creek and graze a little. As soon as they had their fill, I hobbled all of them in a small clearing inside a grove of trees then I settled in to get some sleep. I was pretty sure that the Indians would not follow me on foot.

I didn't build a fire for fear it might be seen. I had bread and a raw potato and an apple for my dinner. It wasn't all that good, but it was filling.

I write this by the light of the moon that shines down between the branches of the trees.

* * * * *

I had to wonder what Isaac was going to do with the four Indian ponies.

September 5, 1867

I woke just before the sun was coming up. I knew that it was not very far to Fort Randall, but I had a feeling that just getting the last few miles might prove to be difficult. Especially if there were Indians between me and the fort. With the number of Indians I had seen over the past couple of days, I couldn't help but think that they might be gathering for a big fight somewhere close. Fort Randall seemed the logical place for such a fight.

I decided that I would spread my supplies over several animals. It would make it so each animal would have a fairly light load. Having a light load would make it easier for them to run faster, as well as further, if I had to make a run for the fort. It would also give me a better chance of getting at least some of my supplies to the fort, if I did have to run for it.

I kept closer to the river using the trees to provide cover, as well as some of the ravines. I took my time and kept my eyes open. It was mid-afternoon when I began to hear shooting. It was rather sporadic, more like someone taking pot-shots just to remind those they were shooting at that they were still there. I tied my animals to some trees, grabbed my field glasses then carefully walked up to a piece of ground that was a little higher than most of the surrounding area.

When I got close to the top of the hill, I could see the fort. It looked like it was under siege by a large number of Indians. I sat down and began to study the area through my field glasses.

After studying the area with my field glasses, I could see that the Indians were pretty well spread out, yet they were taking pot-shots at the fort. There were very few shots coming from the fort. I was sure the soldiers had been given orders not to shoot unless they could hit their target.

I could see two reasons for this. Probably the most important one was to conserve ammunition. The second was to avoid giving the Indians someone to shoot at.

In my searching of the area outside the fort, I noticed what looked like a weak spot in the Indians' position. It would be the best place for me to rush toward the fort. I would be able to get a lot closer to the fort before I could be seen if I was careful. It would make my run to the fort shorter, giving me a better chance of getting in the fort.

I would take my time to get ready for my run to the fort. I was also trying to think of some way to distract the Indians enough so I could get to the fort. It was at that moment I remembered that I still had five sticks of dynamite and enough fuse to make them effective.

I left the little hill and returned to where I had left my animals. I prepared for my run to the fort. Once I had the dynamite ready and my animals ready, I sat down and wrote this. It was also time to wait until the Indians settled down for the night and when there would be only a few standing guard. The Indians didn't seem to like fighting at night. They would wait for the morning light.

September 6, 1867

It was very dark, a little past midnight. It seemed that some clouds had moved in shutting out most of the light from the moon. There were a few fires some distance from the fort. The Indians were gathered around them. They must have been confident that they were far enough from the fort that they were safe from gun fire.

I could see torches along the top of the fort's walls. I was sure they were there so if the Indians attacked at night, the torches would light up the area in front of the wall so the troopers could see to defend the fort.

As quietly as I could, I gathered the reins of my animals then stepped into my saddle. Hiding the match as best I could so no one could see the flame. I struck it and lit a cigar that I got from the same place I got the dynamite. As soon as the cigar was burning well, I kicked my horse and started off across the ground toward the fort with my mule and Indian ponies in tow.

As I got closer to the Indians, I held the reins of my horse in my teeth leaving my hands free. As I approached the first group of Indians, I touched the fuse of one of the sticks of dynamite to the tip of the cigar. It began to burn. I threw the dynamite toward a group of Indians. I didn't bother to see the results, but I heard it explode. I could also hear the Indians scrambling for cover as well as some screams of pain.

As I rode toward the fort, I continued lighting the fuses on the sticks of dynamite from my cigar and threw them toward the Indians.

As I approached the fort, I heard some one yell to open the gate. I heard a few shots behind me. When I reached the gate, it was open enough so that I could ride into the fort. The gate was closed right behind me as I reined in my animals. There were also a few shots from the fort.

I pulled up in front of one of the buildings and stepped down off my horse. I found several soldiers with rifles looking at me.

"Thanks for opening the gate. I wasn't sure you would," I said to the officer as he walked up to me.

"I didn't figure the Indians had any dynamite," he said with a bit of a grin.

I introduced myself to the officer. His told me his name was Captain William Booker, and he was the fort commander.

"I was in sort of a hurry getting in here, but did I see a cannon next to the flag pole?" I asked.

"Yes, you did. The problem is they didn't send anyone who knows how to use it, or a manual on how to use it."

I sort of chuckled, then told him that they did send someone in sort of a round about way. He looked at me as if I just might be a little bit crazy so I thought it might be a good idea to explain.

I told him that I know how to use a cannon. I also told him that I had been an Artillery Officer during the Civil War, and that I was trained in the use of cannons, then I trained other soldiers how to use them and how to position them for the most effective results.

He looked at me for a minute, then began to smile. I told him I would be happy to train a few of his soldiers in how to use the cannon effectively.

He had a couple of soldiers take my animals to the stable, then showed me to the Officers' Barracks. He suggested that I get some sleep, that it was going to be hectic come day light.

I write about this day before I lay down.

* * * * *

It looks like Isaac was going to be an Artillery Officer again.

September 7, 1867

I was up early. I didn't get much sleep. I had a quick breakfast with Captain Booker. He had already selected three men to learn to use the cannon.

The first thing we did was move the cannon from in front of the flag pole to a place just behind the main gate. At that position, we could also see the back gate.

Sergeant Matterson was assigned to me along with privates Jones and Dixon. Since I didn't think we had a lot of time to learn about the cannon, I had them do everything required to get the cannon ready to fire, one step at a time. I explained what we did while we did it, and explained that was what they needed to do to fire the cannon as fast as possible and as effectively as possible every time we shoot it.

When we loaded the cannon, we used scraps of metal. I explained that it was very effective on anyone charging the place. Once the cannon was ready, it was time to wait. We rehearsed each and every move that each member of the crew was to do in order to reload and fire quickly. As soon as I felt they were ready, I told them to relax a bit.

One of the privates asked me how I knew so much about cannons. I told him I had been an Artillery Officer during the war. I chose not to tell him on which side I fought on as he had a bit of a Southern accent. Besides, the war was over, at least that one.

It wasn't long when there was an alarm sounded that the Indians were attacking the fort. I told them to open the gate just enough that we could see out and the barrel of the cannon was clear of the gate. I told my crew that the open gate might get them to focus their attack on the gate. We waited. I could see the men with me were not sure about what was going to happen.

Just as a large group of Indians headed toward the open gate, I signaled for the sergeant to touch his fire to the cannon. Within a second the cannon fired. There was a big bang and a cloud of smoke. As the smoke blew away, we could see ten to twelve Indians lying on the ground with several horses. The cannon had stopped the advance toward the main gate instantly. We could also see the confusion among the Indians. They quickly withdrew from that area in front of the fort. It was clear that they had never seen a cannon and what it could do when used by someone who knew how to use it.

I took a place on the fort wall. I noticed that they seemed to be building up a good size bunch of Indians as if they were planning on attacking the fort from the rear.

I quickly had the cannon moved toward the back gate, and got it ready to fire again. It wasn't long and the Indians started to attack the fort at the rear gate. We did the same thing at the back gate we had done at the front.

When the Indians charged the back gate, we opened the gate just enough for the cannon to be fired at them. Again, we cut them down with the cannon, leaving several Indians and horses lying in the field.

It wasn't long before the Indians were leaving the area. It looked like the battle for the fort was over, at least for now. However, we did not let our guard down. We loaded the cannon, then placed it in the center of the fort where it could be quickly moved to where it was needed should they decide to attack us again. Guards were posted on the walls twenty-four hours a day.

Captain Booker thanked me for making the cannon useful. I reminded him that it was probably not over for the Indians. Just because it worked this time didn't mean they wouldn't change their plans and try to take the fort some other way. The fort had to be ready which might mean they would have to keep the cannon ready and mobile.

I made a visit to the warehouse to see what they had for shells for the cannon. I explained that there were a good number of longer range explosive artillery shells in the warehouse. They could be used by shooting them over the walls toward the Indians and would explode some distance from the fort. They were good for several hundred yards. If they should gather again, it might be a good idea if we were to fire several out there. They might get the idea it was not a good idea to attack this fort. Captain Booker thought it might be a good idea to let them know we could attack them even if they were out of range of the guns they had. I certainly agreed.

The rest of the day I spent relaxing, but where I could be found if they needed me. I was pretty satisfied that the crew for the cannon could handle it alone. I did give them some instruction on the placement of the cannon, and on the different ammunition they had at the fort. They had several different kinds of shells for the cannon. I explained what each one was used for, and why.

After the evening dinner, I went to the barracks where I had a bed and wrote this.

September 8, 1867

I had breakfast with Captain Booker and another young officer. We talked about the current Indian situation in the area. It was not very good. They were attacking small ranchers in the area, and small wagon trains.

I explained that I was planning on finding a place to hole up for the winter. I had heard that the weather could get pretty nasty out on the plains.

Captain Booker said it could, but it might not for several weeks. He also said that they had had snowstorms as early as mid-September in the past few years.

He told me that I was welcome to stay the winter here. However, I would have to work for my keep and the keep of my animals.

I asked him what would he have me doing.

He said that since I had been an officer, I could best be useful as an officer; and I would be in charge of the cannon and those I trained in the use of it. He also said that he might have other duties for me from time to time, such as training new soldiers, but only in relation to my rank of First Lieutenant, the same rank I had had when I was injured. In other words, I could help train the enlisted men, and I might have to lead an occasional patrol.

It didn't sound like too bad a tradeoff, so I agreed. He said he would order uniforms for me. I guess I'm in the Army again.

After dinner, I was moved to the Officers Barracks and wrote this.

* * * * *

I didn't see that coming. The winters on the plains can be rather harsh. Staying at the fort would be better than being out on the plains during a blizzard.

September 10, 1867

The last couple of days I have been learning the general routine at the fort. There were guards to assign to the duty of watching for anyone approaching the fort. There were daily inspections to make sure the men were ready for battle at all times, and their equipment was also clean and ready to use.

I was assigned to carry out the inspections every other day. The other young officer was new to the Army. I sort of took him under my wing, so to speak, and helped him get used to Army life at the fort. His name was David Sarton. He was from Boston and had just graduated from a military school back east. This is his first duty station. He seems like a nice fellow, but he has a lot to learn.

Second Lieutenant Sarton sort of reminded me of myself when Colonel Patrick McHenry took me under his wing and taught me about the military and especially about cannons. He also got me to fight for the Union during the war. I would train the young officer on the uses of a cannon so they would have an officer who knows how to use it after I moved on in the spring.

I have to get up early for the change of guards on the fort's walls. I think it would be a good idea if I got some rest. I will close for now.

September 11, 1867

I was awakened by Master Sergeant Mulhanny just before the sun was up. He informed me that there was about three chiefs and fifteen Indians standing about two hundred yards in front of the fort. When I asked him what they were doing, he said they were just sitting on their horses and looking toward the fort. "They seem to be just waiting out there," he said.

Needless to say, I scrambled out of bed and got dressed in the uniform that I had borrowed from the captain. He had put his old first Lieutenant bars on the shoulders for me.

As soon as I was ready, I went out to the front of the fort and got up on the wall. I could see why Master Sergeant Mulhanny was concerned. The Indian chiefs had full war bonnets on while all the Indians had war paint on.

As soon as I got off the wall, I told the sergeant to have the cannon moved up close to the front gate, and have the gun crew standing by as if ready to fire. I just want them to see it when we open the gate.

I also told him to double the guard at the back gate, just in case they decided to attack from the rear while we were talking to the chief in front.

I told the sergeant we were going outside to talk to them. I don't think the sergeant liked the idea of going out, but he didn't say anything.

As soon as the cannon was in position, I had the sergeant slowly open the gate, but just far enough that the Indians could see the cannon clearly. I then stepped through the gate with the sergeant and two other soldiers at my side. I stepped only about six feet in front of my men and stopped.

Two of the chiefs looked at the others, then at us. It looked like they were trying to decide what they were to do.

One of them said something to the others, then turned and looked at me. He then stuck his lance in the ground and moved toward me. I stepped forward away from my sergeant. I only moved about ten feet, then stopped.

I had no idea what was going to happen next. I didn't know if he was going to ask us to surrender or tell us that he was going to destroy the fort. I sort of doubted it was either. We had hit him pretty hard yesterday with the cannon. I also doubted that he was here to surrender.

When the chief got about twelve feet from me, he stopped and got off his horse. Dropping the leather strap around his horse's neck, he walked up to me and stopped, then spoke to me.

"We do not wish you any harm. We want you off our land. We want you to stop killing the buffalo."

"This fort was built to stop you from killing our people."

"You have big gun. It killed many braves."

"Yes, we do. And we will use the big gun to protect the fort."

The chief turned and looked back at the others. I had no idea what was going through his head. He turned and looked back at me.

"We will not fight against the fort, but we will continue to fight for our land," the chief said.

"And we will continue to do what is necessary to protect our people, that includes using the big cannon," I said.

The chief looked at me for a moment, then turned his back to me. He got on his horse, then rode back to join the others, grabbing up his lance as he rode by it.

As I turned around to join my men, the sergeant told me to look out. I turned around. One of the young braves, had kicked his horse in the sides and was coming toward me with his long lance in his hand. I stood my ground. I drew my gun and took careful aim at the brave as he came at me. I was ready to kill him if he decided that he was going to throw that lance at me. He suddenly pulled up and tossed the lance into the ground, then quickly retreated back to the others. The chiefs and the others turned around and rode off the same way they had come.

I let out a sigh of relief then turned and walked back inside the fort with the others. Captain Booker came up to me. The look on his face gave me the impression that I was in deep trouble.

"You took a big chance with that Indian with the lance," he said.

"No, sir, I didn't. If he drew it back in a position where he could throw it at me, I would have blown him right off his horse. I was ready to shoot him."

"Well, I would prefer you didn't do that again."

"I understand, Sir."

"There's a freight wagon due in this afternoon. It has your uniforms on it," he said.

"Thank you, sir."

He was right. The freight wagon did have my uniforms on it. It also had a detachment of fifteen new soldiers to reinforce the fort. It was a cavalry unit led by a sergeant. Captain Booker told me I was to take command of the cavalry unit.

Since it was late afternoon when they arrived, I told the sergeant to have the men take care of their horses and then get the men settled in the barracks. After they were settled in, I told the sergeant, he and his men could relax tonight. We would get together tomorrow morning to work out our training routine, and any other duties that they would be responsible for. I also told him he could teach me some of the tactics used by the cavalry. I thanked him.

The rest of the evening I spent just talking to the cavalry sergeant. His name was Billy Montrose. He was from Georgia. He had been a confederate cavalry officer. He had come out west after the war and joined the U.S. Army to get away from Georgia.

He told me his men had been attacked by a small group of Indians on their way to the fort, but it didn't amount to much. As soon as they turned and took them on, they scattered.

Taps is playing, so it is time for lights out. I said goodnight to the sergeant. As soon as he left for the barracks, I sat down and wrote this entry in my journal before turning in.

September 12, 1867

I was awake before reveille and dressed for the day. All the troopers gathered for morning inspection. After I did the morning inspection, I released them to get their breakfast. After breakfast, I called them to order in the dining hall. We gathered around, then I introduced myself. I had the sergeant lay out the training for the morning. He was kind enough to brief me on some of the tactics used by the cavalry. Things like how to forcefully dismount an enemy while remaining on one's own horse, and while riding at almost a full run.

I must admit, I ended up on the ground a few times before I caught on. A couple of the soldiers got a good laugh, but they got a little concerned when I looked at them. I laughed also, just to show them that I was human, too.

But as I learned some of the tactics, things became a lot more serious. Sergeant Montrose made it clear that the troopers had to take their job as soldiers as a serious business, and that they had to count on each other and work together.

By the end of the day, I was more than ready to get some sleep after dinner. After dinner I excused myself and went to the Officers' Barracks. I didn't feel much like writing, but I thought I should. I'm sure it will not be difficult for me to get to sleep.

*****

It seems that Isaac is getting into military life rather quickly. It is a lot different being a cavalry officer, than an artillery officer. It is good that he has a sergeant who is willing to help him learn the tricks of the trade, so to speak. It is important not only to him, but the rest of his men.

September 15, 1867

The last few days have been spent in training. Our cavalry unit has become a well-organized unit. They are all working well together. It's a good thing.

At the evening meal, Captain Booker got a message from a couple of farmers just north of us. It seems they are having problems with the Indians killing and stealing some of their livestock. The fact that there was plenty of large game in the area gave rise to the idea they were doing it to get the people to leave. I am sure they were not killing the farmers for fear of retaliation by the Army. However, if that didn't work, they would not hesitate to start killing the settlers.

Captain Booker has given us orders to go there and see what is going on. We are to take whatever steps we deem necessary to put a stop to it. He said that we have not been having any trouble in that area for some time. We are to leave at first light in the morning.

I told the men that they should get a good-night's sleep. It will be a hard ride to get where we are needed. I am also ready to get some rest.

September 16, 1867

This morning we were up before the sun. We had a good breakfast, then got ready to leave the fort. We left the fort shortly after the sun came up over the horizon. It was about thirteen miles to where the incident was to have happened. We did not have enough information to give us any idea what we might be getting into.

It was just before noon when we first heard shots being fired. I sent one of our troopers on ahead to see if he could find out what was happening. He rode on out ahead. It wasn't long before he returned riding as fast as he could.

He reported that there was a small cabin that was under attack by about two dozen Indians. He also reported that there was gunfire coming from the cabin. There was at least someone putting up a fight.

I motioned for the men to follow me. We took off at a run. I motioned for our bugler to sound charge, and to do it loud so everyone could hear it. He did it as we charged toward the cabin. I think we were kicking up so much dust that it looked like there were more of us than just a regular patrol. The Indians quickly broke off the attack on the cabin and made a run for it to escape us.

The sergeant and the rest of the patrol chased them for a bit while I pulled up in front of the cabin. When I stopped in front of the cabin, a man and his wife came out. They had a couple of little ones with them. There was little doubt that they were glad to see us.

I talked with the man and his wife while I waited for the rest of my patrol to return. I suggested that they might want to move into the small town just about a mile west of them. It would be much safer with more people to fight off an attack. I did notice that there were four dead Indians near the cabin. The man did not want to leave his cabin.

I also noticed that there were several arrows in the sod roof. The roof had protected the cabin from burning. It crossed my mind that the Indians might come back and set the cabin on fire if the man and his family left it. I reminded the man that there were too few of us to provide protection all the time. He said he understood, and that he was grateful that we had come when we did. He also said he was not going to be run off his farm.

He asked me how we knew he needed help. I told him we got word that there was trouble with the Indians out here, but I didn't know who it was that told the officer at the fort. I told him that I was just assigned to get out here and stop it.

As soon as the rest of my patrol returned, we left. I decided that we might follow the Indians that we ran off for a little while, just to make sure they had left the area. I knew it was possible that they would return once we were gone, but there was nothing I could do about that.

We made a wide turn just to make are presence known before we headed back. It was almost dark by the time we returned to the fort.

After taking care of our horses and reporting to Captain Booker, we had a good meal and turned in. I write this just before getting ready for bed. It has been a long day.

September 17, 1867

First thing in the morning, I was called to the captain's office for a briefing on what duties were to be assigned to the cavalry unit. It turned out that Captain Booker had decided that it might be a good idea if we made our presence well known outside in the field and that we were not just staying at the fort.

I was given orders to take my cavalry unit and make a wide circle of the area generally west of the fort. By a wide circle, that meant that we were to make a ten to fifteen miles circle west of the fort. It meant scouting that area west of the Missouri River. We were to stop and talk to any farmers or ranchers who have settled in the area and advise them of any Indian movements and where they might be holing up. It was also to help the ranchers and farmers figure out how to help themselves in case they are attacked by Indians, because the Army could not be everywhere at the same time. It would also be for us to get information on the movements of the Indians.

After my briefing with the captain, I went to find Sergeant Montrose. As soon as I found him, I explained to him that we would be gone from the fort for the better part of a week, maybe longer. I directed him to get the supplies we would need for such an undertaking. I suggested we include some winter clothes, extra blankets and coats for the men, just in case it should turn cold.

He assured me that he would make sure we were well prepared for fighting, and for any changes in the weather. Sergeant Montrose immediately began gathering everything we might need.

One of the troopers had been a cook, he was assigned to make sure that there was enough food to feed the entire patrol. He would be preparing meals for the troopers.

Every trooper was given a job to do to get ready. By nighttime, Sergeant Montrose reported to me that they were ready, and that we could move out first thing in the morning.

I thanked him and suggested that he have the men get a good night's sleep because they would be on alert all the time we are gone from the fort. I also reminded him that there was a likelihood that we just might run into some hostile Indians looking for a fight. Sergeant Montrose agreed, said that he understood, then left for the barracks.

I returned to the Officers' Barracks to write this and to get some sleep.

* * * * *

It looks like Isaac had now become a cavalry officer. I was sure that he would make as good a cavalry officer as he did an artillery officer.

September 20, 1867

The eighteenth and nineteenth we roamed around the prairie west of Fort Randall. Our objectives were to find where the Indians were causing trouble and try to stop it. We didn't see anyone or anybody the first couple of days. However, to-day we came across a small farm. The cabin and barn had been burned to the ground. A wagon had also been burned. Sergeant Montrose and I dismounted and walked around the farmyard looking for anyone.

After about fifteen minutes, I came upon what looked like a man. He had died in the fire. From what I could see, there had to have been at least two children and a woman, but we could not find the bodies. I became concerned that the Indians might have taken them.

We walked around behind where the cabin had once stood. Sergeant Montrose, stopped suddenly. I watched him for a moment. He looked like he was listening for something. I got the feeling that he was trying to figure out where the sound was coming from. I asked him what he thought he had heard.

He looked at me and put his finger over his lips, then pointed at what appeared to be a dugout in a hillside. It looked like it might be a vegetable cellar. I moved up close to him. He whispered to me that he had heard something in the cellar. I moved close to one side of the door to the cellar while he got on the other side.

As soon as we were ready, I reached out and jerked the door open, ducking back away from the door in case there was someone in the cellar ready to shoot whoever opened the door.

Just as the door opened, a shot was fired from inside. I yelled for them not to shoot, that we were U.S soldiers, and we were here to help them.

It was only a moment or two before a woman and two small children came out of the cellar. They were dirty and scared.

I told Sergeant Montrose to take them over to a tree that was next to a narrow creek. I told him we would set up camp there for the night as soon as he was sure the area was secured. I also told him to place guards in the area. As soon as the camp was set up, the trooper who was our cook fixed a meal for all of us.

Sergeant Montrose had a couple of the troopers bury the man. He took me aside and asked me what do we do with the woman and kids? I told him we would have to take them with us. I don't think he liked the idea. I told him I didn't like it any better than he did. He admitted that he didn't have a better idea.

As soon as the woman was ready to talk, she told us what happened there. I didn't really have to be told, it was very clear. We talked about what to do with them. I didn't want to end our patrol as we were only out a few days, but we couldn't very well take them with us.

After some discussion between the woman, my sergeant and myself. It was decided that we would take them to a little settlement where she knew a few of the people. She was sure her friends could take her and the children in.

The settlement was only about a day's ride from where we were. The sergeant and I agreed that was probably the best option. We would take her to the settlement of St. Charles. We settled in for the night, and would leave in the morning.

After posting the guards, I went over to a tree to write in my journal.

September 21, 1867

By the time the sun was up, our cook had breakfast ready. The woman, Mrs. Helen Archer, had helped the cook. She said it was the least she could do since we were going out of our way to take her and her children to St. Charles.

As soon as breakfast was over and everything had been packed up, I helped the children up on the seat of the wagon. Private Hughes tucked the kids in close to him to make room for their mother. He put his arm around the little girl so she would not slip off the seat of the wagon. I had to smile because Private Hughes was a big burly sort of man, but with a big heart. He seemed to want to protect the children.

We headed out toward St. Charles. Sergeant Montrose, at my orders, sent outriders to keep an eye out for any trouble that might cause problems for us. They rode about two hundred yards away from the wagon, two in front, two on each side, and two in the rear.

The trip into St. Charles was pretty uneventful. We arrived about five-thirty in the afternoon. We were greeted by several of the town folks. We set up camp behind the blacksmith's shop and stable in an open area, then posted guards.

Sergeant Montrose and I visited with the town mayor in an effort to find out if anything might be going on in his part of this vast prairie.

The mayor told us that they had a little skirmish with a small band of Indians about a week ago, but it didn't last long. He said that other than that, it had been pretty peaceful.

"We have been keeping our guns close at hand, and some of the children who are old enough, stand watch in the church bell tower," the mayor said. "They are to ring the bell if Indians approach. They can see for miles from up there. In *fact, they called down from the church tower to tells us that a military patrol was coming our way."*

It was good to see that they were keeping watch and were prepared for a fight if necessary. Sergeant Montrose and I had dinner with the mayor and his wife, and his daughter and son.

After dinner, the sergeant checked on the troopers. As soon as he was done, he turned in.

I laid out my bedroll under the wagon, then sat on the back of the wagon to enter to-day's activities in my journal. I used a lantern for enough light to write by.

All is quiet, so it is time for me to turn in.

September 22, 1867

We didn't get a very early start because the local people wanted to make sure we had a little home cooking. Several of the women had baked and cooked a good part of the night so that we could have a good breakfast. I have to admit I didn't mind.

We left the settlement of St. Charles and headed west. The main body of our patrol was kept close to the wagon. I continued to keep outriders in positions around the wagon.

I'll make a note here. One of the young privates asked me if I thought it was a good idea to have so many outriders so far away from the wagon. He told me he had always seen patrols in columns with the officer in the lead.

I told him that was the usual way, especially if there was more than one wagon. But I felt since we were on fairly flat land with only a few places where the Indians could hide, it was better to be able to see them from further away. I also told him, that if the outriders saw a large group of Indians, the outriders could get back here pretty fast. And two hundred yards, a horse can cover very quickly. The young trooper walked away thinking about what I had told him. It was probably not what he had learned during his training.

We spent the whole day without seeing a single person, white or Indian. We camped next to a narrow creek. I think to-morrow we will head north for a while, just to see what is going on up that way.

* * * * *

The next couple of entries were rather short and there was nothing of any real interest. It was pretty routine. However, the last entry in Isaac's journal showed that they might be a little short on supplies.

September 24, 1867

We continued to travel in generally a northerly direction. We didn't see any Indians or anyone else for that matter. All we saw where some deer, a couple of coyotes, and a lot of Prairie Dogs. Sergeant Montrose took a hunting party out and got two deer. It was nice to have some fresh meat for a change. The men were getting a little tired of seeing nothing but a few animals. I have to admit, I'm a bit bored too.

September 25, 1867

To-day was a lot different from yesterday, and it wasn't a pretty sight. It was about ten o'clock in the morning when one of the outriders from in front came racing back to us. His partner was right behind him. I could here him yelling, but couldn't understand what he was saying.

I quickly gave the signal for all outriders to join us at the wagon. We quickly set up a defensive ring around the wagon. It was only a matter of less than a minute when I saw the reason for the outriders' swift return. They had a fairly large group of Indians right behind them.

I had the men form a line. I had them kneel down and be ready to open fire as soon as I gave the command. The outriders rode by then dismounted from their horses and quickly joined the line.

The Indians continued toward our line until they saw a line of troopers ready to take them on. They tried to hold up, but it was too late. I gave the command to open fire. The men fired a volley at the Indians. Several Indians and horses fell to the ground. In a matter of seconds, a second volley was fired and more Indians and horses fell. The Indians that remained were doing the best they could to get away. Since they were running away, I told the men to "hold your fire" and had them regroup around the wagon.

I climbed up on the wagon with my field glasses in an effort to see what the Indians were going to do. They were well out of range. From what I could see through my field glasses, it looked as if they were trying to decide if we were worth the losses they might have if they tried to take us again.

While we waited for them to make up their minds about what they should do, I got the feeling that they had expected the 'horse soldiers' to come after them. It was probably the *first time they had seen 'horse soldiers' dismount, form a defensive line, and shoot all together.*

I knew Indians liked to fight from the back of a horse, and they were good at it. Most of my cavalry unit was made up of young, inexperienced troopers. There was also the fact that we had no place to retreat to if they overwhelmed us. Fighting from the ground made it easier to make every shot count.

It took some time before there was any movement by the Indians. It seemed they had decided that it was not worth the losses to continue the fight. They moved off toward the west.

As soon as they moved off, I had Sergeant Montrose have his troopers mount up. I also had him put a scout out to keep an eye on the Indians to make sure they were not going to circle around and attack us again. I took the rest of the patrol and moved north. It was the last we saw of them.

It was getting late when we reached a small creek with some good cover. I had them set up camp in among the trees, and posted guards for the night.

It was almost dark when the scout returned. He reported that the Indians returned to the site of our fight with them. They tended to the wounded and carried the dead off the field of battle. He reported that they were headed west the last time he saw them.

After our evening meal, I posted a few additional guards around the camp with orders to change the guards every two hours. I had them in places where it was hard for them to be seen.

While I was writing in my journal, the young trooper came up to me. He said that they had not been trained for fighting on the ground. I told him that fighting from the best position you can get against the enemy is the position you should use. Fighting from a horse has it's place. When you are greatly out-numbered, it is sometimes better to fight where you can get the best results. With so many Indians, who are well trained fighters from a horse and are attacking so few of us, it is better to shoot from a stationary position so each shot counts.

The young trooper looked at me for a moment, then smiled and walked off. I couldn't help but smile.

I'll close my journal and get some rest.

September 26, 1867

We started out this morning. By mid-afternoon, we could see the Missouri River. I figured we were about thirty or thirty-one miles north west of Fort Randall. I didn't want to get too close to the river as it is rough country with lots of ravines and gullies. There were also places where there was a lot of cover. It was time to turn straight west for a little while.

We turned west for the rest of the day. We found a quiet place beside a stream. I told Sergeant Montrose that it looked like a good place to stop for the night. He agreed.

While we were setting up camp for the night our scout came riding in. He drew his horse up next to me and jumped down.

"Are you sure you want to set up here?" he asked.

I asked him what was the problem camping here. He said there was a group of about a dozen Indians just about a mile and a half up stream from where we were camping. He went on to tell me that there were six adults and about seven or eight children. He quickly added that several of the adults were old. He didn't see but maybe two who were of the age to be warriors.

I called Sergeant Montrose over to discuss the situation. The scout told him what he had seen. After questioning the scout, we came to the decision that we would still camp here. However, we would make sure there were guards well posted around our camp so we would know if anyone tried to come into our camp.

We passed the word to keep the noise to a minimum. I'm sure there will be a few troopers who will sleep lightly tonight.

I will try to get some sleep. I finished writing in my journal.

September 27, 1867

Just as the sun was coming up, Sergeant Montrose came over to me. He told me that one of his troopers had seen a young boy in the stream. The trooper had said that the boy had seen him, then ran back into the trees.

I told Sergeant Montrose to saddle two horses for us. We were going to pay our neighbors a visit. He returned in a few minutes with two saddled horses and two mounted troopers. My sergeant and I mounted up and rode over to where the Indians were camped.

When we rode up to their camp, they just stood there and looked at us. The leader stepped up and said something I didn't understand. Sergeant Montrose translated.

It seems the small group of Indians were on their way to Fort Thompson. They had camped there for the night. Sergeant Montrose asked them why they were going there. One Indian said they were going to spend the winter there because they could get food and shelter for his parents and his old uncle and his wife. He said they were too old to hunt for themselves. He also said that he did not want to fight the 'blue coats'. It was a useless fight.

I thought about what the leader said. He was young enough to be a warrior. But when I looked over the rest of the those in this group, I doubted that they represented a real threat to us, or anyone else.

I told Sergeant Montrose to tell them that they were free to go on their way. He looked at me, then smiled. He told the group of Indians that they could continue their journey to Fort Thompson.

I sat there on my horse and watched them for a minute. The two little boys looked up at me. I reached in to my shirt pocket and took out a couple of cookies I had saved for a snack. I leaned down and offered the cookies to the boys.

They looked at their father to see if it was okay. He looked at me. Sergeant Montrose saw what was going on and said something to the boys' father. The boys' father told them they could accept the cookies.

They took the cookies, smiled, then ran back to their mother. The boys stood behind their mother, then smiled at me. I smiled back and watched them as they ate the cookies.

I turned my attention to the leader for a moment. I smiled, then turned my horse around and headed back to our camp.

When we got back to our camp, the troopers had it ready to travel. We continued to head west.

The rest of the day was pleasant. I was reminded by Sergeant Montrose that not all Indians were like those. A lot of the young ones didn't like us on their land. A few of the older leaders were accepting of what was happening. However, the younger leaders were not so accepting.

We managed to cover about twenty miles or so without incident. We camped in an area that had a few trees.

I couldn't help but think of the two boys and what their life would be like in the future. It is late, and time to put my journal up.

* * * * *

In among all the fighting and distrust, there was one moment of kindness shared between people who didn't trust each other.

September 28, 1867

I was awakened by one of the troopers. He said that there was a group of Indians just to the north of us. He also said he didn't think they had seen us.

My first thought was it was the same Indians we had seen yesterday, but they had moved on. The trooper said it was a different group of Indians.

I quickly got up and told the trooper to wake Sergeant Montrose. He told me that the sergeant was already up, and he was out in a gully watching the Indians. He had sent the trooper to get me.

I followed the trooper to where Sergeant Montrose was hiding. I joined the sergeant in the gully and looked over to see what was going on. The sergeant told me he had been watching the Indians for only a short time. He said he thought they were headed toward Fort Thompson.

I watched them as I counted them. There was about twenty-five to thirty of them. I asked the sergeant what his thoughts were. He said he thought they were probably headed for Fort Thompson to spend the winter. The group is made up mostly of older men and women, those most likely to have difficulty surviving the winter on the plains.

Sergeant Montrose looked up at the sky, then looked at me. I looked up at the sky. It was clear that it just might snow before long. A September snow could produce a good amount of snow, but it usually didn't last very long. It was more of a hint of what was to come later in the winter.

Sergeant Montrose asked me what I wanted to do. I told him to let them go, but keep an eye on them. It didn't look like they knew we were there, and I hoped to keep it that way.

I told the sergeant we would stay where we are for now. He seemed to agree.

I returned to where the other troopers were camped. I told them that we would be staying here for awhile, and they are not to make any noise. We would let the Indians pass in peace, as long as they didn't start anything.

By mid-afternoon, the Indians had continued to move north toward Fort Thompson. It has also started to snow. The snow was not very heavy, and it melted almost as soon as it hit the ground. I discussed our present situation with the sergeant. We decided that we would stay here for the night. We had everything we would need if the weather turned worse and produced heavy snow during the night. If it snowed so much that travel was hard or impossible, we would be safer staying here.

I settled in after posting guards. I had a couple of the troopers gather and cut wood so we could keep a fire going all night.

As night comes, I write about to-day's activities before I turn in.

September 29, 1867

We woke to find everything covered with a heavy, wet snow. It was about six to eight inches deep. The only saving grace was the sun was bright and it had turned fairly warm. After talking with Sergeant Montrose, we decided that we would stay in place for the day.

The troopers spent most of the day relaxing or standing guard duty when it was their turn. The cook kept a pot of coffee ready for anyone who wanted it.

As the day went by, a good part of the snow melted away. If all went well, we would be on our way in the morning.

As darkness fell upon our camp, the temperature turned cold again, but not so cold as to make it terribly uncomfortable. We had come prepared for cold weather. I think we will be able to continue on our way in the morning.

September 30, 1867

The sun came up and it almost immediately began to warm up the morning. After a good breakfast, we got ready to move on. I decided that we would continue on west for one more day.

As soon as all was ready, I sent out the outriders. We started west.

It was shortly before noon when one of the outriders came racing back. I was a little concerned when his partner didn't return. It was cleared up quickly.

The outrider reported that there was dark smoke drifting off to the south, and it looked like there was a barn or possibly a cabin burning. He also reported that his partner was on a hill with his field glasses watching it and looking for anyone who might be around. He said they had not seen any Indians.

I told Sergeant Montrose to stay with the wagon while I rode on ahead with two more troopers.

As soon as we were mounted, we headed out. As we passed by the hill, we were joined by the outrider who had been watching the situation. He reported no movement that he could see. We rode toward the burning building.

It turned out that there were two buildings burning, one directly behind the other. It was a barn and a small cabin. We rode around the area of the buildings, but didn't see any bodies, or any animals.

I dismounted and began walking the area close to the buildings. I was looking for bodies, but didn't find any. I began looking for tracks.

It wasn't very long before I found a number of tracks. There were two of what appeared to be adult boot prints and three that looked like small boot prints. I found no prints to indicate that there had been any Indians at the site.

I called Sergeant Montrose to come take a look. I wanted his feelings about what had happened there.

After he looked around and came up to me. He asked me what I thought. I told him that it looked like the buildings had been set on fire by a woman and a man, not Indians. He agreed.

He thought that whoever had lived there, had destroyed the buildings and left in a fairly heavy wagon. The hoof prints showed that there were at least eight horses, four of them pulling a wagon. The only question was why? Sergeant Montrose suggested that the settlers had been having trouble with the Indians, so they packed up, burned the buildings so they would be no use to the Indians, then moved on.

From the look of the tracks left behind, it looked like they might be headed south toward the Oregon Trail.

The wagon pulled up with the remaining troopers escorting it. Once we had finished with the site, we moved on a few miles further before I decided that we would spend the night near a narrow creek. It had a few trees where we could put up a shelter. I had troopers assigned to guard with a change of guard every two hours. The cook fixed our evening meal.

It is getting dark, so I write to-day's activities in my journal.

October 2, 1867

The past two days had been rather boring. We saw no one. The roads were a bit muddy making it hard for the horses to pull the wagon. We only made about eleven miles yesterday and about the same to-day.

To be honest, there was almost nothing to report. To-morrow we will turn generally south. This will put us on the last half of our circle out from the fort. The temperature was fairly mild yesterday and to-day. From the looks of the sky, it could very well be the same to-morrow.

October 3, 1867

It was fairly cold this morning. It took us a while before we could get moving. The wagon wheels were frozen to the ground. It had been very wet where we stopped. Once we broke the wagon wheels loose, we were able to get on our way. As the day went on, the wind seemed to increase. It was out of the northwest and had a bite to it. Since we had our backs to it, it wasn't too bad.

The one thing I noticed was there was very little movement on the plains. Most of the animals had hunkered down. Maybe if we had been smart, we would have hunkered down, too.

After traveling only about nine miles, I told Sergeant Montrose to find I place where we could get out of the wind. That was not an easy request out here on the plains.

However, he did know of a place about two miles east of our location where we might be able to get out of the wind. I told him to lead the way.

It was more like three miles when we came upon a deserted old stage stop building with a barn. We drove the wagon into the barn where the men unharnessed the horses and put them in stalls.

I went in the stage stop building and found it to be in fairly good shape. We gathered in the building. The cook built a fire in the fireplace after making sure the chimney was not plugged up. While he started cooking, I had the men cleanup the place a little and make room on the floor for as many of us as possible. It worked out that there was room enough for everyone, but only if three were on guard duty. I had two troopers do guard duty in the barn, and one in the cabin. I also had them change guard duty every two hours so that those in the barn would not get too cold.

I took a turn at guard duty in the barn, while Sergeant Montrose took his turn in the cabin. After I did my turn, I sat down at the small table to write to-day's activities in my journal.

* * * * *

It was clear that Isaac was showing his troopers that he was looking out for his men. He certainly didn't have to stand watch at all, but he made it clear that he could do his part to make it as comfortable as possible for all.

October 4, 1867

The wind had settled down a little and it had actually turned a bit warmer. After everyone had been fed and we were preparing to leave, one of the young troopers came running into the cabin. He was very excited.

It took a minute to get him settled down enough to tell us what was the matter. He finally said that there was a large group of Indians not more than half a mile from our location, and they're coming this way. He estimated that there were at least a hundred of them.

Sergeant Montrose grabbed the field glasses then left the cabin to get a look at what was coming. In the meantime, the rest of the troopers grabbed up their rifles.

I went outside and stood by Sergeant Montrose. I could not see anything except what appeared to be a lot of dust and dirt from horses. I looked at Sergeant Montrose. I asked him what could he see.

Sergeant Montrose, turned and looked at me. He was smiling. He said that I should get everyone inside the barn and cabin as quickly as possible. There was a very large herd of Buffalo stampeding toward us.

I asked him if he could see any Indians. He said he could not.

I turned and gave the order for everyone to get inside, and stay away from the door and windows.

It wasn't long before we could feel the ground shake under us. As the buffalo ran between and around the buildings, we could hear some of them actually hitting the buildings. A couple of the buffalo broke into the barn door, and were quickly shot by the troopers.

Although it seemed like it took hours for the buffalo to run by, it was only a matter of a few minutes. It took longer for the dust to settle.

Once it was over, Sergeant Montrose went outside to see what damage was done. Two of the troopers in the barn were injured by the two buffalo that broke in through the door. Luckily, their injuries were minor.

The two buffalo that broke into the barn were killed in the barn. They would provide us with meat for several days. While the two injured troopers were taken care of, several of the troopers skinned and cut up the dead buffalo.

I gave the order to stay at the cabin and barn for two days to allow the troopers to mend, and to allow for the preparation of the buffalo so it would last longer. I also had a couple of the troopers fix the broken door to help keep some of the wind and cold out.

The young trooper who had said it was Indians was a bit embarrassed, but felt a little better when he was told that his warning may have actually saved a life or two.

Things settled down for the rest of the day. We posted guards just in case we were attacked by Indians. By evening, they had the buffalo butchered. We all enjoyed buffalo steaks for dinner. Most of the men went to sleep early.

I sit at the table and enter to-day's activities in my journal before I go to sleep.

October 6, 1867

The two troopers who had been injured by the stampeding buffalo were unable to ride. We fixed a place for them to ride in the back of the wagon.

Once we were ready to move on, I decided that we would head south for a day or two then head back east toward Fort Randall. I would keep an eye on the injured troopers to make sure they continued to recover. If it looked like they needed more medical aid than we could give them, we would head back to Fort Randall by the shortest way possible.

We covered about sixteen miles to-day. The two injured troopers seemed to be doing well.

The weather had turned warm during the day, but was cold at night. Most of the snow had melted, and the wind was just a breeze out of the south.

We found a place to camp next to a small pond caused by a dam on the creek. There was no indication as to who had built the dam and why. I didn't find any sign that someone had even started to build a farm or ranch near it.

The assignment of guards had been given and all the guards are posted. There is a bit of moon to-night. It looks like there is going to be a clear sky.

Since all is well, I'll turn in as soon as I finish writing about to-day's activities.

October 7, 1867

We were all up early. After breakfast we got packed up and continued to head south. We continued south for part of the day. We didn't see any Indians during our move south.

Shortly after noon we headed back east, the last leg of our circle from Fort Randall. I figured that it would take us about two, maybe three days to get back to the fort, if the weather cooperated for us.

To-day we didn't see any Indians. We didn't see any signs of them where they might have been crossing the prairie.

After traveling about eighteen miles, we came upon a small farm. I could see a cow grazing peacefully just to the left of the small barn. There was smoke coming from the chimney, which indicated that there was someone there. I had not seen anyone; but I was sure if there was someone, they would have seen us.

I instructed Sergeant Montrose to take four troopers and go on ahead to see if anyone was there. I also told him to be careful.

I had the rest of my patrol continue to move toward the cabin. We were still about two hundred yards from the cabin when I saw Sergeant Montrose, knock on the cabin door. Apparently, there was no one home. Sergeant Montrose stepped inside the cabin.

The next thing I saw was Sergeant Montrose, come back out of the cabin. By this time, I was close enough to see his face. He looked a little pale as he leaned against the cabin.

He looked up at me as we rode into the yard of the cabin. From the look on his face, he had seen something that really disturbed him.

I asked Sergeant Montrose what was the matter. He told about what was inside the cabin. There were three people, a man, a woman, and what appeared to be a teen-age son, in the cabin. From what he said, they had been tortured before they were killed. He also said they had been dead for several days.

Due to the situation, I gave the order to set the cabin on fire. One of the troopers had a Bible. He asked if he could read a passage from the Good Book.

I had the troopers gather together. We bowed our heads while Trooper Clarkston read from his Bible. As soon as he finished, Sergeant Montrose poured some coal oil on the cabin and set it on fire.

As soon as the cabin began to collapse, I had one of the troopers tie the cow to the back of the wagon. I suggested that he milk the cow before we left. It looked like it needed to be milked. As soon as the cow had been milked, we headed on our way.

It was a pretty quiet group of men when we left. I could certainly understand. I know it was nothing I wanted to talk about.

We set up camp about five miles from the cabin we set on fire. The term Funeral Fire sort of sticks in my mind as I write to-day's happenings in my journal.

October 8, 1867

All of the men in my patrol were very quiet last night, and this morning. I'm sure what they had seen yesterday will stick with them for a long time.

We were ready to move out shortly after dawn. The weather was fairly warm and there was a gentle breeze out of the south. The snow was gone and the prairie was once again dry enough that the wagon moved along well.

We had no trouble at all. In fact, everything went well. I have to admit, it was nice to have a bit of milk at breakfast. That was one thing we rarely got.

We rode into Fort Randall shortly after six o'clock. While the men took care of the wagon, horses and the cow, I reported to Captain Booker.

As soon as I finished my report, I returned to the Officers' Barracks. I write about to-day's activities. It is now time to turn in.

October 9, 1867

This morning we had real pancakes made with milk, something we almost never have. The cook had milked the cow.

As I walked toward the mess hall, I noticed that several of the troopers had built a pen complete with a place to put hay. The cow was in the pen eating the hay. I don't know if they asked for permission to build it, but I wasn't going to be the one to tell them they shouldn't have built it.

Captain Booker walked by it and saw me looking at it. He smiled and said it was nice to have a little milk. I told him how we came to have the cow. He told me the men could keep the cow as long as they took care of the animal on their own time. The men were glad to hear that the captain would let them keep the cow. The men worked out a schedule for taking care of the cow and cleaning the pen.

I spent several hours writing a complete report of our circle around the prairie over the past 22 days.

The rest of the day, I spent overseeing the troops to make sure everything had been cleaned up, equipment was put in order, and everything was ready for the morning inspection.

I also took some time to visit our two injured troopers. I am glad to report that they will be able to return to at least light duty within the next few days. The doctor seems to think they should be ready for regular duty by the end of next week.

It has been a busy day. I will turn in and get some rest as soon as I finish updating my journal.

October 11, 1867

This morning was the first time that we were awaken by reveille. After breakfast, the troopers gathered for morning inspection. The orders of the day were read, and assignments were given. The duty rooster was posted so they could check it any time during the day.

After my inspection, I told Sergeant Montrose to dismiss the troopers to their assigned duties. Once he had made sure they were at the assigned duties, I had him meet with me in the office where we were to meet with Captain Booker.

It wasn't long before Sergeant Montrose came into Captain Booker's Office. We spent some time discussing the situation with regard to the Indians.

There was little doubt that we could not properly cover that large area we had been assigned as the fort's district. We discussed several options, but none of them would help us protect all the settlers in the area.

Captain Booker suggested that we pray for a lot of snow. He knew from experience that it slowed down the Indians activities greatly. We discussed the lack of manpower, but it didn't do any good. We could talk about it, but it didn't change the fact we were severely short on manpower. It was not likely that we would get the additional manpower we needed.

We even discussed the results of our last trip. We had not stopped anything. About the only thing we could say about it was that we had seen a couple of groups of Indians headed for Fort Thompson where they planned to spend the winter.

The one thing we did know was when it starts to snow and the snow stays, there will be a lot less activity by the Indians.

We left the Captain's Office. I made rounds to make sure the troopers assigned to me were doing what they were assigned.

I spent a lot of the day in the office, with a trip around the fort every once in a while to make sure all was well.

It's evening now. I have finished my rounds. I'm in the Officers' Quarters writing about to-day's activities. I will soon go to bed and get some rest so I can start all over tomorrow.

* * * * *

It was well known that there were too few soldiers on the Frontier to deal with any large scale problems with the Indians.

October 12, 1867

I woke from a sound sleep to reveille. Once I was ready to face the day, I went outside for inspections. Much to my surprise, it was snowing. From the look of it, it had been snowing for some time. There was at least three to four inches of snow on the ground, and it was still coming down. Visibility was limited to one hundred yards most of the time.

When I looked around, I could see soldiers shoving snow off the guard walks along the fort walls, stopping every so often to make sure there was no one outside the fort that might cause trouble for us.

I was just about to go into the office when Sergeant Montrose called to me. He was smiling. I waited for him to join me before he said anything. His first words were, "you prayed for snow, and snow you got.". I couldn't help but smile as we walked into the office together.

Captain Booker was sitting at his desk. He smiled at us and said, "You must have it in good with God. You asked for snow and we have snow."

"If you recall, it was you who suggested that we pray for snow, sir. I just followed your orders," I reminded him.

"You are right. Even so, it is nice to see."

"Yes sir, it is," I replied.

The sergeant and I sat down in front of Captain Booker's desk and began discussing to-day's activities. We would keep a steady watch over the walls of the fort with regular changes of the guard. We would also have shoveling duty to keep the walk ways clear and the porches of all the buildings clear of snow.

As soon as Sergeant Montrose had his instructions and had left the office, I spent most of my time in the office with paper work. I did make rounds of the fort several times during the day. The one thing I noticed was that the snow was beginning to pile up. By night fall, we had received at least six to seven inches of new snow. I also noticed that the temperature had dropped steadily all day. By night fall, it was very cold.

I just finished my rounds and found all was well. It was time for me to turn in. I took one more look outside. It is still snowing. I'll finish my entry in my journal, then get some rest.

October 13, 1867

I woke to at least a foot and a half of snow and it was still snowing. It was fast looking like the only thing we could do was to try to keep walkways open so we could get from one building to another, and from the barracks to the guard posts around the fort.

The only thing the guards were reporting was it was snowing. It had been a long time since I had seen snow like this.

About the only activities were taking care of the horses and the cow, and standing guard duty. It gave the soldiers time to mend uniforms, clean equipment, and in some cases write home to loved ones. Although there were not very many of the men who had someone to write to.

I guess I'll write in my journal, then get some sleep.

* * * * *

For the next five days, Isaac's entries were pretty much the same. It snowed every day, although there were a few times when it stopped snowing for a few hours; but the sky never cleared so the sun could shine.

It seemed his biggest problem soon became a question of what to do with all the snow. Isaac began having some of it hauled outside the walls of the fort.

October 18, 1867

To-day, we got a surprise. We woke to the sun shining brightly. It was so bright that it hurt your eyes if you didn't shade them. The temperature seemed to be a little warmer than it had been for the past five days. Where the walkways had been shoveled off and the sun could get to it, I could see the snow was starting to melt a little.

Spirits seemed to improve with the sun and little bit warmer temperatures. The guards reported no movement outside the walls of the fort. The snow was still very deep.

The activities in the fort didn't change much, except there seemed to be a change in the men. They were more upbeat and in a little better mood. It wasn't that they were at each other's throat's or anything like that, they just seemed more talkative. There was talk of being able to get out more with the sun and warmer weather. It still had a ways to go before we would be getting out or doing any traveling. It would take a few days of good weather before enough snow would melt to make travel any distance possible.

It is getting late and I have made my rounds. As soon as I finish writing in my journal, I'll get some sleep.

* * * * *

Isaac had several entries in his journal that were pretty much the same. It seems the weather had improved and a lot of the snow had melted. It wasn't until I got to the entry dated October 23, 1867, that there was anything of interest written.

October 23, 1867

I had just finished my breakfast when a young trooper came into the mess hall looking for me. He said that there was a body, well, the hand of a human body sticking out of a pile of snow.

I grabbed my coat and followed the trooper out of the fort to a pile of snow about fifteen feet from the front gate. All I could see was a human hand sticking out of the snow pile. I carefully dug the snow away in order to see who it might be. It turned out to be a young Indian woman. From the look of things, she had tried to get to the fort for cover, but was either too weak to pound on the fort wall, or she never knew how close she had come to finding protection from the snowstorm.

We dug the body out and took it into the fort. I asked if anyone knew who she was, but no one could identify her.

Since we had no idea what tribe she was from or even where she had come from, we kept her until we could bury her.

Several of the men wondered how many more Indians would we find frozen to death once the snow melted away. Of course, we had no answer.

Two of the men went out and dug through the snow pile near the fort to make sure there was no one else there. It was pretty quiet around the mess hall that evening.

Taps has been sounded. I need to put up my journal and get some rest.

October 24, 1867

This morning I sent out several soldiers to check out the area around the fort for any more bodies. The snow had melted enough that if there were any more bodies, they would be able to be seen. It seemed likely that if there was one woman found in the snow, there might be others who had tried to get to the fort for protection from the storm.

After covering an area of about two to three hundred yards from the fort walls, it was reported that no other bodies were found. There was nothing to indicate who the woman was we had found, or what tribe she was from.

It seemed unlikely that we would ever know who the woman was or what tribe she belonged to. I did have one of the soldiers make a marker for her. He asked me what name he should put on the grave marker. I suggested that he put "Snow Flower". He thought that was a good name for her.

Later that afternoon, several of the soldiers gathered around the grave. One of them read a passage from the Good Book while another placed the marker at the head of the grave.

It was nice of the soldiers to do that for her. Even Captain Booker thought it was nice.

It was pretty quiet around the fort the rest of the day. After dinner and guard duties were posted, a lot of the men turned in. I returned to the Officers' Barracks. As soon as I get finished entering to-day's activities in my journal, I will also turn in.

October 25, 1867

This morning I walked into the mess hall and found two soldiers having an argument. It was between Corporal Olson and Private Jones. It looked like it might come to blows, so I decided to break it up.

It didn't take long for me to find out what the argument was about. Corporal Olson resented the fact that the Indian woman was buried close to the military cemetery. Although the Indian woman had been buried in the civilian cemetery, which was adjacent to the military cemetery, the corporal felt it was too close to the military cemetery. In fact, he said she should have been buried out on the prairie, not with any white people.

I told the corporal that she was properly buried where she was, and it had been Captain Booker who had told them where she was to be buried. I reminded him that she would have been protected from the storm if we had known she was there.

Corporal Olson didn't like what I told him. I strongly suggested that he get over it, or he might just have a problem with me. I'm sure he took that to mean he might lose a stripe and some pay, and he would have been right.

Corporal Olson requested to leave. I dismissed him. He left the building.

I didn't see much of Corporal Olson the rest of the day. When I did, it seemed that he was making a point of avoiding me. It didn't bother me.

The rest of the day was pretty routine. When it was time to turn in, I went to the barracks. I wrote about to-day's activities and will get ready to turn in.

* * * * *

The next five days showed the boredom that was pretty common during the winter months.

October 30, 1867

To-day the sun was out and it was rather warm. I knew it would not last, but I intended to make the most of it. With Captain Booker's permission, I formed up the cavalry unit; and we left for a patrol to check to see if there were any bodies in the area of those who might have died during the latest snowstorm, and to see if there was any movement by the Indians.

We left the fort shortly after breakfast. We headed out west from the fort for a mile or so, then turned north toward the Missouri River.

Once we got in sight of the river, we moved along the river staying just outside the tree line along the bank of the river. I knew that there were Indians who had camped along the river on their way to Fort Thompson. With the snowstorm we had a few days ago, there was the likelihood that there might be some Indians who took shelter in the trees along the river. The Indian woman we found outside the fort may have been from one of the tribes. I knew it was a long shot, but it might also give us some idea of how the Indians faired during the storm.

We hadn't traveled very far when we came across a small group of Indians. There were only about six tepees.

I halted the troopers, then rode toward the tepees with Sergeant Montrose. As we approached, three Indians came out of one of the tepees. They had rifles in their hands, but did not point them at us. They did seem to relax a little when they saw the rest of my patrol just a few yards behind us.

Sergeant Montrose talked to them in their language. I only understood part of what he was saying. It was enough to know he was asking them how long they had been there, and if they were missing any of their women. From what I gathered from their conversation with Sergeant Montrose, all of their group were there and doing well.

We wished them safe travel, then rode back to the rest of my patrol. They watched us as we rode away. We rode on a little further but didn't see any other Indians.

Shortly after noon, we turned and headed back toward the fort. The sun was about to set when we rode into the fort. I dismissed the troopers to take care of their horses, then made my report of our activities to Captain Booker.

Once I had made my report, I went to the mess hall for dinner, then went to the barracks to write about our activities.

* * * * *

It looked like Isaac was not going to find out who the Indian woman they buried was or even what tribe she belonged to.

The next ten days entries showed that they had settled into the winter routine. They went out on patrols two or three times a week, spent a lot of time doing menial things. The soldier assigned to the cannon did regular drills. The troopers spent most of the time in the fort pulling guard duty and taking care of their animals.

It wasn't until November 9, 1867 that I found something interesting.

November 9, 1867

On this day, the daily boredom was disturbed. We had just finish breakfast when one of the guards yelled out that there was a wagon coming toward the fort with a dozen or so Indians right behind them.

I ran to the gate and told the guards on duty to open the gate. I also called out to the men assigned to the cannon to bring it up toward the gate. They were to be ready to fire on my order.

We could hear gunfire, but we were not sure where it was coming from until we saw an Indian fall from his horse. I yelled up to the guard on the wall to provide cover for those in the wagon.

As soon as the wagon got close, I ordered the gate to be opened so they could get into the fort quickly. The wagon came into the fort. As soon as it was in the fort and out of the line of fire from the cannon, I ordered them to fire the cannon.

When the cannon went off, several Indians fell to the ground with their horses. I gave the order to close the gate.

One of the guards yelled down from the wall that the Indians were retreating rather quickly. I told the guards to keep an eye out to make sure they left the area.

I walked over to the wagon. Sitting on the wagon bench was a woman. She said her husband was in the back of the wagon with their two children.

I walked to the back of the wagon and saw two teenage boys with guns in their hands. I told them they were safe and they could put the guns down. It was then that I discovered that the man in the back of the wagon had been shot. I called for the post doctor. After the doctor had finished examining a couple of soldiers who had been taken to post infirmary, he checked the man. The woman quickly followed them into the post infirmary.

I took the two boys aside. It was then that I found out their family name was Ashley. I asked the boys what happened. They said they were attacked by the Indians just a short distance from the fort. They said that they made a run for the fort. Their father was hit by a shot from one of the Indians.

I took the boys to the mess hall and sat down with them. We just talked while we waited to find out how they father was doing. The older boy was sixteen and the younger was fourteen.

The doctor sent a soldier over to the mess hall to tell the boys about their father. Their father's injury was not life threatening. The post doctor said he would recover, but it would take some time before he would be up and around.

I talked to Captain Booker about where we would put these people up. He said the woman could stay in the extra room in the office, and the boys we could put up in the barracks with the men. They were too young to be soldiers, but old enough to room with the soldiers.

Once everything had settled down, it was time for everyone to turn in, except for those on guard duty. I went to the Officers' Barracks to write about to-day's activities before turning in.

* * * * *

It seems that the fort did not have housing for women, but they were able to work it out at least on a temporary basis.

November 10, 1867

This morning we had our guests have their breakfast in the mess hall. Captain Booker joined us. Mrs. Ashley joined us as well. I was proud of the soldiers' use of good manners while Mrs. Ashley was in the mess hall.

She informed us that her husband was doing well, although it would be awhile before he was be able to travel. It seems they were on their way to Fort Pierre Trading Post. They were to meet Mr. Ashley's brother there. Mrs. Ashley said they were going to settle on some land just across the river from the trading post. They had heard there was land there open for farming.

I had not heard of any open land for farming in that area, but then we got very little news out here. The last time I saw a newspaper was in Omaha, and it was just one page of local news, most of it about what was going on in Omaha with a little about Lone Tree Crossing.

After breakfast, the soldiers returned to their usual duties. I found it interesting that one of the boys was interested in the cannon. He apparently had never seen a cannon. His name was Johnny, and he was the older of the two boys.

He followed me around most of the day. He showed a lot of interest in what life was like for soldiers. I have to admit I enjoyed his company.

Since it is almost time for taps, I will take a few minutes to bring my journal up to date before turning in.

* * * * *

It looks like Isaac had found a new friend. I'm sure Isaac is enjoying his company.

Isaac's writings in his journal for the next few days were short and to the point. There wasn't very much going on. The slower pace in the fort's activities had shown that there was not much going on. It did show that the weather had improved considerably.

November 14, 1867

This morning was like most mornings in the fort except for one thing. It seems that the Ashley family was getting a little impatient to get a move on toward Fort Pierre Trading Post. The doctor had told Mr. Ashley that he could travel as long as his boys did most the hard work, like lifting and carrying things.

Due to the nice weather, the ground was clear of snow, and had dried enough to make it possible for a wagon to move along fairly well.

Several of the soldiers helped the boys pack up their wagon, and put in a few supplies to help them on their way. They made a comfortable place in the wagon for Mr. Ashley.

Just before they left Johnny Ashley came over to me. He wanted to know what he should do if he was to become an artillery officer. I suggested he get as much schooling as he could, then apply to a military school. I went to my room in the Officers' Barracks and got the book that Colonel McHenry had given me. I suggested that he study it. I told him it just might help him get into a military school, and help him become an artillery officer.

Johnny smiled and thanked me. He then got up on the wagon, looked down at me and smiled. He then saluted me. I returned the salute and watched them as they left the fort.

I felt that there was very little chance that I would ever see him again, but I hoped his dream would come true. I couldn't help but think that he would make a good artillery officer someday.

The rest of the day was pretty routine. I thought of the Ashley family, especially Johnny, often during the day.

Taps has just sounded. It is time to turn in. I'll finish this entry, then turn in.

November 15, 1867

I had just finished my breakfast when a trooper came in and told me that Captain Booker wanted to see me right away. I left the mess hall. When I arrived, the captain was looking at a map on his desk. I sat down. It was only a second before he looked up at me. I could tell by the look on his face that there was some sort of problem.

The captain told me that he had received a report that there was a large group of Indians gathering up along the Missouri River about a mile north of where the Platte Creek flows into the Missouri River. It was in a location that the Ashley family would be passing through on their way to Fort Pierre Trading Post.

He ordered me to get a cavalry unit ready to travel as quickly as possible and make every effort to catch the Ashley family before they rode right into the Indians.

I immediately left and found Sergeant Montrose. I briefly told him what he was to do and why. He had a cavalry unit mounted and ready to go within the hour. I also left instructions to have a wagon with supplies and extra ammunition and additional troopers to follow as quickly as possible.

I set out with the cavalry unit at a pace that would cover a good deal of ground without taxing the horses too much. Hopefully, we would catch up with them before the Indians spotted them.

It was about a two-day trip in the wagon to where the Platte Creek flowed into the Missouri River. I was hoping to catch up with the Ashley family before they started out in the morning.

It was starting to get dark, and we had not caught up with the Ashley family. I was pretty sure we were not very far behind them.

I suggested to Sergeant Montrose that we spend the night in a grove of trees about fifty yards off the trail left by the Ashleys' wagon. He agreed.

While the men set up camp for the night, Sergeant Montrose and I walked up to a little rise in the ground that might offer us a chance to see if there were any fires up ahead.

I thought I could see a fire some distance away. Just as I turned to tell Sergeant Montrose what I saw, he pointed off to the west of our location. I turned with the field glasses to look at what appeared to be another fire. This one was only about three hundred yards from us. I could see several people moving around the fire, and a single wagon. I couldn't help but think it was the Ashleys.

The sergeant and I quickly returned to where the troopers were setting up camp. I immediately told them to put out the fire, they had just started.

Sergeant Montrose and I discussed what we needed to do. We decided that I would sneak over to where we saw the wagon. If it was the Ashleys', I would have them put out their fire so the Indians would not see it. As quietly as possible we would have the Ashleys move over to where the troops were camped. It would make it easier for us to protect them. If it was not the Ashleys, one of us would sneak over to see if the other fire was them.

I began my walk over to where the fire was located. When I got closer, I could see it was Mrs. Ashley standing next to the fire cooking something. I was also glad to see the fire was on the side of the wagon away from where anyone at the other fire would be able to see it.

I explained the situation to them and that it would be necessary to keep as quiet as possible. I helped them pack up their things and put out the fire. As quietly as possible, Johnny and I harnessed the horses to the wagon. I walked in front of the horses leading them to where my troops were camped.

Johnny walked along beside me. I knew he wanted to talk to me, but he kept quiet.

While I was away, Sergeant Montrose had guards posted and had built a shelter for our fire to cook a meal for all.

I spent some time with one of the guards who was keeping an eye on the fire that was some distance away. I reminded everyone to keep as quiet as possible.

It was pretty late when everyone, except the guards, finally got some rest.

November, 16, 1867

The previous entry, was actually written on this date, but it happened yesterday.

I didn't want to risk anyone seeing the fire I would have needed for light enough to write.

To-day we stayed in the grove of trees while we kept watch on the group of Indians just a little north of us. I talked to Mr. and Mrs. Ashley and tried to convince them that it would not be safe for them to move on north at this time.

After hearing about the group of Indians just north of us, they decided to go south to where they could cross the river, then head north on the other side of the river. Mrs. Ashley said it would put them closer to where the land they planned to settle was located.

I reminded her that we could not go with them. They would be on their own. She said she understood that, and thanked me for my concern.

We stayed where we were keeping an eye on the Indians while the Ashleys moved on south. Once it was clear that the Indians were moving northwest along the river, we headed back to the fort.

* * * * *

The entries for the next six days once again showed how the routine of the fort slowed to a snail's pace during the winter months. It frequently snowed, and the temperature remained fairly cold. About the only thing going on was the regular changing of the guard, which was more frequent than it was when the weather was warmer.

Some of the soldiers not on duty would often sit in the mess hall and play cards. A few of the soldiers wrote letters home even though they would not even get out of the fort for days if not weeks. And some of the soldiers kept busy with taking care of the animals and helping in the kitchen.

November 21, 1867

There was a lot of activity this morning. Several of the soldiers from the fort went out to do a little hunting. They went down along the river to hunt in among the trees for turkeys. They got six real nice turkeys for tomorrows dinner. They also prepared the turkeys for cooking.

The cook, with the help of a few soldiers who normally didn't work in the kitchen, baked several pies over the past couple of days.

I felt good about the soldiers who pitched in and did whatever was needed to make a Thanksgiving dinner for all. Even Sergeant Montrose pitched in by making a potato salad like his mother used to make for Thanksgiving dinner.

By night fall, all the soldiers could talk about was tomorrow's dinner. I certainly could not blame them, as I was excited about it, too.

I had made a special bread for the occasion. It was sort of a cinnamon bread like my mother would make from time to time.

As I sat writing in my journal, I can still smell the food that was cooking in the kitchen. I will close for now. I'm sure I will think of past Thanksgivings. Maybe even dream about them.

November 22, 1867

I sat down at the table and thought about today. It was Thanksgiving Day. Although in the past, the day for it had not been set, it still was a day that most of us at the fort would not soon forget. Only four years ago, President Abraham Lincoln had set the date to celebrate Thanksgiving Day on the fourth Thursday of November.

For some of us, it had a bit of sadness because we could not be with our families back east. For me there was a bit of sadness, too. It was times like this that my thoughts turned to Susan and the child I never got to know because they were both taken from me a little over five years ago.

After I had my dinner, I went out and relieved a soldier from guard duty so he could get to enjoy his dinner, too. I told him that he could take his time. I didn't tell him that I wanted a little time to be alone.

I noticed that Sergeant Montrose also relieved a soldier from guard duty. I could see him looking out over the prairie as if he was thinking.

It is late and I have been relieved of guard duty. I returned to the barracks. When I finish writing in my journal, I'll turn in.

November 23, 1867

Things had turned back to pretty much normal for winter duty at the fort. Several of the men talked about yesterday and how much they enjoyed getting a break from most of the daily routine. I couldn't have been prouder of my troopers for all the help they were in putting on such a great meal. Most of them pitched in helping with preparing the food as well as helping to clean up.

Almost to the man, they praised the cook for all his work in making sure the soldiers had a good Thanksgiving meal. It certainly was not like most meals we get here at the fort.

As for a good part of the day, it was back to the routine of guard duty and caring for the animals, and generally trying to keep busy.

I have just finished my rounds of the guard posts. I will turn in as soon as I finish my journal entry of the day.

* * * * *

It looked like Isaac had enjoyed most of the day. I could understand his sadness on Thanksgiving Day.

The next few entries in his journal were pretty routine. Things had quickly returned to the normal activities during the winter at a fort on the plains in the eighteen hundreds. It wasn't until November 29, 1867 that there was anything of any real interest.

November 29, 1867

The day began like most days at this time of year. It wasn't until mid-afternoon that things seemed to change. Although the past few days had been unusually warm, we had not seen anything moving on the prairie. That was until this afternoon.

One of the guards yelled down from the front wall that there were two wagons and what looked like a small column of cavalry men. There were several horses that didn't have riders led by troopers.

I went up on the wall to see what was going on. It quickly became obvious that the wagons and column had been attacked. It was also clear that they had taken a beating. I called for the gate to be opened, and for someone to get the doctor out here.

The column came into the fort and they drove the wagons over toward the Post Infirmary. I quickly found the young lieutenant in charge of the column and asked him what happened. His name was Second Lieutenant Sam Petrey.

He said that the column was attacked by a large group of Indians. He said they got the better of the fight, but his men held them off. There were seven of the original twenty troopers who were injured, and three dead. One wagon driver was also killed in the fight.

I had our men take the injured into the Post Infirmary. The four that were dead were taken to the storage building until they could be buried.

While the horses and wagons were taken care of by our troopers, I took Second Lieutenant Petrey over to the post commander's office to give Captain Booker his report of what happened. I stood by to listen to what the young lieutenant had to say.

He reported that they had been surprised by at least fifty to sixty well-armed Indians. I was a little surprised they had survived at all since there were only four wagon drivers and twenty troopers. That was until he told me they got the upper hand when they started throwing sticks of dynamite at the Indians. He said that they seemed to be afraid of the dynamite, at least more so than he thought they would normally be.

Captain Booker looked at me and smiled. Second Lieutenant Petrey looked a little confused by the captain's reaction. It wasn't until the captain explained that I had used dynamite to get into the fort while it was under siege. He thought that some of the same Indians who had attacked the fort might have been among those who attacked them. They would certainly have a healthy respect for what a stick of dynamite could do.

Second Lieutenant Petrey said that he had never transported dynamite before. The captain explained that he had ordered it after I used it on the Indians. The lieutenant also said that he had some gunpowder and artillery shells for a cannon. He didn't know why we wanted artillery shells until he came into the fort and saw the cannon. He said he didn't know any of the forts on the Frontier had cannons.

Captain Booker told the lieutenant that I was an artillery officer during the war. The lieutenant just smiled.

As soon as all the troopers and driver who were injured were under the care of the fort doctor, and all the supplies and animals had been taken care of, things once again settled down at the fort.

After my evening duties of making sure the guards were at their posts, I went to the officer's barracks. I update my journal before turning in for the night.

*****

During the next ten entries everything was pretty routine. Very little activity. The boredom of guard duty and the routine of caring for the animals filled most of their days. It had also snowed off and on during the past ten days.

December 10, 1867

To-day started out with the usual assignments of duty, some had guard duty while others took care for the animals.

The day started out with the sun shining and a gentle breeze. However, by the noon hour it was overcast and the breeze had turn to a pretty good wind out of the north. All during the afternoon, the temperature dropped so by the evening meal it was getting darn right cold. I reassigned the guards to two hour shifts instead of the usual four hours.

By the time it was dark, it had begun to snow. It was snowing hard when I went to the Officers' Barracks. As soon as I finish my entry into my journal, I will set the fire in the fireplace so it will heat most of the night. I will probably have to add a few logs to it before morning.

December 11, 1867

I had breakfast with the new lieutenant this morning. I found out that this was his first assignment after military school and his commission as a second lieutenant. He had been trained as a cavalry officer. I told him about having the troopers dismount and form a line when attacked by Indians when they were greatly out numbered. I could see that he took a minute to think about it. I knew he had not been trained to fight that way. We discussed it in detail.

I had to remind him that Indians like to fight on horseback, and that they were good at it. I could see he was thinking about what I told him. I suggested that he talk to several of the troopers who had been with me. He said he would.

As I was leaving the mess hall, I saw the young lieutenant looking around. I saw him get up and walk over to one of the troopers who had been on patrol with me. It looked like he might have taken my advice.

Later that day, I saw him talking to Sergeant Montrose. From the look of things, he was seriously thinking about what I had told him.

The rest of the day was pretty routine. We had a meeting with the captain, assigned duties to the troops, and held the usual inspections. During the evening, we had time to read, talk to others, or just relax.

When it was getting close to time for taps, I returned to the Officers' Barracks to write about to-day's activities before going to bed to get some sleep.

* * * * *

It seems the new lieutenant had listened to Isaac. It was yet to be seen if he would take Isaac's advice.

The next five or six entries in Isaac's journal were about the boring routine at the fort.

December 17, 1867

I woke to the first morning in over a week that the sun was shining. As I walked to the mess hall, I noticed that some of the piles of snow that were in the sun showed signs of melting a little. The temperature was still below freezing, but the sun's warmth had a nice feeling on my face.

As I entered the mess hall, I noticed that the sun had an effect on those having their breakfast. There was much more talking among the men, and they seemed happier.

There was still a lot of snow out on the prairie, enough to make moving around somewhat difficult. A couple of days like to-day and we might start going out on patrol again. Although the patrols would be short and stay fairly close to the fort, they would get us out of the confines of the fort's walls.

Sergeant Montrose stopped by the table where I was seated. He told me that the captain wanted to see me as soon as I finished eating.

As soon as I finished eating, I went to the captain's office to see what he wanted. It seems he was thinking the same thing I was about patrols being able to move around the prairie in a couple of days if the sun continued to melt the snow.

The captain asked me to take Second Lieutenant Petrey along to get him familiar with the area. He reminded me that Petrey was new to the West and some of his thoughts about the Frontier were not correct.

I told him I would work with him starting to-day. It might help him once we resume patrols. The captain agreed.

After I finished with the captain, I went looking for Petrey. I had already heard from a couple of soldiers that Second Lieutenant Petrey was not willing to listen to soldiers who had been on the Frontier for several years. I didn't think it would be a problem for me since I had the advantage of having spent a lot of time on the Frontier, and I outranked him.

One of the soldiers, a corporal who had been stationed on the plains a few years ago, came up to me and asked if he could talk to me about Petrey. I agreed to listen to what he had to say. We went and found a quiet corner in the mess hall where we could talk without being overheard by others. The corporal told me that Petrey's actions on the way to the fort were responsible for the deaths of the troopers under his command when they were attacked by the Indians. The corporal said he tried to tell him that with so many Indians, we should not take them on head first by charging into them, but he did it anyway. The corporal told him that under the circumstances they would be better off taking a defensive position.

"He insisted we were better trained then those 'heathens', and we would show them a thing or two. You saw the results of that decision," the corporal said.

I thanked the corporal for his information, and asked him why he took so long to tell me about his actions. He said he was afraid that it would cause him problems with the lieutenant. I assured him that I would not tell the lieutenant where I got the information. However, I felt it was my responsibility to share what I had been told with the captain.

I went back to the captain's office and reported what the corporal had told me. The captain just looked at me for a moment or so before he talked. He asked me if what I was told was what really happened. I said I didn't know, but the corporal had experience on the plains and dealing with Indians. The lieutenant had no experience in any kind of combat, Indians or otherwise. He was fresh out of a military school and this was his first duty station.

The captain told me that I was to take him on patrols with me. I was to make sure the decisions he made were the right ones, or I was to override any of his orders. I agreed with his instructions. I was also told to keep an eye on him to see how he talks to the soldiers and his attitude toward them. The captain thought it might give me some idea of how the soldiers felt about him. I agreed.

I began watching Second Lieutenant Sam Petrey immediately. A lot of the time from a distance. I wanted to know how he treated the men under him, and what they thought of him.

During the day, I could see by the soldiers' actions around Second Lieutenant Petrey that they had little respect for him. They did what they were told, but it was clear they did it because he ordered them rather than out of respect for him. They seemed to obey his orders when given because they had to or face discipline.

I decided that it might be a good idea to go over to the post infirmary and have a talk with the soldiers who were injured in the battle with the Indians. Two of the men were willing to talk to me. They were convinced that Second Lieutenant Petrey had not listened to the soldiers who had been in fights with Indians before. One of them said flat out that Petrey was responsible for the deaths of those who died. The other one said the only reason they survived at all was their sergeant disobeyed Petrey's orders and had us dismount and form up to defend ourselves. "We eventually forced the Indians to break off the fight. If we had stayed on our horses, we would not be here to-day. And there was a good chance that Sergeant Williams might still be alive," the corporal said.

I left the infirmary and reported back to the captain what I found out from those who had been in the fight. The captain said he would keep my report to himself for now. He also said that I was not to let Petrey out of my sight when on patrol. The captain was pretty upset as well as mad. As I left his office, I got the feeling that he was thinking of charging Petrey with failure to use good judgement under stress.

I noticed that during the time after dinner, none of the men had anything to do with Petrey. No one talked to him or even looked at him.

It is getting toward time for taps, I'll put my journal up for to-night. I wanted a record of what I had been told.

* * * * *

It looks like Isaac is going to have his hands full. Over the next couple of entries in his journal, the only mention of Second Lieutenant Petrey was that Isaac was keeping an eye on him.

December 20, 1867

I got up early as we were to head out for a short patrol to the east and south along the Missouri River. With all the snow earlier, there was a good chance we might find Indians camping in the shelter of the trees along the banks of the river.

I was just about to finish my breakfast when Second Lieutenant Petrey came up and stood beside me. I looked up at him. From the look on his face, he was not very happy.

"Is there something on your mind?" I asked.

He said there was, but didn't say anything more. I asked him what was on his mind. He said that I was, then hesitated. I just looked at him.

Petrey took a deep breath and began by saying that he didn't like how close I was watching him, and wanted to know why. I decided to tell him.

I told him that his actions while engaging the Indians on his way to the fort did not appear to be a case of good judgement on his part, resulting in the death of several troopers.

I could see he didn't like what I said. I added, "When outnumbered by so many, it would have been better for you to set up a defensive position. Those 'heathens', as you called them, are some of the best light cavalries in this country, and maybe in the world. They know how, and when, to fight on horseback."

Petrey looked at me for a minute, then said "You weren't there. What gives you the right to make calls on my judgement?"

"You are right, I wasn't there, but some experienced troopers were. And as for my right to discuss this with you is two fold. One, I am a First Lieutenant which means I outrank you. Second, Captain Booker asked me to find out what really happened out there. When I talk to him again, I can assure

you that I will report your attitude now as well as your actions in the field. There are a lot of things you need to learn that you could not learn in a classroom in some military school back east. I only hope you live long enough to learn them. Dismissed."

I knew I should not have lost my temper, but his arrogance did not set well with me. And it would not set well with Captain Booker, either. I wrote all this down in my journal just in case I needed it in the future. I got up and went directly to the captain's office to report what had taken place.

After reporting my confrontation with Second Lieutenant Petrey, the captain asked me how I thought Petrey should be treated. I suggested sending him back east, or court marshal him for dereliction of duty which caused the deaths of several soldiers. Neither was to my liking. The only thing it would do would be to reduce our manpower at the fort.

I asked the captain to give me some time with him. I felt that Second Lieutenant Petrey was not stupid. If he took what I said to him to heart, he just might make a good officer.

Captain Booker told me that he would give him a chance, but if Petrey didn't change, and change quickly, he would take care of the matter, permanently.

I would give Petrey the rest of the day to think about what I had told him.

To-morrow I would have another talk with Petrey and ask him if he was willing to learn what he needed to learn to survive in this part of the world, or would he prefer being sent back east with a recommendation for him to be released from the Army.

I didn't see Petrey for most of the day. When I did see him, he looked like he had a lot on his mind. I only hoped he was thinking about his actions in the field and not spending his time just being angry with me. I decided that I would not tell him about sending him back east.

When it was about time for taps, I returned to my quarters to write about to-day's activities. I wanted a written record of my dealings with Second Lieutenant Petrey.

* * * * *

It will be interesting to see how things turn out with Second Lieutenant Petrey.

December 21, 1867

I woke early and started toward the mess hall. Had a lot on my mind, most of it concerning Lieutenant Petrey. I mulled over in my mind what the captain had said. I had to agree with his assessment of the situation. He told me that whatever recommendation I would make on Petrey's future in the military, he would support.

I entered the mess hall and immediately saw Sergeant Montrose. He was just sitting down to breakfast. I had a lot to talk to him about, so I decided to join him. I asked him if I could join him. He invited me to sit down with him.

We talked about Petrey. It was decided between us that Petrey would go on the next patrol with us. You might say we thought it was a test for Second Lieutenant Sam Petrey.

I told Sergeant Montrose to put together a patrol as soon as possible. We would be leaving as soon as it was ready to move out. I would notify Petrey.

It was mid-morning when we left the fort. I had Second Lieutenant Petrey leading the column. I rode along behind him next to Sergeant Montrose. Although I had not told Petrey what to do, I was sure he realized that this was his final exam. I had told him he was in charge of the patrol. The sergeant had relayed the overall orders of what he was supposed to do and where he was to patrol. It was now time to see if he could carry out those orders.

It wasn't long before we were close to the river. At that point, Second Lieutenant Petrey had the column turn generally southeast along the river. We were fairly close to the river. I had the sergeant recommend to Petrey that we move a little further away from the river where it would be easier for us to have room to move if attacked from the trees along the bank of the river. Second Lieutenant Petrey listened to the sergeant and we moved about two hundred yards away from the treeline. Petrey had accepted the suggestion from the sergeant. He also sent a trooper out in front of the column as an outrider.

The first day went without a hitch. Second Lieutenant Petrey did a good job and took suggestions from the sergeant. I knew a lot of it was because I was there. I only hoped that he would listen to other soldiers who had been on the Frontier when things happened fast and decisions had to be made quickly, and I was not around.

December 22, 1867

We had camped at the edge of some pretty thick woods. The sun was up and the air was feeling warmer than we had experienced for some time. The cook had breakfast going.

We had just finished eating when one of the troopers yelled out that Indians were approaching us. I didn't say anything. I wanted to see what Petrey was going to do.

He called the men to arms, then had them take a defensive position at the edge of the woods. He stood out in front of his men while he looked for the Indians. He saw them as they came over a slight ridge. There were at least twenty-five or so. There were men, women, and children. They were all walking.

Second Lieutenant Petry told the men to stand at ease, but be ready for anything. He walked out in front of his men to greet the Indians.

It wasn't long and the Indians stopped and looked at the soldiers. After a moment or two, they cautiously approached Petrey and raised a hand in peace. They said something to Petrey, but it was clear the lieutenant didn't understand. He called Sergeant Montrose to join him.

Sergeant Montrose quickly realized that Second Lieutenant Petrey didn't understand what the Indians had said. Sergeant Montrose walked up beside the Lieutenant Petrey and translated what was said by the Indians.

After a few minutes of conversation between the Indian leader and Petrey, Petrey told them they could go on their way and wished them well on their journey.

We watched them as they walked on by us. It pleased me that Petrey handled the encounter well. I did take a minute to let him know that he had handled it well. I also reminded him that he still needed to learn how to know when to fight, when to take a defensive position, and when to talk. I told him a few things to look for when talking to Indians. They could be just checking out his forces. I told him the Indians like to know what their chances of winning are before they start a fight.

Second Lieutenant Petrey said he took his que from Sergeant Montrose. That was good thinking on his part. Sergeant Montrose was an experienced soldier. I was beginning to think that Second Lieutenant Sam Petrey just might make a good field officer, yet.

We moved out as soon as the Indians were out of sight. We continued along in our southeast direction for the remainder of the day. We set up camp near the Missouri River.

After we were settled in and had guards posted, I sat down to write about to-day's activities. I have to admit I was feeling a little better about Petrey, but he had not been tested in a fight.

December 23, 1867

We were up with the sun and having breakfast when Second Lieutenant Petrey came to me. He asked if we would be out away from the fort on Christmas Day. I told him that we were going to head west for a little while, then north on back to the fort. In fact, those were his orders of the day.

He nodded then turned and returned to where Sergeant Montrose was standing. From what I could see, he had given the sergeant orders for the day. It wasn't long and we were on the move again.

We moved west for a couple of hours before Second Lieutenant Petry gave the order to head north toward the fort. The going was not too bad. There was a little snow on the ground, but not enough to make it difficult for the horses to move along at a reasonable pace.

It was two-thirty in the afternoon when an outrider came racing back toward the column. He was yelling that the fort was under attack by Indians. The outrider said there were a large number of Indians at the fort, and they were firing at it, but it didn't look like they were trying to get inside.

I called Petrey and Montrose to come to me. I asked Petrey what he thought we should do. He immediately said we needed more information, but we should send a few troopers on ahead to make sure what we were up against. He said that he should take them. He needed to know firsthand what we were dealing with.

I agreed, but told him that he was to lead the troopers, but I would go with him. Without comment, we took twelve troopers and headed toward the fort.

When we came to a slight ridge, we stopped. Using our field glasses, we scanned the area. I glanced over at Petrey to see what he wanted to do.

Second Lieutenant Petrey called up Corporal Jones. I heard him ask if we had any dynamite. Corporal Jones said we did. He was given orders to get it, and have the rest of the troopers come to our location. I asked Petrey what his plans were. He said you got in the fort using dynamite, maybe it would work again, only this time we will be attacking them instead of trying to get in the fort.

He added that he was going to have the troopers spread out so it looked like there were more of us, and had the bugler sound charge loud and strong.

Second Lieutenant Petrey looked at me as if he was looking for my approval of his actions. There was no place in the manual for such an action, but under the circumstances it looked like something that might work. It might work really well if some of the Indians had had dynamite thrown at them before. It would also help if the men trained to use the cannon in the fort would start shelling the Indians from inside the fort.

Suddenly, there was a load explosion that hit near some Indians. It was clear that the cannon was being used. I told Petrey to hold up on sending our troopers in. I wanted to let the cannon do its job first, which was to add a certain amount of fear into the Indians thinking.

It wasn't long and the Indians started to spread out, that was when we charged in. The Indians decided that it was time to get out of there. We pursued them for about a mile before we broke it off and returned to the fort.

As soon as we were in the fort, the men took care of the horses and equipment while we reported to Captain Booker. He was glad to see us. He also approved of Second Lieutenant Petrey's actions.

After completing our report, I returned to the officer's barracks to write to-day's activities in my journal.

* * * * *

It seems that Second Lieutenant Petrey had passed his test. Taking a page from First Lieutenant Madison's playbook paid off.

December 24, 1867

I was up early and went to the mess hall for breakfast. As soon as I stepped into the mess hall, I was greeted by five troopers. They requested permission to go out of the fort to a shallow creek nearby where they could get a tree for a Christmas tree.

I gave them permission but only if they had at least ten troopers as escorts. With the Indians attack on the fort just yesterday, I felt it was justified. They agreed.

I took a position on the wall and scanned the area using my field glasses. As soon as I felt it was clear, I gave them the signal that they could go. I watched them all the way out.

As soon as they had a tree, I watched them as they hurried back into the fort. I have to admit, it was a nice-looking tree.

I spent the rest of the day doing my routine chores. After the dinner meal, I went to the Officers' Barracks. I spent a lot of time thinking about the last time I had seen a Christmas tree, and the Christmas I had had with Susan.

I will turn in for the night as soon as I bring my journal up-to-date.

December 25, 1867

I woke this morning and looked out the window. It was snowing. The snow flakes were drifting down and covering everything in white. I got dressed and went to the mess hall for breakfast.

When I entered the mess hall, I could see several of the soldiers hanging strings of popcorn around a pine tree. Some of the soldiers had made different decorations out of paper, with a few of them made from cans from the kitchen. One of the soldiers had made a star for the top of the tree from a piece of metal.

It was nice to see them all working together. It was sad for me as it was times like this that I really missed Susan.

I sat down and ate my breakfast while I watched them decorate the tree. One of the soldiers, Private Smith, came over to me and asked if I would like to join them in singing when I finished my breakfast. I told him I would like to, very much.

It wasn't long and they gathered around the tree and began singing Christmas songs. I joined in.

After awhile, I noticed that several of the soldiers seemed to look a little sad. I could certainly understand. It was a time when we missed those we had left behind. I decided that it was time for me to leave the mess hall.

I went outside and made rounds of the fort to make sure that the guards were at their posts. I took a minute to wish each one of them a Merry Christmas.

During the evening, they had a special dinner for all the soldiers. Several of us went out and relieved the guards so they could enjoy the Christmas dinner.

While standing guard, I couldn't help but look up. The snow had stopped and the sky was so clear that I could see thousands of stars. I didn't know what the name of the star *was that seemed to be just a little brighter than the rest. Even while standing guard on the wall, I could hear the songs being sung in the mess hall.*

As things quieted down for the night, and I was relieved of guard duty. I went to the barracks. I couldn't help but think of Susan and our baby boy.

I decided to take a few minutes and write about to-day in my journal before I blow out the lantern to get some rest.

December 26, 1867

I woke this morning feeling pretty good about yesterday. It was nothing like the Christmases I had in the past, but it was enjoyable.

As the day went on, it seemed to me that it was taking on the feel of a routine, almost as if it was a sample of things to come. The regular changing of the guards, the inspections, and taking care of the animals.

By the end of the day, things seemed to be back to normal. With the heavy snow last night, there was little chance that we would be taking any patrols out for some time.

At taps, I have just finished entering to-days activities in the journal.

* * * * *

The next four or five entries in Isaac's journal showed just how slow things were at the fort. Every other day it snowed just enough to keep the patrols from going out. But there was very little movement out on the prairie anyway.

December 31, 1867

To-day was pretty routine at least most of the day. We did have a very nice dinner of venison steaks, boiled potatoes, corn and apple pie. A few of the soldiers sang songs. At midnight, the cannon was fired to enter in the New Year. A toast for the New Year was given by Captain Booker to the men.

Taps was sounded at twelve-fifteen. The latest it had ever been sounded.

Needless to say, most of us were ready to get some sleep.

January 1, 1868

Today seemed to be a day of rest for the men. About the only activities were those that were required to maintain security of the fort, to take care of the animals, and make sure the soldiers were fed.
Several of the soldiers wrote letters to friends and family back home. Most of them played cards in the mess hall when not on duty or had other responsibilities.

* * * * *

The New Year was upon them. There was a lot of wondering what it would bring. Being a soldier at a fort on the Frontier was one of never knowing what might happen at any minute.

The next few entries showed just how boring it could be during the winter months. There was little to do outside of the everyday routine.

It wasn't until January 14, 1868 that there was anything of interest.

January 14, 1868

The past few days we have been experiencing a few days of warmer weather. It had melted the snow enough that a patrol could get out and move around a bit. Captain Booker thought that it would be a good idea to send out a patrol to check along the river to see if there was any movement by the Indians. It was to be a fairly short patrol, just one night out. He suggested that Second Lieutenant Petrey take charge of the patrol.

It didn't take long for the patrol to be ready to move out. Sergeant Montrose would go with him.

I stood on the walkway on the fort wall and watched as they rode off toward the woods along the Missouri River. It felt good to know that Sergeant Montrose was going to be on the patrol. He, at least could talk to the Indians. I had learned a lot from him so I was able to converse with most of the Indians.

I, like most of the men at the fort, was a little worried about them. But then we all worried about any patrol that left the fort. One never knew what they were going to run into out there.

Just because we worried about them, didn't mean we didn't have work to do at the fort. I reported in with Captain Booker, then held inspection of the remaining soldiers, scheduled the men who were to stand guard duty, and made sure that the animals were taken care of and the barns cleaned. There was always something to do.

As the general routine of the day went by, I thought about the patrol, as did many of the others at the fort.

When it was time to turn in, I went to the barracks to bring my journal up to date before going to bed.

January 15, 1868

The morning had been pretty routine. Nothing out of the ordinary. It was just shortly before the noon hour when I was called to the wall. When I got there, the soldier pointed to an Indian on a horse several hundred yards away from the fort. He had a horse in tow, and it looked like there was a body slung over the horse's back.

I took the field glasses from the soldier and looked out at the Indian. What I saw made me angry. Slung over the horse's back was a soldier. It looked like an officer. I could hear him yelling something. It sounded like get off our land.

I reached over and took the rifle from the soldier. Using the wall for support, I took aim at the Indian and slowly pulled the trigger. The Indian fell off the horse with a bullet hole in his chest

I ran down off the wall, grabbed a horse tied near the gate as I told them to open the gate. I rode out to where the Indian laid dead. I grabbed the reins of the horse with the body over it, and rode back into the fort.

It wasn't until I was inside the fort that I took the time to see who was over the saddle. It was Second Lieutenant Samuel Petrey.

By this time, there were several soldiers, mounted and heading out to where the Indian laid dead. One of the soldiers dismounted to make sure the Indian was dead. He grabbed the Indian's horse, put the Indian over the back of the horse and took him into the fort.

One of the soldiers asked why he brought the Indian into the fort. He looked at me and said he wanted to make sure that when we caught up with the Indians, we had the right ones. He also said, "what he is wearing will help identify the tribe he was from."

Captain Booker was standing nearby. He saw it was Second Lieutenant Petrey. He wondered what had happened to the rest of the patrol. He told me to take a patrol and find out what happened to them. He reminded me that I should go prepared to fight.

I got a patrol together in record time. All we had to do was follow the trail left in the snow by the Indian. I had a patrol of twenty well-armed and expert cavalry men. All of them ready for a fight. We wasted no time in getting underway.

It didn't take us very long to get to where the fight had taken place. What we found made me angry. There were thirteen men dead. There were signs of one hell of a fight. I could see in the snow where there had been bodies of Indians, but those bodies had been taken away.

As Corporal Jones came over to me, I thought I heard something. For some reason I will never understand, it suddenly came to me that there had been fifteen men on that patrol. We found thirteen dead plus the one returned to the fort, which left one missing.

I yelled out to be perfectly quiet. It was then that I heard something coming from behind a bush. I ran to the bush and quickly looked behind it. There on the ground curled partway under the bush was Sergeant Montrose. He was in pretty bad shape.

He was able to tell us that they had been attacked during the night. The only reason that he had been able to hide was after he was shot, he was able to crawl under the bush. He was also able to tell us what tribe they were from, and where they talked about setting up camp. Sergeant Montrose could hear them talking. They would be camping about eight miles south near where a creek flowed into the Missouri River.

I had three of the men fix up a stretcher so they could take the sergeant back to the fort. I also told them to tell the captain that we were going after those who killed Petrey and the men in his patrol.

I took the rest of my patrol and began following the Indians. It was just about dark when I was about ready to stop for the night. In looking around I noticed what looked like the glow of fires in the darkness in the woods some distance away.

We stopped and dismounted. I talked to the men about how we would attack them. Corporal Jones reminded me that he had brought along a few sticks of dynamite.

We carefully sat down and planned out our attack. But first, I needed to make sure we had the right ones. I didn't want to attack Indians who had nothing to do with the attack on Petrey's patrol.

One of the soldiers told me he had been a scout in the Confederate Army. He could sneak up close enough to find out if they were the same Indians who attacked Petrey's patrol. I gave him permission to find out. I also told him to be careful.

I watched him quickly disappear into the darkness. It seemed like forever before he returned.

When he returned, he told me they had several Army horses and Army issued rifles. He also said that he recognized Sergeant Montrose's hat. One of the Indians was wearing it.

I told the men to settle in and to remain quiet. We were going to wait until the Indians settled down and were sleeping.

January 16, 1868

It was after mid-night before the Indians settled down and their camp was quiet.

When Corporal Jones returned, he reported that there were twenty-five, maybe twenty-seven Indians, all of them warriors. He also reported they were all pretty well bunched together, with two sitting up close to the fire.

Corporal Jones drew a plan on a piece of paper. It showed us where the Indians had guards. There were only two, and they were sitting close to a fire. They were wrapped in buffalo blankets to keep warm. Jones was sure that he and one other could get to them and end their lives without a sound. He picked a private who had been with him in the war.

We had planned our attack on the Indians very carefully. However, it didn't go off as smoothly as we had hoped. In taking the two who were at the fire, one was able to make a little noise. The noise alerted the rest and it quickly turned into a shooting match. A couple of sticks of dynamite were used which confused as well as killed many of the Indians.

When it was over, we had two soldiers injured, but not seriously, and one dead. The Indians had twenty-one killed or dying of their injuries. The three left were quickly put in irons.

We settled in for the rest of the night with three soldiers keeping watch. We will head back to the fort in the morning. I sat next to the fire and wrote my report of our activities.

*****

That must have been some fire-fight as the soldiers were outnumbered. It was apparent that their surprise worked.

January 17, 1868

We were up early. Once we had breakfast and fed the surviving Indians, we headed back to Fort Randall. It was mid-afternoon when we got back. The three Indians were locked up in the brig to wait for the captain's decision on what to do with them.

After I gave Captain Booker my report of our patrol. I went to the Infirmary to check on Sergeant Montrose. It was good to see that he was awake and sitting up a little in bed. I walked over to him and handed him his hat. He reached out with one hand, took his hat and set it on his chest. He looked up at me and said "thanks". I told him I was glad I could get it back for him.

We talked for a few minutes before I checked in on the wounded from yesterday. They were all doing well even though one of them had a serious wound. The doctor assured me that he would survive, but it would take him awhile.

The last couple of days had been hard. I was tired, but I had one more thing to do before I could get some rest. That is to make my entry in my journal.

* * * * *

It was good to see how the battle with the Indians turned out.

The next six days in Isaac's journal showed that things had returned to normal. Inspections, taking care of the animals, keeping uniforms clean, and standing guard duty, were the major activities.

January 23, 1868

To-day I woke to the sun shining in the window of the Officers' Barracks. It was the first sun we had seen for the past five or six days. The general tone of things in the mess hall was much lighter. It seems the sun lifted a few spirits.

After breakfast, I reported to the captain's office for morning briefing. Although it was sunny and the temperature was a little warmer, there was still too much snow to send out a patrol. Captain Booker suggested that we practice drills inside the fort. The open area inside the fort was large enough that the troopers could practice going from horseback to a defensive formation, then remounting to attack on horseback again.

The crew that was responsible for the cannon and it's uses could also do dry runs practicing shooting and moving exercises. Since the fort had both a front and back gate, the gun crew would have to be ready to reposition the cannon quickly if a full-scale attack on the fort should happen.

I have to admit that there were a few who thought it was a waste of time to practice what they already knew. I reminded them that it was very important that each soldier knew what he was supposed to do, how to do it, and frankly when to do it. The few who sort of objected to the practice suddenly found themselves doing more practice until they got it right at least three times in a row.

It was also important that they knew at least a few of the other jobs that needed to be done in case they had to fill in for someone who might have been injured or killed.

At dinner, it seemed that a number of the soldiers were still talking about the exercises. I heard a couple of soldiers say that they felt better, if for no other reason than it gave them something to do.

After dinner several of the soldiers gathered in the mess hall to play some cards, or some other game or to just relax

and talk. As it was getting late, I made rounds of the guard posts to make sure all was well. It was quiet.
I returned to the Offices' Barracks. I will turn in after I finish entering to-day's activities in my journal.

* * * * *

It was good that the captain had kept the men busy. The next two entries I read showed that the weather had started to warm up a bit.

January 26, 1868

After a couple of days of fairly warm weather, it once again turned cold. The wind blew in from the north, and the cloud cover became thicker as the day went by. It was about three in the afternoon when it started to snow again. By six o'clock it was snowing very hard. In fact, it was snowing so hard it was difficult to see all the way across the fort.

The captain kept the two-hour limit on the length of time a guard was to stand watch. Since it was my night to have the duty, I was responsible to make sure the guards were changed every two hours.

In between checking to make sure the guards had been changed, I decided to write a letter to Colonel McHenry. I was sure that he would get a kick out of hearing I was once again in the Army, to say nothing of the thought that he would be surprised to hear from me as I had failed to keep in touch with him.

Since we were short a Sergeant, Sergeant Mathers from the Cavalry Unit came to take over Sergeant Montrose's duties until he recovered from his injuries.

I'm now back in the barracks. Since I wrote this while on duty, I'll just put up my journal and get some rest.

*****

It sounds like they are short of Officers in the fort, but that was often the case.

The next seven entries in Isaac's journal were mostly about the weather, which was not good. The snow had gotten pretty deep and made any kind of movement outside the fort very difficult.

February 3, 1868

Nothing much has been happening around here. A couple of the men got into a fight over a card game and had to be pulled off each other. They spent a couple of days in the brig. Tempers are a little short around here mostly because there is not enough to kept the men busy. It is hard to hold exercises when there is almost a foot of snow. We have shoveled paths from one place to another. Even the mail has not been able to get through to us.

The guard duty is still limited to only two hours due to the cold. The guards have little to watch as nothing is moving around outside the fort, either.

* * * * *

Over the next month or so, the days were much the same as the previous days, cold, windy, and most often snowing.

March 31, 1868

Today started out with the clouds slowly drifting off. By mid-morning, the sky was clear and the sun was shining brightly. Moods seemed to improve with the weather. Even some of the snow is beginning to melt.

Although it was a great improvement in the weather, it made for a lot of mud in the fort. If the weather holds for a few days, it well make it so we can start making patrols around the area again.

A couple of the men were talking about getting out and doing a little hunting. It would be nice to have a little fresh meat from a couple of deer or maybe a buffalo.

We are still restricting the time spent on guard duty as it is still pretty cold at night. We will need a few days like today before we can really get out and about.

It is about time for taps. I have to make rounds to make sure the guards are at their posts.

I finished my rounds. It is time for me to get some rest.

* * * * *

The next few entries showed where the weather continued to improve, slowly. It wasn't until I got to the April 10, 1868 that anything really changed.

April 10, 1868

With the improvement in the weather, I am getting the urge to continue my trek into the Frontier of the Dakota Territory.
It was a beautiful day to-day. The sun shined all day and there was a gentle breeze out of the south. The temperature was up to a point where a light jacket was all that was needed to stay comfortable.
I decided that it was time to tell Captain Booker that I would be leaving soon. When I told him I would be leaving in a week, he tried to get me to stay on. I told him that I was not supposed to be in the military in the first place due to my leg injury. I had only agreed to it to help him, but more to help me feel useful while staying here for the winter. He thanked me for all the help I had been to him, he said he would miss having me around, and that he hoped I would find whatever it was I was looking for. I thanked him, then left his office.
In a way, I felt I was letting him down, but I had done what I had agreed to do. It was time for me to move on. It was time to start gathering the things I would need in my travels across the plains of the Dakota Territory.
I went to the Officer's Barracks and started making a list of what I would need. I had many of them from before I came here, I just needed to get them together and make sure they were in good condition.
It was just before the evening meal when there was a knock on the door to my room. When I opened the door, I found Sergeant Montrose, Sergeant Mathers, and Corporal Jones standing there. They had big smiles on their faces. I noticed right away that Sergeant Montrose was still having some difficulty moving around.
I will never forget Sergeant Montrose's words. "We came by because we heard that you were getting ready to

move on. We have a gift for you. It is from the cavalry unit that you spent so much of your time helping to learn how the cavalry works best out here in the Frontier. It didn't always go along with the manual, but it works here."

They handed me a package all wrapped up in brown paper. They insisted that I open it. I thanked them, then opened the package. Inside was a buckskin shirt and pants. On the shirt was the lieutenant bars the captain had loaned me. They wished me well, then left me standing there.

I can't remember when anyone had done so much for me, with one exception, and that was Colonel McHenry.

I closed the door to my room and sat down at the desk in the corner. I can hear taps while I am writing this. This was a day I will never forget.

* * * * *

Isaac had made a lasting impression on at least some of the men at the fort.

The entries for the next week were rather short. They were mostly about the weather and how it was gradually improving, and about getting his supplies together.

April 17, 1868

This morning the sun was up and the air was comfortable. I had my horse saddled and my mule packed. I decided that I would wear the buckskin pants and shirt as I left to show the men that I appreciated their thoughtfulness.

As I rode toward the front gate of the fort, I had to pass between two rows of cavalry troopers as well as four soldiers who were saluting as I rode by. When I got to the gate, I stopped, turned around and returned the salute. I then turned back around to leave.

As I left the fort, I couldn't help but think of the men who had become friends. I had this same sort of feeling a couple of years ago when I was discharged from the Army.

It was both a sad day and a good day. I was leaving some friends behind, but I was going out to fulfill my dream.

I had decided to head northwest along the Missouri River. Again, I stayed far enough away from the river to avoid the deeper ravines and gullies to make it easier on my horse and mule. I made about twenty miles to-day. I found a small creek where my animals could relax and get some water and green grass.

I finished my entry in my journal, before I laid down to rest.

* * * * *

Isaac is finally back on his way to the Black Hills. His delay at Fort Randall had been planned. What happened there had not been planned, however. He had made some friends at the fort.

He is once again on his way to fulfill his dream.

April 18, 1868

It was cold this morning. I took my buffalo coat and a pair of pants out of my pack and put my buckskin pants and shirt in the pack. After my breakfast, I put out my fire, saddled my horse and put my gear on my mule. I started out in the same direction I had traveled yesterday.

There was a cold breeze out of the west, but with the buffalo coat it was not at all uncomfortable. There was very little to see out on the plains. The ground was fairly level with only slightly rolling hills. There were a few gullies.

The further I got from the Missouri River, the fewer trees. It was easy to see for miles out here. The best way to describe it would be to say there was nothing for miles and miles.

I did see some antelope. However, they stayed some distance away. I also saw some buffalo off in the distance.

I spent the night in a shallow gully to get out of the wind. I also used the gully as a place to hide my fire. A fire could be seen from miles away out here. I'm writing this by the light of my small fire.

* * * * *

Isaac is taking precautions to avoid being seen. It is understandable since he is now all alone.

The next three or four entries gave little information except that it was a wide open and lonely land. The weather had remained cold at night, but fairly comfortable during the day.

April 21, 1868

I got a good start to my day. It was cold and there was a breeze out of the west. My horse and mule were glad that I had decided to stay far enough from the river to make it easier on them.

It was just about noon when I saw a fairly large group of Indians who were moving south. From the look of them, there were a fairly large number of them who were warriors.

I had no desire to get into a fight with them. Off to my right was what looked like a ravine that ran down toward the river. It was deep enough that I could hide in it, and move further down it toward the river.

I turned into the ravine and quickly moved along the bottom of it until I was sure I was far enough away and around a bend in the ravine where I could hide. I stayed there ready to put up a fight if I had to.

I hunkered down and waited for them to pass. I'm not sure how long I was there, but it seemed like a long time. I found a place in the ravine where I could spend the night. I built a small almost smokeless fire before dark to fix my dinner. I put out my fire out after dinner. I write this before it was too dark to see.

April 22, 1868

To-day I am camped close to what I believe is the White River. From the look of the river, I don't think that the water is very good. It is almost as white as the ground here. Since I have enough water for now, I will stay here. To-morrow I will cross the White River in the hope of finding better water. I will continue on keeping the Missouri River to my right.

I have built a lean-to in among the trees as it looks like it might rain. If it does, I will try to capture some rain water to refill my canteens.

It has started to rain. It is also getting too dark to write any more to-night.

* * * * *

It was good to see that Isaac was being careful and that he was making sure he had plenty of water, although he was probably only a mile or less from the Missouri River.

The next week or so shows he is making pretty good time. It had rained a couple of afternoons and the weather had been cool. However, he had not had any problems that he had not expected. That was until May 2, 1868.

May 2, 1868

I am standing in the bottom of a gully watching about twelve Indians who had chased me for almost a mile from where I had camped before I found a place that would provide me with cover and a place where I could make a stand.

Since I took cover in the gully and shot three of them, they have taken cover in a shallow ravine. Every once in a while, one of them will pop up to see if I was still there. I got the feeling that they expected me to run at my first chance.

I'm hoping they don't try to work around behind me as my back is not covered very well. I've looked up and down this gully for a place where I might be able to get away without them seeing me. I have learned that Indians can be very sneaky. I didn't want them sneaking up behind me.

It looks like the gully makes a sharp turn to the north about a hundred yards east of where I am. It also looks deep enough that I might be able to walk my animals down the gully and around the turn, and hopefully be able to escape.

It will be dark soon. Just before dark, I will make an effort to shoot one of them in the hope of giving them the idea that I plan to stay and fight.

May 3, 1868

I made it as far as the bend in the gully. I saw two Indians had worked their way around to the gully and were working their way to where I had been. Luckily, I saw them first and had my pistol in my hand. I was able to shoot both of them before they could react to seeing me.

I decided that it might be a good idea if I got out of there. I took my animals out of the gully, mounted my horse and rode away from there as fast as I could. I had to be careful racing across the plains in the dark. I didn't want to have my horse or mule fall in a ravine or gully, or step in a prairie dog hole.

Once I was sure I was out of the area, I slowed down. As the sun started to come up in the east, I could see a little better. I started looking for a place where I could hole up. I needed to give my animals a little rest.

As the sun came up, I could see a creek that looked like it had good water in it. There was also a place where I could hide and hopefully get some rest. I curled up behind a bush and kept my animals close so if anyone came around, they would let me know.

It was mid-afternoon when I woke. It was a clear day. I took my field glasses and scanned the area looking for anyone or anything that might cause me harm. I saw nothing. My horse and mule were grazing at the edge of the creek and looked content to be there. I decided that I would stay here and give them a chance to get a good rest. I would also try to rest, but would still keep an eye out for any danger that might befall me.

If I figured right, I was only a day or two from Fort Pierre Trading Post.

May 4, 1868

After getting up, I took time to scan the area using my field glasses. I saw nothing that would cause me any problems. After a good breakfast, I packed up, saddled my horse and started out toward the Fort Pierre Trading Post. The day was rather pleasant. We, that is my animals and I, were well rested.

We had traveled for a good part of the day when I thought I saw what looked like a sod house. It surprised me since I had not seen a living soul, other than the Indians a couple of days ago.

I stopped and took a minute to scan the area with my field glasses to see if there was anyone around. I saw what looked like an Indian woman come out of the soddy. I was a bit surprised as I had not seen any Indians who lived in sod houses.

It was a moment or so later that I saw a man come around from behind the house. He was dressed like the pictures I had seen of mountain men, but I was a long way away from any mountains.

I decided to ride toward the house and not make any move that might make them think I was a danger to them. As I did, I noticed the man go behind the house.

When I got closer, the man came out from behind the house with a rifle this time. He held it loosely, but still pointed in my direction.

After I introduced myself, he relaxed a little. We talked for awhile. He offered to let me spend the night there.

We visited during the evening. I found out his name was Franklin Grover and he had been from Ohio. He left Ohio because he didn't want any part of the war. I didn't bother to tell him that I had been in the war.

It turned out he was there to hunt buffalo. He kept most of the hides to sell, but gave most of the meat to one of the local tribes. His wife was from that tribe. It sounded to me like a good trade-off.

I also enjoyed an evening meal of buffalo steaks with them. As soon as it was getting dark, I camped behind their cabin.

May 5, 1868

I woke early and had breakfast with Mr. Grover and his wife. Mr. Grover was very nice and offered some advice if I was going to the Black Hills. He suggested that I go directly west from the Fort Pierre Trading Post. If I did that, he told me I would end up in the middle of the Black Hills.

He also suggested that I not say anything about going to the Black Hills. The Black Hills were closed to white men, especially miners. I had not said anything about going to the Black Hills to mine gold.

He reminded me that the Army was trying to keep miners out of the Black Hills. He also said that there were not enough soldiers to prevent anyone who really wanted to get into the hills from doing so.

I got the feeling he knew where I was going, and what I planned to do there. I simply smiled and thanked him for his advice.

Mr. Grover also told me that I should make sure I had plenty of water because there was little water in the area called the Bad Lands, an area I would pass through on my way to the Black Hills.

I thanked him for the information, then headed out. I continued on toward the Fort Pierre Trading Post. I made about twenty-five miles today. It was rolling prairie land with several ravines and gullies. I am sure that I will get to the Fort Pierre Trading Post to-morrow.

May 6, 1868

I got a good start to the day. It was a little past the noon hour when I arrived at the Fort Pierre Trading Post.

The man running the trading post was a pleasant man. I purchased a few things from him including a half dozen sticks of dynamite, fuses and a few cigars. He asked me what I wanted the dynamite for. I told him how helpful they were against thieves and Indians when they wanted to attack me. He got a good laugh when I told him about the general store owner who tried to steal my horse and mule, and how I used the dynamite to get away.

* * * * *

It seems that Isaac has been able to get some good advice along the way.

The past couple of weeks of Isaac's journal showed how lonely it was, but little else. The entry dated May 19, 1868 proved interesting.

May 19, 1868

I got an early start this morning, but it proved to have been for nothing. I had only traveled about two miles when it started to cloud up. It wasn't long and the wind was blowing hard only minutes before a storm blew in. I barely had time to find shelter near a creek before there was such a downpour of rain that my shelter could not keep me dry.

My animals didn't like it either. I had to hold onto their reins to keep them from running off during all the thunder and lightning. During the heaviest rain, I could not see more than about ten feet. Just off to the north of us, it sounded like the water rushing down the creek. If the conditions were right, it could be a flash flood. I was sure that I was up above the creek far enough that it would not affect me.

After the heaviest part of the rain, the wind died down and the rain settled into a fairly steady rain for about two hours. By the time it was done, almost everything was soaking wet. The only things that were dry, were a few of the things that were under the packs on my mule.

By noon, the sun was out again. It made it difficult to work in order to get things dried out because it was so hot and humid after the rain.

I found it interesting how fast the rain water soaked into the ground. The ground was almost dry by the time the sun was beginning to set.

There is no dry wood to build a fire. I will have to make do with what I can eat that does not require cooking. I will also have to put up my journal as the light is fading fast.

May 20, 1868

I spent to-day getting everything dried out. It was also a day of rest for my animals, and for me. The weather had improved. It was not as hot and humid as yesterday.

I was able to shoot a rabbit for my meal. It took a while to find enough dry twigs from some bushes near the creek to build a fire and cook the rabbit.

I think I will be on my way tomorrow. It is getting dark so I will close my journal for to-day and get some rest.

May 21, 1868

I got a good early start this morning. However, I didn't get very far.

About noon, I came over a slight rise in the land. I stopped suddenly. There in front of me were so many buffalo that it seemed that they covered the land for miles.

I don't know much about them, but I do know if they were to stampede, I could easily end up as part of the earth. I had also heard that it didn't take much to cause them to stampede.

I took my field glasses out of my saddle bags and scanned the area. It looked like the best way around them was to move north. There was a slight ridge that would keep me out of their sight.

I moved off the slight ridge and began moving north just down on the side of the ridge out of sight of the buffalo. I did stop fairly often and rode up close to the top of the ridge to see if I had gotten past them.

I must have traveled almost five miles before I thought it was safe to turn back west toward the Black Hills. I only went a few miles further before I found a place where I could spend the night. It was along a fairly shallow creek.

It was still fairly early, but I had no idea how far I would have to travel to find a place to camp. The water in the creek looked good, and there were enough twigs from the brushes along the bank of the creek to use for a fire.

I will close my journal for now and get some rest.

* * * * *

The next month of entries in Isaac's journal were not very interesting. They were short and mostly about the weather. It seems that he had a storm almost every other afternoon. Summer storms are very common on the plains.

June 26, 1868

I got a pretty good start to the day. I was moving along on what looked like a trail in among some high gray outcroppings of what I was sure was the beginning of the Bad Lands. They reminded me of gray clay that had been washed by heavy rains.

As I came around a bend in the trail I was following, I came upon a young Indian girl. She couldn't have been more than sixteen or seventeen years old. She was limping. Her left leg looked as thou she had been bitten by some animal, maybe a wolf or a coyote. As I approached her, she was scared of me and tried to run away. I'm sure she had been told about the bad white men. She couldn't move very fast.

Once I caught her, it took several minutes of talking softly to her before I was able to convince her that I only wanted to help her. I got her to sit down and be still. I took some of my water and washed the wound on her leg as best I could, then bandaged it.

I tried to find out where she was from, but she wouldn't talk to me. I looked around but didn't see any encampment of Indians. I had no idea what to do with her. I couldn't just leave her there, all alone in this vast wild land.

As I walked over to my mule, she followed me. She tried to tell me something, but I could only understand a few words. It sounded like she wanted to go with me.

I tried to find out where she was from, but she didn't understand me. I couldn't just leave her there all alone. I saw a couple of trees only a few hundred yards away. I decided that I would go there and camp for the night. As I started to leave, she began to follow me again. She limped along. I could see she was in pain, so I stopped and lifted her up on my horse and took her with me to where I planned to camp.

I built a fire and made dinner for us. She helped the best she could. I fixed her a place to sleep. Since all I had for a shelter was a small lean-to, she would have to sleep next to me. I sat down next to her and tried to talk to her.

Using sign language, some Indian words I had learned while at the fort, I was able to find out a little of what happened. She told me in her own way that she did not know where her family was, or if they were even alive. I figured out from what she was saying that her tribe had been attacked and she had been taken prisoner. She had escaped.

I also found out that her name was Little Dove, or something like that. I would call her Little Dove.

My fire is about to go out. Little Dove is sound asleep. I will put my journal up and try to get some sleep.

June 27, 1868

To-day is a day that I will never forget. It started out with me waking up. It felt good as Little Dove was curled up along side me. But the good feelings quickly turned to fear for my life.

I woke to see four Indian warriors standing there looking at me. They looked like they were about ready to kill me, or at the very least injure me by cutting me up.

I woke Little Dove. When she saw the warriors, she said something that I didn't understand. The one who seemed to be the leader, said something to her that made her mad. Little Dove jumped up and began talking to him so fast that I could not understand one word of it. It sounded like she was chewing him out for what he said.

The warriors backed off a little. Little Dove turned and looked at me. From what she was saying, I got the impression that the leader was her brother. He might have been accusing her of more than just sleeping next to me.

After a few minutes of their discussion, the leader settled down. He and the other warriors stepped back. One of the other warriors built a fire. We all sat around and had breakfast together. I had to wonder if this was going to be my last meal.

After breakfast, Little Dove told me that she had to go. I wished her well and watched as she rode off on a horse with the warriors. I have to admit that I will miss Little Dove, but I was glad to see she was back with her people.

As soon as they were gone, I packed up and headed west again. The rest of the day was rather uneventful. What little excitement I had in the morning was enough for one day.

I made only about fifteen miles today. I am sitting next to my fire thinking of Little Dove, and writing an account of the day.

June 28, 1868

I made about eighteen miles to-day. If what I have been told is correct, I am camping on the bank of the Cheyenne River. To-morrow I will cross the river and keep moving west. I don't know how much further I have to go, but it really doesn't matter. I have come this far, there is no turning back for me. I will say this much, with only a few exceptions, this has become a very lonely trek for me. I spend most of my days alone. Only finding someone I can talk to on occasion. It is very lonely out here. In some places I can see for miles, in others, not more that a few hundred yards.

* * * * *

It seems that Isaac might be having doubts about coming to the west. The next few entries added nothing new. He continued to mention about how lonely it was out on the prairie.

July 2, 1868

It was about mid-day when I saw a man on a horse coming toward me. He had two Indian ponies that had rather large packs in their backs in tow. I rode closer to him, then waved at him. He stopped. I noticed that he put his hand on his gun as I approached him.

I rode up to about fifteen feet from him when he called out for me to stop. I stopped then told him who I was. The man looked like a mountain man.

After I explained who I was and where I was headed, he seemed to relax a bit. It took a little while before he decided that it might be all right if we sat down and built a fire and had a meal together. That seemed to be the thing to do.

His name was George Peters, and he had come out to be a mountain man some fifteen years ago. The packs on his horses were beaver pelts and a few hides from deer, elk, and bear. He said it was his third trip to sell his beaver pelts, and that he planned to make it his last. He said he was hoping to buy up some land and settle down somewhere in the eastern part of the Dakota Territory and farm. During our time together, he said he had been alone too long and it was time for him to find himself a wife. I certainly could understand.

We camped together beside the creek, and talked until it was pretty late. As soon as he was asleep, I write in my journal by the light of the fire.

July 3, 1868

We were up early and had breakfast together. I stood there and watched him as he rode east. I wished him well. As he rode away, I almost wished I was going with him.

I packed up and continued to head west. Since the river I was headed toward ran more south than I wanted to go, I headed west. George told me that if I was looking to find gold in the Black Hills, I should go to the northern part of the hills.

He suggested I travel as straight west as possible and I would end up close to the northern part of the Black Hills. He also reminded me that I should be very watchful of the Indians in that area. They didn't like strangers in the hills.

I took his advice and headed straight west. I made about sixteen miles to-day before I found a place where I could camp for the night and enter to-day's activities.

* * * * *

Based on what Isaac wrote in his journal, he was probably only about four or five days from entering the Black Hills. The next few days of entries showed that he continued on west, they were rather uneventful days.

July 8, 1868

I have been watching what I believe to be the Black Hills for the past two days. They don't seem to be getting any closer, however, they do seem to be getting bigger. I can see why they are called the Black Hills. They look black from miles away.

I think I will have two days before I actually enter the Black Hills. I will have to be very watchful.

I made about nineteen miles to-day. I have hidden my fire from view by building it in a gully so hopefully I will be able to sneak into the hills, unseen. I will put out my fire before it gets dark.

July 9, 1868

I am about five miles from actually being in the Black Hills. I am camping in the bottom of a gully that appears to run up into the hills, and where I will have cover in among the pine trees.

I have had a cold dinner as I do not want a fire that might draw attention to me. My horse and mule don't seem to mind being in the gully. As soon as it is dark, I will take them out of the gully so they can graze on the buffalo grass. When they are done, I will bring them back into the gully.

July 10, 1868

To-day I entered the Black Hills. I am now surrounded by pine trees. The gully has gotten deeper the further up it I go. I'm looking for a place where I can get out of the gully. I must have traveled two miles, maybe three before I found a small gully off to my left. It was short and looked like a way out of gully I was in.

I started to look for a place I could hide for the night. I found a place along a creek that has a rocky outcropping where I will hide my horse and mule. It will do me for to-night.

It is my plan to move deeper into the hills. I hope to find a place where I can make a shelter that will hide my animals and myself while I look for gold.

I built a small fire to cook on. I will put it out before it gets dark. I am writing this entry before it gets dark.

July 11, 1868

Working my way deeper into the Black Hills, I came upon a little valley. It stretched out for about a half a mile. It was rich with green grass, and a narrow creek that followed the length of the valley. It was the most beautiful place I think I have seen in a long time.

As I looked out into the valley, I noticed something move on the far side, in among the trees. I pulled back into the cover of the trees and watched.

It was but a minute or so before a group of Indians, men, women and a few children, walked into the valley. They immediately began to set up camp near where the creek entered the valley. There were seven teepees being set up.

There were three rather large warriors sitting on their horses and looking around while the others worked to set up camp. It was clear they were there to protect the others.

I slowly moved back deeper into the forest to avoid being seen. As I did, I noticed one of the warriors rode over to one of the others. While they talked, I noticed one of them looked over toward me. I was sure that I had been spotted, but they didn't make a move toward me.

I slowly moved deeper into the forest to a place where I was sure they would not find me. I found a place where I could hide my animals, and where I could get some rest. I chose not to have a fire for fear the Indians would see it, or smell it.

As soon as it gets dark, I will settle in to sleep. In the meantime, I will keep watch, and write in my journal.

July 12, 1868

The Indians I had seen setting up camp in the little valley had seen me. They had waited until I had settled in, then approached me where I had camped. They took me prisoner and took me to their encampment where I was tied to a tree.

I was questioned by one of the women who spoke pretty good English. She looked like she might be at least part white. It was easy to talk to the woman they called Pale Doe. She explained to the Indians that I was not there to do them harm.

During the day, we had a chance to talk. Her real name was Marguerite Holder. She had been found by them almost three years ago when she was walking along a trail after the 'sickness' had killed everyone in the wagon train except her. They had fed her and allowed her to stay with them. She said they had taught her their language and treated her well.

By the end of the day, they allowed me to be untied. They also returned my animals to me. I built a lean-to near the edge of their encampment. They also returned my journal to me.

July 13, 1868

To-day, I spent most of the day with Marguerite. Although she was dressed like an Indian woman, her features were those of a white woman. Her skin was tanned from spending a great deal of her time out in the sun.

About noon, I noticed that the leader of the warriors came by my lean-to and asked Marguerite something that I didn't understand. She said that she would be back later, then walked off with the warrior.

I had no idea what they would be talking about, but I was sure it would be about me. I had not given them any reason to think that I would try to harm any of them in any way.

When Marguerite returned, she sat down next to me. She told me that the warrior she had just talked to had asked her if she wanted to go with me. She said "he called me 'one of her kind'."

I asked her, "what did you tell him?"

She looked at me for a minute before she said anything. She finally said,"I told him I would go with you if you asked me".

I looked at her for a minute, then smiled. I told her that I would like to have her go with me. She leaned over and kissed me, much to my surprise.

Marguerite then went to the Indian encampment. She returned shortly with two ponies, one with a pack on its back and one with just an Indian blanket on its back.

She had gotten all her belongings, as well as a few gifts from members of the tribe. She said they were wedding gifts.

As soon as I was packed up and ready to travel, we left the small tribe and headed deeper into the Black Hills. We found a nice little clearing about three miles from where I camped last night.

I set up camp while Marguerite built a fire and cooked our dinner. It was nice to have someone to talk to as well as someone to help with what had to be done.

July 14, 1868

With Marguerite at my side, we continued to travel deeper into the Black Hills. It was late in the afternoon when we came upon what looked like a cave. We tied our horses and my mule to a tree. I got a lantern from the packs on my mule, and lit it.

As soon as I was ready, we walked over to the cave. Marguerite held my rifle in her hands while I drew my pistol. I had no idea what might be in the cave.

I walked up to the entrance of the cave and carefully bent over to look inside. Lying on the floor was the body of a man. From the look of him, he had been dead for five or six days.

The man was lying face down. I turned him over and discovered that he must have been killed by a bear or some other large animal. Looking around the cave, it became apparent that he had not been mulled there. Tracks in the floor of the cave showed that he had crawled to the mine to die.

I continued to look around the cave and realized that it may have been a cave to start with, but it had been dug further back by a human, probably the dead man. I also found some of his tools.

I worked my way back into the mine where I discovered a wooden box. It was a box similar to the boxes used by the military officers. I opened the box and found dynamite, fuses, and nitroglycerin, as well as tools for mining. Inside a leather pouch inside the box, I found a C.S.A. Army uniform of a lieutenant. The dead man had apparently been a Confederate officer. There were other things that led me to believe, or rather, confirmed that he had fought in the Great War. It also provided me with his name, First Lieutenant Jeffery P. Butler.

It was clear that Butler had come here to mine for gold. I wondered if he found any.

When I stepped out of the mine, Marguerite was still waiting for me. I sat down with her and told her what I found inside the cave, and that it wasn't a cave, but a mine.

We decided that we would set up camp over among the trees about thirty feet from the cave entrance. We would take some time to decide what we would do.

After setting up camp, Marguerite built a small fire to cook our dinner over, while I tried to follow the tracks of the bear. I had my doubts that I would find the bear. It would be good to know if the bear was still in the area.

In tracking the bear, I noticed a few places where there was what looked like blood on the ground. Moving slowly, in case the bear was still in the area, I moved along the tracks. It wasn't long before I found the bear. It had crawled off into some brush to die. Butler had apparently gotten several shots in the bear before he died, which eventually killed the bear. The bear had been dead long enough that there was nothing useable to us.

When I got back to our camp, dinner was almost ready, and I told Marguerite about the bear. It seemed to please her to know the bear that killed Butler was also dead.

After dinner, I took Jeffery Butler out of the mine and over to a place at the edge of the woods where I buried him. I made a small cross with the name, Jeffery P. Butler carved into it. I had no idea where he was from, but it mattered little. I said a few words over him before I covered his grave, and placed the cross at the head of his grave.

After dinner, I sat down and wrote this entry in my journal so if someone should find me like I found Butler in the mine, they would at least know who I was, and maybe a little about me.

July 15, 1868

To-day, I started going through the mine. I was looking for anything that might tell me if Butler had been successful in finding gold. I found two bottles of gold, one of the bottles was full of gold dust and small pieces of gold. The second bottle was only about half full.

I also found two narrow veins of gold running through the rock wall of the cave. It would not take long before I could finish filling the one bottle and start on a third. I went to work on doing just that.

Marguerite and I kept our camp just inside the edge of the forest. We decided that we didn't want to live in the cave. I split my time between working in the mine, and hunting. I did save the evenings for writing in my journal.

July 16, 1868

Marguerite and I went hunting together. We had gone some distance from our campsite when we were spotted by several Indians. They were not of the same tribes as Marguerite had been staying with when I found her.

It quickly turned into a running and shooting fray. I dropped one of the Indians, then turned to run. Just as I turned to run, I saw Marguerite fall. I ran to her, but when I got there, she was dead.

I was also hit in the arm with an arrow, but it wasn't much. I broke the arrow in two, and pulled it out of my arm, then ran toward the mine.

I was able to fend them off at the mine because the only way at me was through the cave entrance, and I had that covered. I could see a couple of Indians were headed toward my horses and the mule. If they got them, they would not get very much as we had stored our supplies in the mine.

For now, it was a stand-off that would probably last until it was dark.

While waiting to see what the Indians were going to do, I caught up my journal.

Just in case I am overrun and lose my life. I will hide my journal in a mental tea box along with some gold and a picture of my wife, Susan. I have also hidden a third bottle of gold behind some rocks on the wall of the mine.

July 17, 1868

The Indians are almost at my front door, so to speak. It looks like this will be the end. I cannot fight all of them off. I am short of ammunitions, and I am injured to the point I will not be able to fight much longer.

If I write nothing more, whoever finds this journal will know that I put up a good fight.

It is time to face my enemy. I will sign my name, then put my journal in the tea tin in case this becomes my last entry. May God have mercy on my soul.

Teacher, Soldier, Indian Fighter, Frontiersman, and Miner.

First Lieutenant Isaac J. Madison, born August 4th, 1840.

Made in the USA
Middletown, DE
20 April 2024